The Wrong Side of the Sky

Gavin Lyall was born and educated in Birmingham. For two years he served as an RAF pilot before going up to Cambridge, where he edited *Varsity*, the university newspaper. After working for *Picture Post*, the *Sunday Graphic* and the BBC, he began his first novel, *The Wrong Side of the Sky*, published in 1961. After four years as Air Correspondent to the *Sunday Times*, he resigned to write books full time. He is married to the well-known journalist Katharine Whitehorn, and they live in London with their children.

Gavin Lyall

The Wrong Side of the Sky

Pan Books London and Sydney

The characters in this book are entirely imaginary
and bear no relation to any living person

First published 1961 by Hodder & Stoughton Ltd
This edition published 1966 by Pan Books Ltd,
Cavaye Place, London SW10 9PG
8th printing 1976
© Gavin Lyall 1961
ISBN 0 330 10488 8
Printed and bound in Great Britain by
Richard Clay (The Chaucer Press) Ltd, Bungay Suffolk

PART ONE

1

I HADN'T BEEN in Athens for at least three months and hadn't reckoned on being there for another three months, but there I was standing breathing the good fresh petrol fumes of Elliniko Airport and waiting for the starboard engine to get cool enough for me to start an appendectomy on its magneto.

When we'd taken off from Turkey – with no cargo – we'd fuel enough to fly clear to Bari and beyond, with plenty to spare for dodging high ground and long sea passages. But these small Turkish fields aren't too particular about how much water gets into the fuel, and when on top of that we got a mag drop of two hundred revs just after clearing the coast, that meant Athens to me. In this world a man gets no more than he puts cash down for, and Hauser wasn't paying me a big enough salary to get me charging out over the Ionian Sea with a load of watery fuel and shaky ignition.

I called up Elliniko Airport and gave them a rough time-of-arrival and asked if they would ring Mikklos, who acted as our Athens agent, to suggest he cable Hauser in Berne and then try and rustle up a cargo for us. *If* it wouldn't take his mind too far off his lunch.

Young Rogers didn't see the point of it all. He still had too much RAF Transport Command blood in his veins; to him, a mag drop was something to watch, not get worried about. He just hadn't been co-piloting long enough on seventeen-year-old Dakotas with clapped-out engines, nor around the sort of business where you got dirty fuel and didn't complain.

The hell with him. While he flew with me he'd stay alive and like it.

Elliniko called back in a quarter of an hour to say they'd contacted Mikklos and would I like a priority landing? I said no thanks; it was just a crack at the state of Aircargo's planes, anyway.

We made Elliniko at about half past one, with me doing a three-pointer to show the control tower that Jack Clay was in a better state of repair than the planes he flew. I don't suppose it impressed them much. It stopped impressing me when I saw what else they'd got to look at in the way of aircraft handling.

We'd got parked and I was standing around in the shade of the wing trying to remember the Greek for *Customs Officer* and waiting for Rogers to break out the overalls and spanners when I looked out along the approach and saw a plane I couldn't identify at first. A small high-wing type with wing-tip tanks. Then it turned head-on, showing me the cranked gull-wing shape, and I had it; a Piaggio 166. A sleek little twin-engined executive job, four big passenger seats, a private bar and still room for the owner to curl up for a cuddle in the back. You don't see many of them; I guessed this one be-longed to one of the Greek shipping bigwigs.

It eased round very smoothly on the final turn. I kept watching. There had been a bit of a bump, an updraught, as you came in off the sea – but the Piaggio went through with never a quiver.

Gradually the feeling began to grow on me, and me trying hard to disbelieve it as it grew.

Only a pilot would have noticed it, and perhaps only a pilot with my number of flying hours in his logbook. But to me it was like seeing a beautiful woman in the distance and watching her come closer and waiting for the inevitable dis-appointment as she came. And then finding her perfect.

You couldn't say what it was about her that made her per-fect. You couldn't say what it was about the way the Piaggio landed. But it was perfect, too. It held the turn until it was a few feet off the runway threshold. Then the wings smoothed out, the nose eased back and it slid on to the ground with no apparent effort to the transition from one element to another.

One in a thousand pilots has it. Maybe less. Screwball Beurling had it, and Ken Kitson, and Zurakowski – though I never saw him, only heard what they said about him. And maybe a handful more in the whole world. Thousands of good pilots, great pilots even, who have every other quality or skill, don't have this: a complete affinity with aeroplanes and the air that makes everything about the way they fly per-fection.

There was no envy about the way I watched. This was some-thing too remote for envy, and it's not every pilot who can put a Dak down on three points without swinging off the runway. I just watched. There are some women you can watch without wanting them.

The Piaggio leant its nosewheel on to the ground, slowed and taxied clear in one flowing movement. I let out a long breath and found Rogers under my elbow.

'Well, how did you like that?' I asked.

'Nice little planes, those,' he said.

A miracle could happen in that boy's hip pocket and all he'd notice would be an itch in the backside.

'Get across and say hello to Control and Customs for us,' I snarled at him. 'And bring me back a bottle of beer.'

I went off to wave my engineer's licences in the face of some young hopeful of a mechanic to convince him that I could scrape the points of a Pratt and Whitney 1830 as legally as he could, and a damn sight cheaper.

I spent an hour and a half crawling over and inside the starboard engine. Rogers spent the same time passing me spanners and fetching me bottles of beer and wishing I'd let him go away and prowl the city. Then, as I was getting the cowlings back into place, he rode back from one beer mission in a big, battered, old yellow Dodge coupé. Alongside him, driving, was Mikklos.

Mikklos was a small, tubby character in thick spectacles and a bristly moustache, pushing fifty but not moving it much. As an agent, he would ship or fly anything anywhere and the fewer the questions, the better he liked it. Essentially, he was a small-time crook trying hard to be an upper-middle-class crook. He wore an expensive black-and-white hound's-tooth check tropical suit, an open-neck cream silk shirt, a snappy straw hat – and looked as if he had swum in the soup in them.

'Hello, Mikky,' I said, getting down off the wing.

'Captain Clay!' He stuck out a warm, fat little hand. But there was nothing soft about this grip. 'I have met your great friend and co-pilot.' He waved a hand at Rogers, who was standing and smiling fixedly at him.

'Sorry to butt in on you like this, Mikky,' I said, 'but I didn't want to press on to Bari with a shaky engine. How's the love life?'

Mikklos liked that question: it saved him the trouble of bringing it up himself. He shrugged and smiled. 'Ah – these

9

young girls, they don't appreciate me. Now – if I were tall and thin and good-looking like you —' He grinned at the idea. Anything that stepped up his pace would have killed him.

I smiled back. 'Did you cable Hauser?'

'Of course. I told him I have a cargo for you.'

'Have you now? That's quick work.'

'Can you fly to Tripoli, tonight?'

'Tripoli, Libya?'

'Yes. Tonight.'

That was 650 miles: say five hours' flying. It would take me over an hour to get loaded and away here – these things always take longer than you can see reason for. So I'd land at Idris airport at nine tonight. Fair enough.

The trouble was that almost all those miles were over the sea, and still using a load of fuel that had too much water in it. I wasn't keen on it – but it was the job I was paid to do.

'I could do it,' I told him. 'What's the cargo?'

'Oil-drilling equipment. 1,400 kilos.'

'About three thousand pounds. Where is it?'

'Right across there, Captain.' He pointed off behind the hangars. 'It is all arranged.' He gave me a quick grin, waddled over to the Dodge and whirled away.

'Extraordinary little chap,' said Rogers.

'Have you got that beer?'

'Yes.' He gave me the fat little brown bottle. 'Are we going to Tripoli?'

'Unless there's a reason why not.' I took off the cap with the opener on my key ring and poured the beer down my throat.

'We could be back in Berne tomorrow lunchtime, then?'

'That's right.' If an engine didn't pack up half-way to Tripoli. I was wondering if I could jump straight across to hit the coast near Benghazi and then coast-crawl. It would add another 250 miles, and nearly two hours, but it would mean only 250 miles of sea instead of 650.

The Dodge swept back around the corner of the hangar, trailing a rickety high-sided lorry in its dust. There was another man sitting beside Mikklos, a big dark bird with a small black moustache and showing a lot of dark hair through the open neck of his shirt. He stayed in the car while Mikklos came across.

'All here, Captain,' he grinned.

The lorry pulled slowly round by the door of the Dak and backed up to within a few feet of it. In the back were ten wooden boxes, about the size of coffins, but built very strongly of battered, inch-thick boards that had gone grey from the sun and dust of a lifetime's travelling. On top of them sat another well-built character in a white shirt and slacks and giving me an unfriendly dark eye.

Mikklos told him something in Greek and he jumped down and pulled the first box to the edge of the lorry.

'All Customed,' Mikklos said, twanging the Customs wire wrapped around the box and sealed with a little lead medallion. He turned away and yelled at the others to come and help.

Then he groped a handful of papers out of an inside pocket and gave me two, a filled-in manifest and a blank load sheet, to be filled in when the cargo was properly arranged.

The manifest specified four cases of drill head bits, and six cases of drill sections and sundry technical odds and sods.

'They want these things in a hurry,' I remarked.

'They stored them here when they brought them out of Iraq. Now they want them fast. American oil companies.' He shrugged. 'All damn bits and pieces and nowhere to put them.'

'Yes,' I said, tucking the manifest away in a shirt pocket. 'Open 'em up.'

'What, Captain?'

'The boxes. Open 'em up.'

'But they've been through Customs!'

'The Customs man can come across and put more seals on them. He's got to come and check over the plane. It won't take him ten minutes to check the boxes again.'

'They're screwed down tight.'

The two big characters and the lorry driver, a short, wiry little man in a vest, had all stopped work and were staring at me. I could feel Rogers staring at me, too. Mikklos had got back his smile by now – a little sadder, perhaps, but still going strong.

'Captain, why are you so suspicious?'

'Because I'm growing old, I guess, Mikky. And because I've flown stuff for oil companies before. Not one in the world needs four whole cases of drill bits so damn fast they have to be flown in just like that. Open 'em up.'

Mikklos smiled wider and even more sadly and shook his head gently.

'Captain.' He took my arm and led me away out to the shadow of the wing-tip. Rogers tagged on.

'Now, Captain. All right, maybe they are not drill parts. But it is all fixed, at both sides. Here *and* there.'

'That's more like it, Mikky. But it ain't fixed in the middle.'

'Five thousand drachma, Captain?'

I heard Rogers pull in his breath sharply. Five thousand of anything sounds like a lot unless you're used to the rates of exchange. To me it sounded like just over £60.

'No, Mikky. I'm not doing it. Let's not waste time.'

'Ten thousand I make it.'

£125.

'No, Mikky.' I turned. He caught my arm. His face looked worried, the first time I'd ever seen him look anything less than sad.

'Dollars. Three hundred fifty dollars. Done?'

'No. I'm not carrying it. If you want to do a deal with me, talk it over first. Don't stand out in the middle of an airfield and try to stuff it down my throat.'

I turned away and walked out around the nose of the Dak. Behind me, Mikklos said sharply: 'You've carried guns before, Captain.'

I kept on walking. When I got to the starboard engine I climbed up the stepladder and started screwing in the last press-screws. On the other side of the plane I heard voices and thumpings. Then the lorry pulled away. A few seconds later Mikklos's Dodge whipped after it. His acceleration sounded angry.

When I climbed down the ladder Rogers was waiting for me. He looked at me curiously and said:

'I've often wondered what you'd do to an offer like that.'

'Now you know.'

'No offence, Jack, but three hundred and fifty dollars sounds a lot of money.'

'Too many things can go wrong. With bad weather we might end up in Malta or Sicily, and I'm not going to be caught with a cargo of guns.'

He picked up the stepladder and walked round to the door with me.

'Where are they for?'

'Algeria, probably. Ex-EOKA stuff that never got to Cyprus. Fly 'em into Libya, take 'em two hundred and fifty miles down

12

into the desert and you can cross into Algeria without even going through Tunisia.'

He nodded.

'I suppose it's a bad business. Still,' he added, 'three hundred and fifty bucks.'

'You wouldn't get much of it.'

He looked offended.

'He said you'd carried guns before,' he said nastily.

'He was just talking.'

I threw the stepladder down into the back of the Dak, slammed the door and started across to Control to cable Hauser for instructions.

I needn't have bothered. When I got back and ran up the engine to test the magneto, the water that had settled to the bottom of the tanks nearly blew the engine out of the wing. I was stuck in Athens for the night whether I liked it or not.

2

WE GOT a couple of rooms in a small hotel just off Omonia Square. Most aircrew in Athens lived up around Sintagma Square, within spitting distance of the Royal Palace. Aircargo crews lived where Hauser's expense allowances let them; in Athens, that meant Omonia Square.

The sheets were patched, the windows gave a good view of the vegetable shop across the street and the doors were the sort that any policeman could knock down with a good sneeze – and probably had. But the place was a lot cleaner than a lot of hotels around there, and it cost us five whole drachma a night more than the neighbourhood rate.

We washed and changed – me into the snappy new light-weight suit that I'd picked up the last time I was in Rome. Then we went out to eat. On the way, I looked in at the Post Office to see if there were any cables from Hauser – there weren't – and then phoned Mikklos. He wasn't in, but I managed to convey to his secretary that I had no hard feelings about the cargo offered and was still in the market for another.

We ate in a small, hygienic café set aside for the poorer tourists up near Sintagma Square. I've got nothing against the *tavernas* – Greek food is pretty much the same anywhere – but I wasn't going to sit in somebody's soup-stains in my good lightweight suit.

'What do we do now?' asked Rogers. It was going on seven o'clock.

'We can go to a movie,' I suggested, 'or maybe go up to the King George for a drink and see if there's any airline boys we know.'

That suited him fine. Airline men were his people, he thought. Give him a year or two with this scruffy little outfit and he'd be all set to take over somebody's big, shiny jetliner. He hoped.

We went to the King George.

The King George lies up on Sintagma, with American bar just below street level. You can get into it either from the street or the hotel itself; we went in through the hotel to see if there was anybody around the lobby that I knew. There wasn't. We went down to the bar, a long, narrow room with a row of stools along the counter on our left and a row of tables on the right, and a lot of smoke and chatter going on in between.

I knew one man there, a big TWA captain who'd had a row with me once after I'd baulked his landing in Rome by blowing a tyre as I turned on to the runway. I didn't know if it had turned funny in his memory by now. Funny enough for him to buy me a drink, anyway.

Then I saw Kitson. It was ten years since I'd last seen him – but only a few hours since I'd seen his flying, in that Piaggio.

He was sitting up on a bar stool at the far end, dividing his attention between something in a tall glass and a smallish, fair, sun-burned girl dressed with that fresh crispness that's as American as the Statue of Liberty and a lot easier on the eye. She had on a tan cotton shirtwaister with a full skirt, a wide black suede belt and what looked like ballet pumps.

Her hair was cut short and swept back over her ears. She must have been twenty-seven or twenty-eight and she had all the figure the dress could take in the places it was built to take it; but alongside Ken she looked like a high-school girl.

He was dressed like the inside of a millionaire's wallet. He had on a cream shirt that, from the way it folded, could only have been chamois leather. Pale fawn slacks held up by a pigskin belt, and off-white Italian suède moccasins.

'Get yourself a drink,' I told Rogers. 'There's a man I want a word with.'

He looked offended, but went off and nudged his way into the bar within reach of the TWA captain. TWA fly jets.

I went over and put a hand on Ken's shoulder.

'Hello, superman. Looking for a job as a Dak co-pilot?'

He turned his head slowly to look at me. He had a long, bony face, with a thin, straight nose and a wide mouth. His black hair was longer than when I'd last seen him, his face was browner and there were more sun-crinkles around his dark eyes, but he hadn't aged ten years. Men in £25 shirts stay younger longer.

I don't know why the hell I thought that. I was very damn pleased to see him.

'So it's still aviating around,' he said slowly, and then he grinned and grabbed my hand.

'Let me introduce you,' he said. He waved a hand at me and then the girl. 'Jack Clay, Shirley Burt.' He waved a hand at the bar. 'And that's the bar. What are you drinking?'

I grinned and nodded at the girl and said: 'Hello,' and then, to Ken, 'Scotch, I suppose.'

'Have an old-fashioned. They're all right here.' He leant across and knocked on the far side of the bar. The barman left young Rogers practically sitting in the air and slid along to us on greased rails. Ken ordered two old-fashioneds and a martini.

'You get service here,' I remarked.

'It's the money that does it,' Miss Burt said. 'He practically sweats the stuff.'

'Don't you love that refreshing, outspoken, down-to-earth New World outlook?' Ken asked me. The girl grinned. She had a nice face. You couldn't honestly say more for it than that, except that you could stand having it around a lot longer than a lot more beautiful faces.

'Is that Piaggio your own?' I asked Ken.

'Nope.' He didn't bother to ask how I'd known he was flying it. He knew how good he was. 'That belongs to my revered employer, the terror of infidels, protector of the righteous, second cousin to the thunderclouds, His Excellency the Nawab of Tungabhadra. May the sun continue to shine from his hip pocket.' He raised his glass solemnly.

'And the money flow from his bill-fold,' said the girl.

I took a gulp of my drink. Ken had been right about them knowing how to mix them.

'I wonder he hasn't invested in a Viscount,' I said.

'Not he. Then there'd be no excuse for not bringing all his friends and hangers-on along. This job's fitted out so there's only room for four – and two up front.'

I looked at the girl. She was stirring her martini with a cherry.

'Are you one of the four?' I asked.

She shook her head.

'Not me. I'm what they call a working stiff. I click a camera for one of the agencies back States-side. I'm doing a picture story on the Raja now.'

'Nawab, dear,' Ken corrected her, swilling his drink around the ice.

'The hell with the captions,' said Miss Burt. 'Let 'em figure it out back home.'

Ken finished his drink with the third gulp and slapped the glass on the bar. 'And another?'

The girl gave him a quick glance that was a lot more old-fashioned than anything they mixed in glasses, but Ken didn't notice.

'My shout,' I said, finishing off my own.

'Don't be silly,' said Ken. 'His Excellency pays the bill.'

'Not for me,' the girl said.

The barman broke the lap record again and Ken ordered two more old-fashioneds. Then he said to me:

'Well, what are you doing now, boy?'

'Oh, flying Daks for a small Swiss outfit. Charter work, mostly. Freight, passengers. Everything anywhere. The old game.'

'How long have you been there?' Ken asked.

'Four, nearly five years.'

'What are you doing at the moment?' the girl asked. She looked honestly interested.

'We've been flying stuff for a Hollywood unit on location in Turkey. They packed up yesterday and we were coming back to Berne and got magneto trouble. So I put in here. Now I've got fuel trouble.'

'Water in it,' said Ken absently. 'I know. Won't take 'em long.'

'Them?' I said. '*I'm* licensed to pick Pratt and Whitneys to bits. *Them* cost a bit much for my boss.'

Ken looked at me. 'Yes, yes,' he said softly.

The girl was looking at me approvingly. She would like a

man to mend his own engines. But if she was thinking anything else of Ken, she was wrong. He could pick a P and W 1830 apart with a rusty hairpin.

Our drinks arrived. Ken put half of his away in one go. His personal carburettor certainly wasn't giving any trouble.

'Who's "we"?' Miss Burt asked me.

'My co-pilot. Young chap down there.' I looked down the bar. Rogers was getting the word from TWA and listening to it all as if it were the first cuckoo.

'Any good?' Ken asked.

'He's all right.' Ah, if that boy only knew how I praised him behind his back.

Looking at Ken parked there, something occurred to me.

'You can't have just got in today?' I asked.

'No. We've been here three days. That was just an air test I was doing this afternoon.' He finished the rest of his drink.

'Stay another three days,' the girl said, 'and they'll be rigging old-fashioneds in machine-gun belts for you.'

'That's an idea,' Ken agreed.

'What's His Excellency doing?' I asked. 'A Grand Tour?'

'Not quite.' He looked at the ice in his glass. 'The dry season's here again. Another?'

'Let me get this one,' I said. 'Just to prove I'm in work.'

Ken grinned. I looked at Miss Burt's glass.

'I'll have one,' she said. 'The last. Then I'm eating. Are you eating here?'

'I've eaten already,' I said.

'That's my boy,' Ken said. 'Get the unimportant business over first. I'll stay here and see you don't get picked up by strange women.'

I looked at Miss Burt. She was nibbling on the cherry with a small frown on her forehead. If she'd appointed herself to seeing that Ken fed regularly, she'd taken on a full-time job. Ken had always been able to soak it up, but he'd acquired a new professionalism at it in the last ten years.

It might have been a habit that you picked up along with chamois shirts. Or it could have been something you did in defiance of them. Being a Nawab's professional pilot isn't everybody's dream of a perfect job, and I couldn't yet see how snugly it fitted Ken.

He summoned up the barman and I gave the orders. The man was going to be disappointed in my scale of tipping, but he'd probably had an unbroken three-day run of luck in this corner.

I shovelled round my cigarettes. Ken lit them with a ribbed gold Dunhill.

'Are you over specially for the Nawab?' I asked Miss Burt.

'No. I'm permanently in Europe – for a year or two, anyway. I'm based in Paris. Every American in Europe is based in Paris; it's getting to look like Fifth Avenue. I was in Beirut on another story and I bumped into the Nawab and company there.' She looked at Ken. He smiled back and reached for our drinks.

I paid and the barman managed to hide his sorrow.

We sipped; Ken gulped. Then the girl said:

'I think I'll take this in with me. If you characters are staying here . . .'

'We'll be here,' Ken said.

She went away with a neat, unhurried stroll. I watched her go, weaving between the clumps of airline men and tourists. The crowd was thinning out for dinner, leaving just those who had eaten earlier elsewhere and those to whom this was home. I climbed up on the girl's bar stool.

3

WITH HER gone, it was as if we'd loosened our ties and scratched under our arms and kicked the dirty crockery out of sight under the kitchen table. It was nothing to do with her. It was just something to do with us. For a while nobody said anything. We gazed into our drinks and dragged on our cigarettes.

Then Ken said: 'Well, how's life?'

'I'm living. And flying.'

'Yes,' he said. 'What else does a man want to do?' Then: 'What's it like as a job?'

'It pays hard cash. Not often and not much, but hell – it's only Daks.'

'What're they going to replace them with?' That was a big topic in the airline and air industry just then. Six firms had planes that were intended as 'Dakota replacements' and any line that still worked Daks was knee deep in shiny brochures and well-cut salesmen-engineers.

'They aren't,' I said. 'We'll still be operating Daks when everything else goes by space ship.'

Ken grinned. I asked: 'What's His Excellency like as an employer?'

Ken spread his hands. 'He pays well. And he's no fair-weather passenger, I'll give him that. He wants to go somewhere, then he wants to go. He assumes I can find a way to get him there.'

'Where d'you live, out there?' I asked. I knew that wherever the Nawab of Tungabhadra lived, it certainly wasn't Tungabhadra. That had been one of the small central Indian states, mainly Hindu, but with a Muslim ruler. The sort of situation that got solved very smartly when Partition came. They'd have to be living somewhere in Pakistan by now.

'He bought a place up near Fort Munro; you know?' I knew it: in the foothills of the Sulaimans, west of the big plain of the Indus.

'Nothing too fancy; just an old Governor's palace,' he went on. 'Just thirty bedrooms and an airstrip in the back garden. But at least there's no spiritual leadership to worry about.'

'Nothing like the simple life.'

Ken nodded and took out a white silk handkerchief and wiped his forehead. It wasn't that hot, not at this time of the year in Athens, and not ever in the American bar of the King George. His rate of drinking had slowed since the girl had gone, but the amount he had taken before was tightening its grip.

Rogers came wandering up, trying to look casual, with a near-empty glass in his hand. He stopped just behind Ken's shoulder and gave the chamois shirt its due attention.

'Tony,' I said, 'I want you to meet an old friend of mine: Ken Kitson.'

Ken swung around and I explained that Rogers was my co-pilot and that I'd flown with Ken in the war. Rogers's glass seemed to remind Ken of his mission. He waved a finger at the barman and ordered three old-fashioneds without even asking Rogers what he wanted.

Rogers asked Ken what he was doing now and when it came out he practically curled his lip. He was prepared to worship the jet men and listen to anybody who flew for the big airlines, but for him a personal pilot was one step down from whoring. In a way, you couldn't blame him, but I did anyhow.

Ken nosedived into the new drink and then started on a line about the Piaggio. It made me smile, but it made me envious, too. In the *Pilot's Notes* the Dak is credited with a cruising speed of 140 knots. Ours missed that by a good ten knots by now. The Piaggio cruised at 180 and had a top speed of over 200.

There was no real comparison, of course. The Piaggio was built as a fast limousine for the millionaire market; the Dak is for carrying people and things at the best economic rate and, in that, it's the best transport aircraft ever built. But there aren't any less than sixteen years old now and occasionally, sitting in a bar with the other birdmen, I get a yen to fly something that doesn't rattle at the joints.

For Rogers, that wasn't just a yen, it was a permanent way of thought. He could make it, too. I knew I probably couldn't. That might account for something.

We had another round. Then Rogers asked: 'What's the Nawab doing, flying round seeing the sights?'

Ken shook his head and wiped his hair out of his eyes. 'Not quite, my son. The Nawab is on the trail of a heap big mystery. The Nawab – may his virility and bank account remain undiminished – is tracking down the family heirlooms.'

'One of his wives run off with a Greek sailor?' I asked.

'Not married, dear boy. A Nawab of the old school.'

'Don't kid me. I saw what some of them learnt in that school.'

Ken grinned. 'Well – if you really want to know – and don't tell anybody I told you – what he's after is jewellery. Real, genuine, sparkling jewellery. Two ammunition boxes' – he spread his hands on the bar, about two feet apart – 'like that, of it. Estimated value getting on for one million and one half – sterling. He wants it back, please, dead or alive. Usual rewards.'

Rogers was looking at him cautiously, not sure when to stop believing.

'When did this happen?' I asked. 'I mean, when did it get stolen?'

'I'm glad you asked that question.' Ken squirmed on the stool and leant himself sideways against the bar. 'It happened, dear friend, back in the days of our youth, in the good old days of Partition, when the Nawab lived in Tungabhadra in his dear old pink marble palace, all safe and secure. Except, of course, for the mob of howling Hindus waiting outside to cut his dear old throat.

'Well, seeing that such an occurrence would be contrary to the established order of things, some jolly Western friends of the Nawab rallied round with a bunch of Dakotas and started flying out the gold dinner sets and necklaces and other items of petty cash, taking them to the safety of Pakistan and the true belief.'

Some of it was Ken and some of it was the whisky but it all came without a slipped syllable.

'They also,' he went on, 'took out the Nawab and the front rank of his court, which was perhaps less of a service to the true belief, but that's the way life goes. Anyway, in the execution of this noble deed one of the pilots involved – clearly a low-class fellow who'd been to the wrong school and probably the wrong squadron too – he looked down the back one day and saw there were these two big boxes of loot and he thought to himself: Why stop at Pakistan?'

He stopped and rattled the ice in his glass and said: 'The fuel state's getting serious again.' While he was summoning up the barman, Rogers gave me a look and wrinkled up his nose. I shrugged.

'Now,' Ken turned back again, 'we left our hero sitting in the cockpit of his Dak realizing that he had on hand all the wherewithal for the good life and no more aviating around in low company. So – observe his devilish cunning, friends – he puts down at Goa, which, you may recall, is a small Portuguese colony on the west coast fairly much untroubled by religion and riots. He has his tanks topped up there and then suggests to his co-pilot, an honourable and upstanding lad, just like our friend here' – he waved a hand at Rogers, who recoiled – 'suggests that he steps down and examines the state of the tail wheel.'

He took a quick pull at the fresh glass.

'The unsuspecting fellow does so, and is surprised – nay, dumbfounded – to hear the door slam and the engines rev up. And before he can say "This is the action of a cad and a bounder", the Dak is away, winging a lonely path across the Arabian Sea into the tropic sunset.'

'There, I confess, I diverge from the facts for dramatic effect, since it was only eleven in the morning; but he went west, anyway.'

'*That* I believe,' I said. 'What did you say his name was?'

'I didn't – but it was Morrison. Ex-flight-lieutenant.'

I shook my head. 'Never knew him. You say this all happened ten-twelve years ago?'

Ken nodded a little harder than he need have done. The sweat was standing out on his forehead and he wasn't feeling it any more.

'Broken up,' I said. 'Melted down. Stones re-cut. The Nawab could stare at a window full of his own stuff and not know it. Beirut was as good an idea as any – you said you'd been there, didn't you? A lot of shady jewellery goes through there, but nobody recognizes it when it comes out.'

Ken shook his head, again rather strongly. 'You're right in principle, friend Hawkeye, but wrong in fact. A couple of months ago the Nawab got two or three pieces of the stuff back, intact. One of his buyers picked it up in Beirut. Don't ask me how His Ex recognized it when he got it, not with all the stuff he still has back at home, but he did. That's what started the hunt.'

'What made you come to Athens?' Rogers asked.

'Picked up a hint in Beirut,' Ken said. 'From a —' but he didn't tell us from whom.

I hadn't seen her coming, but suddenly Miss Shirley Burt was standing alongside Rogers, ignoring him and looking at us two. Ken's long black hair was hanging damply down over his ear, his face was streaked with sweat, his shirt neck had opened another button and his sleeve cuffs were turned back. At some stage my shirt collar had got unbuttoned, I'd opened my jacket and loosened my belt.

They had all been perfectly natural moves at the time, but I could see what impression she was getting.

'My God,' she said, 'the monsoon's come.'

'Martini for you?' Ken asked calmly.

'Old war-time buddies,' she snorted.

I dumped the last of my drink down the hatch and slid off the stool. 'I think I'd better be getting along,' I said.

'Not without seeing he gets to bed, you don't,' said Miss Burt grimly.

I thought of saying that she was quite capable of seeing to that for herself and then decided I wouldn't. I stood there, more or less on my feet and more or less upright.

Ken looked at me, made a hopeless expression with his eyebrows and slid off his stool. He staggered as he hit the floor. That seemed to surprise him.

I moved in to brace him if he needed it – and if I could manage it. But he jerked himself upright, wiped a hand across his forehead and shoved his hair back out of his eyes.

Then we looked at each other.

'Suppose I'll be seeing you,' he said.

'I'll be around.'

He nodded and started towards the door to the hotel stairs, with Miss Burt closed up on one side and me lagging at the other. Rogers, reckoning, rightly, that this was none of his fight, had faded away.

The crowd round the bar was piling up again. Some of the men watched us with wry hell-that's-life smiles. It must have been the third night running they'd seen this show.

We reached the stairs up to the lobby, almost ramming a tall, solid gent in his doorway. He frowned at us, then stepped back from the door.

'Mr Kitson,' he said harshly, 'so you have been drinking again.' His voice had a guttural Germanic note in it.

I had just enough whisky inside me to want to bop this party and just enough not to dare risking it. I'd need to be stone sober to tackle a job like that.

He was tall – I'm six feet and he topped me by an inch or more – and was built like a guardsman. His new grey suit was cut ten years out of date, double-breasted and hugging round him tightly so that it bulged where it touched, but the bulges were all up around his chest and shoulders.

He had a thick, fleshy face on a wide neck, thin lips and short, curly brown hair. The only non-combatant touch about him was a pair of square rimless spectacles. But he could always take those off.

Ken told him where to go in two short words.

The girl heard them without blinking. The tall party rocked and coloured behind his tan. Then he reached out, twisted Ken by one shoulder and shoved him towards the stairs. Ken sprawled in the air, recovered and ended up on his two feet and a wall.

The big man passed on into the bar, marching as if he were going in to collect the orders of the day from Bismarck.

'Maybe I should have hit him,' I offered feebly. The girl looked me up and down and said gently:

'No, not tonight.'

Ken was back in the middle of the landing, staring at the bar

23

door with a tight, flushed look on his thin face. An elderly couple came out of the door, edged delicately around us and went on up the stairs, giving us sharp looks over their shoulders.

Ken loosened up suddenly, gave us a quick grin and said: 'Bed, I suppose. See you, children.'

Drunk as he was, he was still light and controlled on his feet. We watched him up the stairs and out of sight. I rubbed the back of my neck and found it damp.

The girl was looking after him with a grim smile. 'I'd like,' she said softly, 'to meet him after 7 pm sober – just once.'

'Are you sure?' I asked.

'I don't know,' she said carefully. Then she smiled. 'But at least I'd find out.'

I nodded as sympathetically as I could with a head that was getting heavy for its hinges, and started up the stairs. I had to pick my way carefully. 'Who was the Prussian Guard?' I asked.

She nodded. 'That's it, all right. That was Herr Herter, the Nawab's private secretary.'

I banked around a corner. 'I'd hate to see his private manner.'

'I suppose you can't blame him too much. I wouldn't like to see my boss's pilot pickled every night.'

We reached the lobby. 'I'm not blaming him, only his manner. How did he get it through Beirut without waking up with a knife in his back?'

That was just stalling. I could see the next line of conversation coming from a long way off. I started to get out my cigarettes.

'What do you think it is with Ken?' she asked me.

I offered a cigarette and she shook her head. I lit my own, carefully and slowly, and blew smoke over her head.

'I never did like this scene,' I said. 'The girl asking the man's best pal what should they do to save him from himself, but really meaning what should they do to save him for her? And enlisting the pal's aid.'

I had her full attention. I ploughed on.

'I first met Ken about fifteen years ago. I wouldn't have told him to lay off drink then, and I'm not going to start now. If he wants to see if he can make whisky come out of his ears, that's his business, not mine. It may be yours – if you can make it yours – but your business ain't my business, neither.'

'Receiving you loud and clear,' she said grimly. 'War-time buddies. Phooey.'

I shrugged and breathed more smoke.

'But there's something there,' she persisted. 'He told me he couldn't go back to England. Would you know about that?'

Suddenly I felt a lot sober.

'That was just talk,' I said. 'He must have been tight, then.'

'Sure he was tight. But he never starts talking wild, no matter how tight he is.'

'He can go back to England,' I said. 'Any time he pays his fare.'

She gave me a long, careful look.

'War-time buddies,' she said again. 'Goodnight, Captain.'

I watched her turn the corner. Then I leant against the wall and chewed on my cigarette.

Mr Herter, that man of a thousand graces, came up from the bar, gave me a sharp look and marched up into the hotel. I leant on.

There was a lot more in that girl's head than just how to click a camera. If it came to that, there was a lot more to that girl than just a head. I gazed up the empty lobby, then dropped the cigarette butt in a big relief brass tub and went out into the cool air.

I took my time walking back to our hotel and stopped halfway down Stadio Street for coffee at a pavement café. I didn't much want it, but I'd be glad I'd done it in the morning. Ken was in much better training with the bottle than I was.

When I got back to the hotel the proprietor was sitting on the front steps getting the word from an Omonia Square Venus in a tight, black frock. He jerked his thumb at the doorway and said: 'Your friend —' She lifted an eyebrow at me to show she was still on duty if I was interested. I thanked them both and went on in.

There was still a lot of light on upstairs. Part of an Omonia Square hotel never sleeps. Part of it is the men who lie half-dressed on their beds staring at the cigarette smoke on the ceiling with empty eyes. There are two or three of them in every cheap hotel in every city in the world. They are always there and you never ask why because you know the answer already. They are there because there is nowhere else for them to be.

There was no light under Rogers's door. I shut my own door, opened the window and lay down on the bed. The window let in muted shuffling sounds from the street outside and reflections moved gently across the ceiling. I lit a cigarette and watched them move.

After a time I got off the bed and undressed and lay down and lit another cigarette. And when I looked at the ceiling again, it was still there.

A Dakota. I saw it sitting in a rusty hangar on rotted tyres, or at the bottom of a green bay, half-covered with sand, or lonely and stark in the middle of a desert. But wherever I saw it, I knew what was in it. Two ammunition boxes. And in the boxes, loot. Diamonds and sapphires and emeralds and rubies and pearls. All set in fussy gold mountings. But the hell with the gold. Break it up and chuck it away and take the stones down to a little man I happened to know in Tel Aviv. And then make mine another Americano and tell the chef I'll come in and tear his ears off if he doesn't put enough tarragon in the Sauce Bearnaise.

I jerked off the bed and walked to the window and stared down at the street, sucking in the cool air. I felt sticky and I felt angry. There are plenty of different ways to spend a night in a cheap hotel and the worst is to stare at the ceiling and dream.

The men who lie and watch the ceiling with empty eyes are dreaming the same dreams. Add together the dreams of an Omonia Square hotel and you can make a take-over bid for Standard Oil. Nobody ever thinks of anything but being rich. You don't need to: in a cheap hotel there are always women and drink that are just as cheap, but there is only one price for becoming a millionaire.

I pitched the cigarette butt down into the street and watched the sparks burst from it, bright as rubies.

4

I FELT BAD in the morning, but no worse than I should have felt. I shaved in cold water, put on my second-best uniform and staggered down to meet Rogers in a café down the road. We ordered yoghurt, bread with butter and jam, and coffee. Oceans of coffee.

He let me get through two cups quietly, then asked:

'What happened to your pal Kitson last night?'

'Went to bed.'

'God, that was a story he was telling.' He chuckled into his cup. 'Does he always get that way when he gets stinking?'

'Ken's all right,' I said.

He stared at me. 'You didn't believe it, did you?'

'You've never done any flying out in India. Ken and I have.'

'I never bought a guaranteed-solid-gold watch at an Oxford Street auction, either.'

I should have shrugged and left it at that. But I didn't.

'It isn't the strangest damn story I've heard from Partition time,' I said. 'And some of them I know were true.'

'Yes,' he said, 'but two box-fulls of jewellery. Over a million quid. I've heard about the "fabulous riches of the East", but my God —'

'Peanuts,' I said. 'Two box-loads. They have it by the roomful out there.'

He was staring at me.

'Between the wars,' I said, 'some of those Princes invited out some Bond Street jewellers to look over their gems and give them a valuation. I once met one of the men who'd gone out there. He'd been in the trade twenty years and he said he just didn't know how to value that stuff; he'd never seen anything like it before – he hadn't got any standards. Remember, these Princes weren't a bunch of oil-well Arabs with a garage full of Cadillacs and a kitchen full of chorus girls. They've been mining gems and gold out there for over three thousand years. It mounts up.'

He was giving me a wary, watchful eye.

I said: 'So what d'you do with it when you've got it? What can you spend it on? These boys had everything already. They've been civilized a long time out there – maybe a bit longer than Greece. They had a poet as good as Homer about the same time as Homer.'

'They also had a few wars and riots and things,' he said.

'Certainly they did. They were highly civilized. They went out and chopped each other up every twenty years. But so what? War doesn't hurt a diamond. It may just shift it around a bit. It's still there, somewhere, at the end.'

I waved for more coffee and lit a cigarette.

'Jewellery is a wonderful way to be rich,' I said. 'We don't appreciate it in the West. We prefer land and limited companies

27

and capital assets. These boys had all there was of that just by being princes. Then they got started on the jewellery. You ever thought about jewellery?'

I let him think about jewellery while the coffee came. The waiter took my money, counted it and sneered at the tin wings on my chest. Pilots are supposed to be rich men.

'Diamonds,' I said. 'Marvellous things. They're about the most stable form of wealth there is. They don't get broken or burnt down. They don't get devalued. They don't go bust when the stock market falls off a skyscraper. And you can't argue title deeds about them. Just stick a handful in your pocket and you're a rich man. It's that easy.'

'Until somebody knocks you on the head,' he said thoughtfully, 'and empties your pocket.'

'Right. And that's what they were afraid of at Partition. You got some odd set-ups before Partition: Muslim states with Hindu rulers, Hindu states with Muslim rulers. The Nawab was one of them. When Partition came it was time for them to depart – with the loot. Not all of them did. A few of the smaller ones got their throats cut and the jewellery went into the bazaars. But the big boys were able to take care of themselves – for long enough to get out, anyway.'

I took a gulp of coffee and wondered how the hell I had got to be giving history lessons in an Athens café at half past eight in the morning.

'That's where you got the aircrew coming in,' I said. 'There were plenty of ex-RAF crews knocking around India after the war, looking for any flying job they could get. Ken and me, for two. Around Partition time, both sides started airlifts, bringing refugees from India to Pakistan and vice versa. And both governments were very anxious for their own particular Princes to hang on to their jewels – to stop the other side getting it.

'On the quiet, the British government backed them up on this. If even a small part of the stuff had come on the open market it would have knocked hell out of the South African diamond market. So the airlifts switched to bringing Princes and jewels out, sometimes flying guns in. And they brought it out by the plane-load. Daks, Lancastrians, four or five thousand pounds *weight* of it at a time: pearls, diamonds, gold plate, the lot. Then back for more.'

He was staring at me.

'Were *you* carrying any of this?'

I shook my head. 'It was a pretty specialized job. I was carrying mostly ordinary refugees. But I knew some of the boys who carried jewels, and *they* knew what they were carrying – at five hundred quid a round trip.'

'There should be some rich aircrew knocking around by now.'

'They weren't the sort of boys to hang on to it. Anyhow, it was only fair pay for the job. They were flying some pretty beat-up old crates, no proper servicing, home-made airstrips – and the other side taking pot-shots at them along the route. They didn't want to die rich. They drank it up.'

He reached slowly for his coffee.

'All right,' he said. 'So, grant it was there, and grant they moved it – what then? What happened to it?'

'Nothing. It's still there. It still belongs to the Princes. If the mobs had caught them with it, then it would have gone on the market. But once they'd got out with it, their own governments couldn't touch it. That's the beautiful thing about a diamond. You can't nationalize it. The only thing you can do is bash the man on the head and take it. And your own government can't do that. So it's still locked up in the back room.'

'Except,' he said slowly, 'for two boxes.'

'Yes,' I said, 'except for them.'

He thought for a while. Then he said:

'It's just a little difficult to believe that, if they had that much wealth, they couldn't afford to have somebody watch where it went.'

'True.'

He looked up at me. 'So it's still an unlikely tale.'

'True,' I said again. 'All I'm saying is, it could have happened. The context is right. The story itself may be pure baloney.'

He nodded. He seemed happier with that thought. It was more his size.

I finished my coffee. 'You'd better go and see if there's any cables,' I said. 'I'll see you at the airport.'

5

I DIDN'T FEEL strong enough to get involved in the Athenian telephone system again, and Mikklos's office was only a few hundred yards away, so I walked down to see if he had a clean cargo lying around somewhere.

He had two rooms above a bicycle shop on the main road to the Museum. You walked up a narrow, dark flight of stone stairs, turned right, bashed on the big, wooden door and waited for his secretary to shout something that you interpreted as 'come in'.

This time she didn't shout it. I waited a moment, then tried the door handle. It opened, and in I went.

The room had the same dusty smell it had when I was last in there, about four months before. Nobody seemed to have touched the row of box files, bundles of paper and ledgers that lay stacked along the wall to my right. Nobody had even dusted them.

The big, dark desk in the middle of the room had everything on top of it and nobody behind it. I reached for the handle of the inner door.

It opened before I got to it. Mikklos peered out. For a moment he stood there, looking at me anxiously, then he started to grin.

'Captain! I am delighted to see you. Please come in.'

He turned quickly away and was back behind his own desk before I was properly in the room. As I turned to shut the door I heard a drawer open and close quickly.

'Sit down, sit down.' He waved an arm at a worn, leather-seated office chair and sat down himself.

I pulled up the chair, stuck my cap on the corner of his desk and sat.

'I am sorry,' he said, flapping a hand towards the door. 'Maria has gone on a little errand. Now – what can I do for you? Your aeroplane is all right again?'

'Not quite. But I'll have it fixed by lunchtime. You got my message last night?'

'Yes. You have changed your mind perhaps about the cargo?'

'I'm sorry, Mikky.' I shook my head.

'I can assure you there will be no trouble. Perfectly all right.

I would not give it to everybody, only to a man I know and can trust.'

'That I'll bet. I'm still not touching it. Have you got anything else on the books?'

'Nothing, nothing,' he waved his hand across the foam of papers spilling off his desk. 'Goats, cows, tomatoes, agricultural machinery, machine parts – nothing to go by air. Everybody in Greece is too poor. What does Mr Hauser say?'

'About your cargo?'

He nodded.

'I don't know yet,' I said. 'But it doesn't make any difference to me.' I stood up again. 'So there's nothing else?'

'Nothing.' He looked up at me very seriously. 'He won't be disappointed in you?'

'Hauser? He's always disappointed to watch a dollar go past. But he might be even more disappointed to see me in jail somewhere; it would reflect on his reputation.'

He nodded sadly. 'I am sorry I cannot do anything for you, Captain.' Then he reached down to a drawer on the left and hiked up the office bottle of *ouzo*. He poured small shots into two glasses, added water from a jug on a shelf behind him and passed a glass over to me.

'Cheerio, Captain.'

I raised the glass and sipped. I don't like anisette drinks much, but he'd been cheap with the portion and there was plenty of water with it. I put the rest away in one swallow and walked around the end of the desk to put the glass back near the bottle. Then I jerked open the top right-hand drawer of the desk. A 7·65 mm. Beretta automatic lay there on top of a sheaf of papers.

I closed the drawer again. He must have had the gun in his hand, behind his back, when he came to see who was visiting him.

'You should clean up your business,' I said. 'It's easier on the nerves.'

He watched me go out with sadness, or worry, or perhaps just disappointment in his eyes.

The secretary was back in the outer office. She was new to me. Mikklos liked to change secretaries every few months – or perhaps the secretaries liked to change Mikklos. It was possible to be narrow-minded about his theories of office relationships.

This one was small, dark and with a cottage-loaf figure, and

31

black hair as curly as a poodle's. She seemed startled to see me. She watched me go past with wide, dark eyes, one brown hand frozen in the movement of yanking a paper from the old steam organ of a typewriter.

The agency Mikklos was all nerves this morning. Perhaps it had had a bad night. I grinned cheerfully and passed on my way.

6

ROGERS WAS still wandering around looking for an Athenian souvenir for his tubby Swiss girl friend when I got to the airport. I stripped down in the plane and put on overalls, then dug out a jar and bled fuel from the starboard tank. When it settled, the bottom of the jar showed an eighth of an inch of good Turkish water. I climbed up on the starboard engine, took off the inboard shoulder cowling and started to work on the carburettor filters.

At half past ten Rogers rolled up with his souvenir; a bright, black, white and red goat's-wool bag that would do her as either a shopping bag or half a brassière. He also had a cable from Hauser. It asked me if I was sure I had done right by refusing the cargo and told me that, failing the finding of another one, I should be back in Berne by nightfall the next day.

There didn't seem to be any answer to that, so I saved his money and didn't send one. I told Rogers to get into overalls and join in the coolie work. He didn't want to, but he didn't argue. I was just about to climb back into the engine when Ken came around the corner of the hangar.

He was wearing a different rig this morning, but it was all in the same income bracket. He had on a heavy, white silk shirt, open at the neck, and over it a suède jacket, half zipped up. Below that was a pair of light cavalry twill trousers and suède chukka boots.

The suède jacket looked a bit much for the day, which was coming to the boil, but that was his business. There was no sign in his face of the evening before. He looked clean, undissipated and very serious.

'When are you taking off, boy?' he asked.

'I don't know,' I said, wondering what the hell.

He glanced up at the starboard engine.

'Can we fix it in half an hour?' he asked.

'Well – why?' I asked. 'What is this?'

'I want to come with you.'

'Well, hold on a minute —'

'Can we fix it?'

'Hold on,' I said again. 'I'm not going anywhere. I've got nowhere to go.'

He seemed surprised.

'I thought you'd got a cargo. Africa or somewhere.'

Had I told him about Mikklos's cargo? I didn't think I had. And I would have told him I'd turned it down.

'I had a cargo,' I said slowly. 'I turned it down. It was one of those cargoes you turn down. Now what is all this?'

He was chewing on his lip and not looking at anything in particular. He was beginning to look too hot for that jacket.

'I've got to get out of Athens,' he said.

'Well, there's a hundred ways out of Athens.' I forced a jolly smile on to my face. 'You can get out any time you like. Cheer up, man.' I gave him a hearty clap in the ribs. And felt the gun stuck in his waistband, under the jacket.

'Get in the plane,' I said. 'We can talk out of sight.'

He stared at me tensely for a moment, then wheeled around and went to the door of the Dak.

Rogers was struggling into his overalls.

'Tony,' I said, 'nip over to the hangars and see if you can borrow a big tin with the lid cut off, or pan or something. I want to wash the filter in petrol when I've got it loose.'

He stared, too, then grunted and went on struggling. I took out a packet of cigarettes and passed one to Ken. We breathed smoke and waited for Rogers to go. Finally he had the overalls on. He gave us a last, uncertain look, then dropped out of the door and walked off.

'Okay,' I said. 'Now give.'

'I talked too much,' he said. 'Last night. The Nawab thinks I've bitched up the whole works. He wanted Herter to give me a working over. I'm not standing still for that – so I want to get out.'

'There's still a hundred ways out,' I said, watching his face

33

in the dimness inside the plane. 'You can get boats, planes, trains even. This time of the year you'll get on a plane at any time.'

'Yes, yes.' He was getting through his cigarette fast.

'You can hire this plane, if you like,' I said. 'Just as soon as we get the fuel cleaned up. That shouldn't take us too long. Then we can change where we're going when we're in the air – that should throw them off the trace for a while, if that's what you're worried about.'

'Yes, yes,' he said again. He pitched his cigarette through the doorway on to the concrete. 'Thanks, Jack. I think I can manage. Thanks, anyway. I'll be seeing you around.'

He dropped lightly through the door and went off towards the hangars in long strides. I watched him through a window until he went out of sight. Then I sat back in one of the double seats and breathed smoke at the roof.

It was thick and musty but still cool inside the Dak. The sun hadn't been on it long enough to get the interior boiling yet, and there was no wind from the door. The cigarette smoke hung in shreds from the roof among the smells in the dimness. The smells of past cargoes and past passengers; of oil and petrol, leather and metal, and beneath them all a smell that is the particular Dakota smell, sharp and unmistakable. And familiar – familiar long after you have forgotten the smell and even the look of a dozen different women.

It was one of those moments for recognizing familiar things and remembering things you know so well as to have forgotten you knew them. I breathed smoke gently and thought.

Mikklos with a gun in his top drawer was one thing, a part of the complicated game of crookery that he played across his crowded desk. The gun was a good-luck symbol, a twentieth-century charm. Ken with a gun was something else, something very different. But I wasn't at all sure what.

I finished the cigarette, climbed out and ground it into the concrete. Rogers was walking back with the sawn-off bottom half of an oil drum. He dumped it in the shade and asked:

'What was Kitson after?'

'Saying goodbye. He's pushing off.' I climbed back up the step-ladder and started excavating for the carb filter.

I got it off and dropped it down for Rogers to wash out. Then

34

I pumped fuel out through the feed until all the water had gone. I'd just about decided it was all good, clean stuff left by now when Rogers said:

'There they go.'

I looked up from under the wing. The little Piaggio was going past around the perimeter track at a tearaway pace, throwing up dust in three tracks from its wheels and then flinging it away with the prop wash.

I knew there was only Ken on board. He'd taken the fastest route out, but he'd also taken one that would ensure the Nawab's continued interest; His Ex might not follow up the matter of a missing pilot, but he'd certainly want to know where the hell that aircraft had got to.

I got up and walked round to the nose of the Dak to watch it take off.

The small plane pulled up behind an MEA Viscount waiting at the head of the runway. The Viscount turned on, ran along and rose into the clear, almost cloudless sky. Ken gave it about fifteen seconds from take-off and started himself.

The little Lycomings raged, then whipped the plane forward as the brakes came off. He was off the ground in under two hundred yards, engines still belting, and into a steep, climbing turn to the right, against the circuit pattern.

'Christ!' Rogers said.

The Piaggio held its turn, passing over the control tower and airport buildings, gaining altitude slowly. It kept going through three-quarters of a circle and then straightened out, heading back across the hangars and the runway at about five hundred feet. It passed almost directly overhead, and I could read the big, green registration letters on the silver wings.

One of the engines seemed to falter. Then it banged loudly, gave a couple of pops, blew smoke, and died. The plane heeled violently into the dead engine, straightened, sagged, then started on a much more gentle climb out over the sea. The dead propeller spun visibly, and stopped.

'Christ!' Rogers said again.

I ran round to the door, jumped in and stumbled up the slope into the cockpit. I snapped on the master switch and then the radio, and dragged my headphones out of the locker while it warmed up.

Out of the side window I could see the Piaggio still limping away over the sea. The radio came alive with a hum and crackle. A voice speaking English with an accent was calling urgently to it.

There was no answer.

Out of the window I could see the Piaggio still. It seemed to be holding its height just under one thousand.

The voice went on calling, asking what had happened, asking if the Piaggio could hear. There was still no answer. The voice tried in French, then another voice in German. Then it stopped. I found it again, in English, on another channel. There was still no answer.

I watched the Piaggio dwindle out of sight across the sea. Then I switched off the radio and the master switch, put the headphones back in the locker and climbed out again. Rogers was still looking at the horizon.

'What the hell happened?' he asked. 'Did he say anything?'

'Nothing I heard,' I said. 'Let's get this filter back on.'

Twenty minutes later two Greek Air Force Thunderjets streaked past low to the west, heading out to sea.

'Search,' said Rogers, half to himself. He watched them out of sight. 'I suppose the Nawab must have ordered him to keep going,' he said slowly. 'You wouldn't have thought that —'

'The Nawab wasn't on board,' I said. 'It was just Ken.'

'Then why did he just keep on going? After he'd lost an engine?'

'I don't know. But in case anybody asks, he wasn't across here first. Got that?'

He looked at me curiously.

'Look,' I said. 'He's had some sort of blow-up with the Nawab. What he's trying to do I don't know, and I don't want to know, and I don't want to get involved. So he never came here. Okay?'

'All right.' He shook his head in a puzzled way.

I got the filter back on and the cowlings screwed back in place and decided to wait getting her refuelled until we were ready to leave. We changed and went across to the control tower about noon.

I asked there about the Piaggio: no news. The Thunderjets hadn't spotted anything. They'd asked one or two planes to keep their eyes open and had passed a message to RAF Coastal Command in Malta.

I went down to the bar.

I was on my second beer when Miss Shirley Burt came in. She must have been looking for me; she came straight across, looking worried.

'Do you know what happened with Ken?' she asked me.

'No more than I could see,' I said. She seemed to want to know what that was. 'He took off and one engine went dead on him. He kept going, out to sea, and not answering the radio. They've got some sort of search going on now; they'll step it up if they haven't heard anything in a few hours.'

'A few hours!'

'They've got nothing definite to worry about yet. Any twin-engined plane can fly on one engine for as long as the fuel holds out; I wouldn't know how long that'd be with that particular plane. But of course it's got no safety margin left, and not many people would choose to fly over the sea like that. And they were worried that he didn't answer the radio.'

It was textbook stuff and I gave it her in a straight, textbook voice.

'Where else could he land?'

'South of here, there isn't much before Crete. All the islands are pretty rocky and you don't get much in the way of long beaches in the Aegean.'

She chewed on her lip. It was none of my business, but she looked good today. She had on a light cream dress, another shirtwaister, with a tan leather belt and tan shoes. She ran her hand quickly through her hair in a mannish gesture, and looked up at me, blinking fast.

The bastard might at least have told her goodbye. But that was none of my business, either.

'Have a drink,' I suggested.

She didn't want to, but there was nothing else to do. Sitting around growing cold inside is part of falling for a pilot. She took an iced beer and a cigarette.

Herter came into the bar and headed straight for us. I put my drink on the counter to leave my hands free, just in case. He stopped in front of me.

'Captain Clay?'

I nodded.

'My name is Herter, private secretary to His Excellency the Nawab of Tungabhadra.'

'In Fort Munro,' I said nastily. If he wanted to start anything

37

I was willing to help get it going. There was a sour taste at the back of my mouth that hadn't come from anything I'd eaten or drunk, and taking a swing at this big thug might help wash it away.

He gave me a small frown and went on.

'Have you seen Mr Kitson this morning?'

I shook my head. 'I saw him take off. Just over an hour ago.'

'His Excellency is very worried about him. It seems he had an engine failure, but did not turn back.'

Luckily I didn't think of a crack there.

'I believe you have an aeroplane for hire?' Herter went on.

I sat back on my stool.

'Yes, I've got an aeroplane,' I said slowly.

'Is it ready to take off?'

'It needs some refuelling first.'

'Will that take long?'

'No. Say half an hour.'

'His Excellency wishes you to fly him out to search for Mr Kitson. Can you be ready in half an hour?'

'If I can hire some help,' I said.

'Do what is necessary. His Excellency will be here in half an hour.'

He turned to go.

'You didn't ask about the price,' I said.

He turned back and looked at me as if I'd sneezed in the ranks.

'His Excellency does not ask about prices,' he said, and went out.

I looked at Rogers, then the girl, then at Rogers again.

'Well,' I said, 'we're flying.'

'Can I come too?' the girl asked.

'On my say-so, yes,' I said. 'I don't know what the Nawab will say, but I'll see what I can do. Get something to eat now. And get us some sandwiches or something. We'll be at the Dakota at the end hangar.'

I finished the last of my beer, then went off to wave the Nawab's name in front of the airport management.

Half an hour later the three of us were waiting by the Dak. His Excellency's name had had all the effect I could want: the plane had had snappier attention than she'd seen in her life. The tanks were filled up again, the windscreen was clean and

38

the tyres were at their correct pressure for once. If the old tub had developed star temperament and blown a hydraulic line I wouldn't have been surprised, but everything I could test seemed to be working, and even the weather report was good.

I shouldn't have been thinking of it that way, but this afternoon we were going to put ourselves back in the profit columns of Hauser's good books.

A big, black Mercedes 300 saloon flowed around the corner of the hangar and stopped at the Dakota's wingtip. I could see Herter behind the wheel and a small, darkish man in the back seat and somebody I couldn't make out sitting next to him.

Where they found that car in Greece, I don't know; the Greek roads didn't deserve it. Or perhaps I just had my scale of values wrong. Probably on a decent road he wouldn't have ridden in less than a hand-stitched Hooper Rolls-Royce.

Herter sprang out, marched around to the far door and let out the third passenger. I took a deep breath and held it.

She was the loveliest thing I've ever seen, and I've spent a long time looking. She was tall, about five eight, with long, dark hair down to her shoulders. She wore a completely plain white dress with an open neck, straight skirt and delicate white shoes. Her figure did the rest. I couldn't imagine it doing more.

Her skin was a warm, honey colour, and that, with the high cheekbones and big, dark eyes, gave me the idea she might be Eurasian. The easy grace as she came around the bows of the Mercedes gave me a lot of other ideas that I won't detail.

The Nawab hurried after her; Herter went round to the boot of the Merc and started dragging out clothes and rugs and hampers.

'You handle the flying this trip,' I said to Rogers out of the side of my mouth. 'I'll tend to the passengers.'

Behind my elbow, Shirley Burt muttered: 'All you need is fifty million bucks.'

'Who wants money?'

'She does.'

The Greek ground crew were gathering like flies. Herter detailed one and handed him the keys of the car. The lad climbed in and slid away in a happy haze.

Herter strode up. I hit Rogers with my elbow and he staggered forward and took the armload of stuff from the German. Herter nodded and started on the introductions.

'Your Excellency, may I present Captain Clay, our pilot.'

The Nawab nodded and smiled faintly at me. He was a short, dark character, about thirty-five, with a long, narrow face and a slight stoop. His lank hair came down to a sharp vee on his forehead, and there were touches of gold at the edges of his smile. He wore a white, short-sleeved cotton shirt with a pair of sunglasses sticking from the breast pocket, fawn slacks and a battered pair of sandals. Millionaire dress.

Herter turned to the girl.

'Miss Brown, may I present Captain Clay, the pilot.'

I nearly shouted with laughter at her name. The classical Indian poets would have split an intestine finding names to describe her, and she had to be Miss Brown. I turned on a sickly grin and grabbed for her hand. It was long and cool and firm.

She smiled at me. My toes started to curl up.

And all the time I had my uniform cap on and should have been handing out snappy salutes all round.

Herter was helping the Nawab on board, up the wooden steps somebody had rustled up for us. Nobody had noticed, or cared to notice, Miss Burt.

'Your Excellency,' I said, reeling off my first salute of the day, 'I wonder if I might make a request of you. Miss Burt is very anxious about Mr Kitson. Would you permit her to come on the flight?'

The little man paused on the steps and looked down at us. His face was completely blank.

Miss Brown took the initiative. 'Let her come, Aly. As long as she doesn't bring her cameras.'

The Nawab nodded briefly and went on board. Miss Brown followed, then Herter.

'You heard the lady,' I said to Shirley. 'Get on board.'

Her lips were set in a hard line and her eyes were sizzling. She wanted to come, but she hated to come as Miss Brown's guest. She turned and sizzled at me for a moment; but I had been smiled on, I was fireproof. I grinned back and she stumped up the steps into the plane.

I looked at Rogers over his armful of luggage.

'What are you staring at?' I asked.

'You,' he said. 'I thought you were going to lie down on the steps and let her walk over you.'

'Get on board,' I said. 'I'm waiting until we're outside the three-mile limit, where the Captain's word is law.'

He staggered up the steps. I shoved them aside, jumped in, slammed and locked the door and started up towards the cockpit. The Nawab and Miss Brown were seated amidships, Herter just behind them, and Shirley Burt right up in the front row of seats before the bulkhead.

'Fasten the seat belts, please,' I said. 'We'll be taking off in about five minutes.'

Herter looked round at me. 'His Excellency will want to sit in the front with you, Captain.'

'Once we've taken off,' I promised. I held myself back from helping Miss Brown with her seat belt, and went forward. Shirley was looking out of one of the windows, her seat belt fastened.

'Okay?' I asked.

'Yes.' She didn't turn her head. I went into the cockpit and banged the door behind me. Rogers started to read off the check list before I was firmly in my seat.

7

I CLEARED THE airport circuit, levelled off at one thousand and set the throttles, trimmers and mixture where I wanted them. Already I saw what I guessed was Kea, the first of the Cyclades, blending on the horizon with the end of the peninsula. And beyond it, stretching eighty miles southwards in a gentle, sickle curve, were the rest of the western Cyclades; five more main islands and as many isolated lumps of rock and goat pastures as you cared to count.

The air was clear, gemstone clear as you get it only in the spring and autumn when there's no heat haze and the *hausfrau* tourists aren't stirring up the dust with their size-nines.

I opened the side window and leant back in the cold blast for a few moments. I felt better. The taste in my mouth was gone.

'Go tell the Nawab he can have your seat,' I told Rogers. 'You can hold Miss Brown's hand if she feels lonely. If she wants anything else holding, send for me.'

He gave me a long-suffering look, but he wasn't too sorry to get the chance to lean across Miss Brown and point out the view. Miss Matterhorn was a long way away.

The Nawab came forward and dumped himself in the right-hand seat. He seemed at home in an aircraft. I shut the window on my side.

He put on his sunglasses and stared out at the sea. I dragged up a tattered map, folded it to show the Aegean ahead and passed it to him.

He nodded politely and studied it a while. Then he asked: 'What direction did Mr Kitson go?' His voice was nicely pitched, more Oxford than Fort Munro.

'Just east of south.' I took out a Biro and scratched a line leading at about 160 degrees from Athens. It filled in the bow-string across the curve of the islands, ending on the last one, Saxos.

He studied the map a while longer.

'We will look at each island,' he decided.

'Wilco.' I eased on the control wheel and swung left for Kea.

Looking at each island wasn't as easy as it sounded. It meant approaching at no more than a thousand feet to get a good look at the shoreline and all the inlets, then climbing to have a look at the valleys inland. None of the islands was more than a few miles wide in any direction, but almost all of them had peaks at over 1,500 feet.

The Piaggio should have shown up as sharply as a gold tooth, but aircraft that try emergency landings in rocky country don't always look like aircraft when they've finished. Sometimes you can pick up the largest piece with just two hands; sometimes they burn down to a black smudge.

In either case, that goes for the pilot, too.

We drew a blank on Kea. Kythnos, too; then Serifos.

After that we cruised around for twenty minutes at three thousand while the Nawab and party got their heads down in the lunch baskets. I let Rogers take the controls while I went back to my second dose of Miss Brown and to see what Shirley Burt had brought for my lunch.

Miss Brown was pure nectar; the lunch was bread, a good sharp cheese and green figs. I sat down beside Shirley and jammed my feet up against the bulkhead. She looked at me anxiously; the time was running out on her. She'd spent too long seeing not much out of a small window but seeing enough to know that I'd been right about there being no landing places on the islands.

'Was there any news on the radio?' she asked.

'I checked a few minutes ago. Nothing then.'

'Will he – have landed by now?'

It was half past two. Ken had been airborne – if he was still airborne – three and a half hours. He would still have a good fuel margin left. I told her so.

She nodded and I stuffed bread and cheese into my face. After a while she said:

'Where are we going next?'

'That's up to the Nawab. We've looked at about half the islands down this side. After he's seen the rest, he may want to try the ones farther east, or jump on to Crete. It's his ride.'

'You don't sound too worried,' she said tartly.

I didn't, either. Maybe I should have been; but it was difficult to worry about Ken's flying. But I'd been unworried about others, before, and been wrong.

Still, I could be sure of one thing: that if Ken had got into a situation where only a handful of pilots could have got themselves out again – he was out. I passed that thought on to Shirley.

'That bastard is one of the world's top pilots,' I added.

She looked at me curiously. 'One of the pilots at the airport said that, too. Just from seeing Ken fly around and land.'

'That's all you need to see with what he's got. I first met him at Advanced Flying Training School, back in 1943, when we were learning to fly Oxfords. The main runway had a big slope on, and when you were landing one way it was going downhill damn near as steep as you were. Instructors used to come out of the huts to watch him land. Instructors, that was, the people who were supposed to be teaching us.'

'That sounds like the old story you hear about every musician. His first music teacher tells him: "Go home, my boy, and tell your father I can teach you nozzink. I can only learn from you."'

'I suppose it does.' I smiled wryly. 'Life's just one damn cliché after another.'

'How d'you like the one down the back? The stubby, little rich guy and the big, beautiful friend?'

'Don't remind me. That cheese has stimulated my vitamins.'

'You need more than vitamins, chum. I told you: fifty million bucks.'

'You did mention it. I'm working on it. You wait till you see the bill I give His Excellency for this trip.'

She smiled and ate a fig.

'Just who is she?' I asked, sort of casually.

'Private secretary.'

'I thought that was Herter.'

'They don't clash. Most of her work is stuff that Herter couldn't possibly handle.' She gave me a completely innocent smile.

I nodded. 'I knew Ken's job must have had something more than just that Piaggio in it.'

It was a damn silly thing to say; it brought us back to topic A with a jolt. Her eyes glistened wetly and she turned her head quickly to the window.

I grabbed a handful of figs and went back to the cockpit.

The Dak seemed to be working perfectly. I tested this and that, opened the gills a fraction, then just sat and waited for the Nawab. We'd been airborne for two hours and we still had a good, safe six hours left in the tanks, plus a trouble margin.

The little man came forward about five minutes later, and Rogers went back for his share of the lunch. We gave Syphnos the once-over, then Milos, and had only Saxos left.

This one was slightly lower and flatter than the rest, as the sunken mountain chain eased off before sweeping down under the sea for the last time. The highest peak, on the north end, was just under one thousand feet, and cultivated in little rough, stone-faced terraces almost to its top. The eastern shore was high, broken ground, but the western side was mainly low cliffs and banks.

The shoreline was fairly well built up: there was a string of large – for the islands – two-storey, white and cream houses stretching along south from the quays and the huddle of square, white buildings and small boats that formed the main village. A road, a dusty, yellowish-grey scar, curled up the slope behind, then ran on for a mile and a half to a village in the centre.

In between the two the road ran straight, almost, across gentle undulating ground that nobody had started hacking up

44

into stone-walled fields the size of small rosebeds. An island farmer will wall off a field that we'd think too cramped to make a decent grave plot.

I beat in a hundred feet above the road, straight across the villages, bringing little brown children in white trousers or frocks spilling out of the houses and standing craning up at us. The inland village was white, pure white, with little square houses that seemed rough-cut from big plaster of Paris blocks, and the occasional finer-cut shape of a church, topped with a little blue dome.

The Nawab had been leaning forward in his seat, peering intently down. There was nothing particular to see, nothing we were looking for, but I knew he must be thinking what I was: that this road gave the only safe chance at a landing that we'd seen in the whole island chain.

I climbed up beyond the village as the ground rose, then let down over the sea on the far side and started to investigate the shoreline.

As I came round the southern point I found that what I'd at first taken to be a little village on the extreme tip was, in fact, a small island, standing south-west, nearly a mile off shore.

I turned around it. It was about half a mile wide and slightly less long, just one small hump at the north-east end and a larger hump holding up the village at the south-west. Between them, opening north-west, was a triangular valley, starting with a sandy beach and trailing off quickly into rough grass and, in the final angle of the vee, a grove of cypresses.

I swung back and finished my tour of Saxos, then climbed to go inland for a look at the valleys on the high ground. Nothing.

I looked at the Nawab. He was frowning carefully at the tattered map.

'There is nothing more, south of here?' he asked finally.

'Only Crete,' I said. 'About eighty miles on.'

'You are sure?'

Sure I was sure. 'What does the map say?' I asked politely.

He went back to frowning at it. We were climbing gently all the while. I pushed on more power and we went up more steeply. He looked up and stared ahead as the horizon rolled back.

At 3,500 feet we were six or seven miles south of Saxos and could see for another forty miles and more ahead. There was nothing to see. I circled showing him, to the east and north, Olos and Antiparos and the silhouette of Paros beyond it. Close behind us, Saxos looked small and impudent on the hard, grey-blue of the sea.

I looked at the Nawab. He was staring moodily out, watching the islands wheel past. I reversed the turn, putting the left wing down to give myself a view, and circled again. Then, looking down inside the turn, I saw it.

A something, a smudge, a stain, a darker grey, a thumbprint on the hard, glossy surface 3,500 feet below.

It would be a bank of floating seaweed. I took off power and kept in the turn, starting to spiral down. The Nawab leant across and peered out of my side. We went on down.

At 2,000 feet it could still have been seaweed; I had seen seaweed before. But I had also seen oil before. It had the dull sheen that this had. I began to get that sour feeling at the back of my tongue.

At 600 feet I started to ease on power again, and held my height at 400, still circling. By then I knew it was oil; not a streak, but a defined patch. In the middle of it two or three small, solid shapes stuck from the dull surface where the waves could not break.

I rammed on full power, plunged and then pulled the Dak up on one wing-tip, a hundred and fifty feet above the sea.

One of the small, oil-stained somethings had the shape and yellowish colour of a lifejacket. Empty. Another might, in the glimpse I got, have been a wheel.

I straightened and climbed and told the Nawab what I thought I'd seen.

'We must land at that island,' he said.

I looked at him. 'If we can,' I said.

We beat back to Saxos in wide zigzags, covering all the sea between the oil patch and the island. Nothing.

The Saxos road was narrow, but it had no ditches. I flew slowly along parallel to it, out to the right, studying the surface and estimating the run I would have. I made it about a third of a mile, almost dead straight, but lengthened in effect because I could come in low over the harbour and meet the road as it came up to meet me. The surface was what I'd expected: crumbled stone. I hoped they'd crumbled it thoroughly.

A good pilot could get down safely. Any pilot would get down alive.

I was a good pilot.

Before I made the final run I said:

'We may not get out before night. It's pretty hot right now and I need cold air to get the best out of the engines for take-off. I can't guarantee leaving before last light.'

He nodded. 'I understand.'

'Another thing: I'd better tell Athens, or they'll start searching for us. Shall I say we think we've found the wreckage of the Piaggio?'

'No. We cannot be sure.'

'Okay.' I hadn't been keen myself: if Ken was waiting to be pulled out of the sea somewhere else, it wouldn't do him any good to call off the search now.

But I didn't think he was waiting to be pulled out of the sea.

I couldn't raise Elliniko at that height and distance, but I hadn't really expected nor wanted to. They were going to start bitching whatever I told them. But I reached a BEA flight somewhere north and asked them to relay a message that I was putting down on a safe landing ground to clean out a carburettor. At second-hand, Elliniko found it difficult to argue, and I always had the reputation of Aircargo's planes to make it sound authentic.

When I had got that cleared up to my satisfaction at least, I asked the Nawab – very politely – to go back to his own seat and send me Rogers.

He objected. 'I can help. I have often flown my own aircraft.'

'My co-pilot's trained for the job,' I said. I didn't ask if Ken had ever let his employer land the Piaggio or merely ride around the big, open sky holding the pole.

He went back and Rogers came up.

8

WE CAME in about three knots above the stall and hit the ground like a wet sponge, which was how I wanted it. There were a few exciting moments keeping the Dak's wheels on a track built for an island bus, and I did some natty steering with the help of engines, rudder, brakes and the power of prayer, and we stopped. We had about a hundred yards of straight road to spare ahead, a quarter-mile cloud of white dust behind and the undivided attention of the entire population.

It takes a lot to excite a Greek islander, but we were a lot. And they didn't even know about Miss Brown yet. I taxied the Dak off, turned to face the road and shut down the engines.

'I hope we can get off again,' said Rogers, that tactful lad.

That would make it a lot easier telling him he was the one who stuck around and guarded the plane.

We had a crowd of kids and youths around the door by the time I got it open. I yelled:

'Anybody here speak English?'

They looked at me and each other.

'English,' I yelled. 'Inglese. British.' They got the idea and started running around, pointing this way and that, and finally produced a man of about thirty in a blue shirt. By that time we were all of us standing outside with everybody over the age of ten having lost interest in the plane as soon as they saw Miss Brown. It didn't seem to worry her.

The bird in the blue shirt shoved his way forward, regretfully decided she wasn't in command and addressed me.

'Welcome to Saxos,' he said briskly. 'I am Nissis Marinos, head of the Saxos Tourist Committee.' Later, I found he was also the whole committee. The rest of the time, he was the schoolmaster. I said who I was, then wondered if I should start introducing the Nawab.

Herter took the whole matter out of my hands. He shoved in, introduced himself, then started explaining what we were there for. Since he wasn't quite sure what I'd seen, nor where, he had to keep on referring to me, and the schoolmaster had to break off to clout a few young heads that had decided to dismantle the Dak for souvenirs.

It seemed Nissis himself hadn't seen anything. He lined the kids up and gave them the gist of Herter's story. Several of them had seen something. He interrogated them for a while, then turned back to Herter.

'About three hours ago an aeroplane came past, very low, going towards the south. It made funny noises.'

'What size of aeroplane?' I asked. He asked the kids. Nobody seemed too sure, except that it was smaller than the Dak.

But probably none of them had been this close to an aeroplane before; anything flying would have looked smaller.

'What colour was it?' I asked.

The general consensus was silver.

'Was it a different shape from this one?'

By now several of the other island males had joined in at the back. One of them, a stoutish character with a thick, white moustache, had definite views on this point. He stumped through the kids and up to the wing root of the Dak. He hit the wing a clout with his walnut fist, then reached and walloped the fuselage as high as he could go.

He explained this to me, but I got the point anyhow. The other plane had been high-winged. Several of the kids seconded this thought.

I shook the old boy's hand and said *'Efkaristo'*, several times, which just about emptied my Greek vocabulary beyond the drinks menu.

Herter went off to pass this information on to the Nawab, who was standing with Miss Brown well outside our little circle. I filled in the conversational lapse with grins all round and reached for a cigarette. I found Shirley Burt under my elbow.

'What does it look like?' she asked.

I lit my cigarette.

'It looks bad,' I said. That was how it did look. She went on staring at me.

I said: 'It seems Ken went past, about three hours ago, flying low and making what they called "funny noises". That could be an engine popping. I suppose you know we found an oil patch about seven miles south of here and I thought I saw a lifejacket floating in the middle of it.'

'If he did come down in the sea,' she said slowly, 'what chance would he have?'

I considered this very carefully. The little, bright-eyed children around were listening intently, not understanding a word, but duplicating my every expression. Now they looked very solemn.

'It wouldn't be as good with the Piaggio as with some aircraft,' I told her. 'When a plane comes down in the sea it floats for a while, but it's the fuel tanks in the wings that keep it up. That means the wings are on the water; with a high-wing job that puts the cockpit under the surface.'

She nodded slowly, then her face crumpled up.

'Why didn't he try and land here?' she wailed. 'The damned, damned fool.'

She turned around and leant on the doorway. The children looked at her with awe, then at me. I looked back; there wasn't any way to explain to them. I felt the louse of the century.

Herter came marching through the crowd.

'Captain. We are going by boat to see this patch of oil. Since you know about aeroplanes it would be good for you to come.' He made it clear that that was the only reason I was being invited. It wouldn't have broken my heart to stay on Saxos: a fourteen-mile ride in a five-knot Greek fishing boat across the open sea isn't my idea of a party.

'The aeroplane will be all right here?' he asked.

'I'll leave my co-pilot to guard it.'

We went over to get Nissis to organize a boat. As Herter was explaining, a little, stooped man with a big beak and wispy white hair arrived. Everybody made way for him. He wanted to know what was going on.

Nissis introduced him as the leading citizen of the island and we all shook hands. The old boy must have been about eighty, but under his wiry, white eyebrows he had a very young clear pair of blue eyes.

Nissis started explaining and Herter started breathing impatiently. Suddenly, the old boy flung out an arm southwards and asked something in what might have been an incredulous tone. Nissis laughed it off and went on explaining. When he had finished, I asked:

'What was he suggesting?'

Nissis grinned. He had a friendly, narrow face, with a smudge of a black moustache and sleeked-back, dark hair.

'He wanted to know if you had come to see the crashed aeroplane on Kira.' He grinned at my frown. 'That is the small island at the south. But the aeroplane crashed there a long time ago.'

'How long?'

He shrugged. 'Ten years. More, perhaps.'

I left it at that and let Herter get on with the orders of the day. Shirley was standing in the shade of the wing, dabbing powder on her face.

'We're going out in a boat to look at the oil,' I said. 'You could wander round the island if you liked. We'll be gone at least three hours.'

She shut her compact with a snap and dropped it into one of the big pockets on the front of her dress.

'I know it sounds stupid,' she said, 'but I've got to come.'

'It'll be cold, probably rough and dull. We may not find the oil and even if we do it may not tell us anything.'

'I'm coming.'

I nodded and went to tell Rogers that he was staying.

We got assembled and started off for the harbour, trailing a long train of children who wanted to stay close to me and older males who wanted to stick by Miss Brown. Aircargo had brought Saxos the double feature of its life.

Nissis sent a deputation ahead to get the boat laid on, and it was waiting when we got there: a twenty-five-foot caique, all undecked. It was painted white, with dark red trimmings and had that exaggerated concave boat-shape that all Mediterranean fishing boats have, making them into caricatures.

There was a stumpy mast forward, an oily old Ford motor aft and nowhere clean enough for fifty million dollars and his girl friend to sit down. Herter wanted it cleaned up, but the Nawab didn't want to waste the time. Herter put a few bits of old fish over the side with a stately disgust and then gave up. We piled aboard.

The Ford sounded old and tired enough to belong in an Aircargo Dak, but the old fisherman in charge whanged it knowledgeably and we chugged off. Five knots had been a good guess at the speed.

We cut across the smooth water of the harbour and hit the open sea with a thump. Miss Brown, whom I happened to be looking at, braced herself against the Nawab. Herter stuck his two hands flat on the gunwales on either side of himself and went on looking like the rock of ages in corsets.

We turned south – left – and headed down past Kira. I stared hard at it, wondering where it could be hiding the remains of a crashed aircraft.

Nissis noticed my interest.

'The aeroplane is in the trees there.' He pointed at the grove of cypresses at the head of the little valley. I still couldn't see anything.

The Nawab got interested.

'What aeroplane?'

Nissis explained.

'It didn't crash during the war?' the Nawab wanted to know.

'No. Ten years ago.'

I asked: 'What kind of aircraft was it?'

'Oh – like yours, perhaps.'

'What happened to the pilot?'

He shrugged. 'I do not know. I was in Athens at the time.'

The Nawab stared at the cypresses. He was interested, all right. So was Miss Brown.

'Let's go and look at it, Aly,' she suggested. She'd have gone ashore to look at a pile of dead fish, just as long as they weren't bouncing around on an eight-foot swell.

The Nawab was intrigued, perhaps more by the idea of getting off that swell himself than by the idea of looking at any crashed aircraft. Finally he decided: he and Miss Brown would look at the crashed whatever-it-was, the rest of us would look at the oil.

I pointed out – very politely – that if they were really interested in the crashed plane, they'd need me to interpret it for them. Shirley looked at me sharply. So did the Nawab.

Finally he said sourly: 'I suppose you know why we are in Athens?'

'I heard something.'

'From Mr Kitson, no doubt.'

I let that go past. He stared for a while and then agreed; I would go ashore with them, Herter would go on to look for the oil.

Nissis passed on the changed orders to the old boy in the back, a calm, wrinkled character with a white stubble on a dark face, a large nose and a gorblimey cap pulled down over it. He was draped around the tiller like a sack of old clothes and he simply leant on it harder and round we went towards Kira.

As we neared the shore – we were going to have to run up on the beach – Shirley said: 'Don't you want to see where —?'

I shook my head. 'It wouldn't tell me anything. Herter can look at oil as well as anybody, and if they can fish anything out they can do it without my help.'

Her eyes glared but she didn't say any more.

'Why don't you come ashore?' I asked. 'There'll be nothing to see out there.'

She stared away at nothing on the horizon.

The inlet to the beach was about two hundred yards across and the water smoothed out as we came between the headlands. The old boy hung his beak over the side, sighted up the valley ahead and then kicked the engine into neutral the moment before we grounded.

We still had eighteen inches of water to paddle through. I wondered if I should offer Miss Brown any assistance, but Herter beat me to it. He stepped over the side, scooped her out of the boat and carried her ashore as calmly as if he were bringing the milk in off the doorstep. The Nawab didn't wait to see if he was going to get the same treatment: he climbed out and got his feet wet. Me too.

As we reached the beach Nissis leant out and called:

'Ask for Nikolas Dimitri. He speaks English.'

I waved. Herter climbed in and the boat dragged itself off again. We walked up across the sand.

Up the line of the centre of the valley the sand was fifty yards across, and mostly firm. Looking back, I could see why: storm waves would have an unbroken reach from the horizon. In winter they probably got the sea half-way up the valley.

Up above us, on our right, the hump and its village of little white houses looked very steep. A narrow, stepped path wound up and vanished behind the first cluster of houses. Ahead of us, another path led through the wiry clumps of grass behind the sand. I had expected to find it marshy: it wasn't. There should have been a stream, but there wasn't that, either. Probably the village had tapped it off, farther back.

I took the lead. The grass reached for about another hundred and fifty yards and was pretty flat and level until, as the valley sides began to close in, it rose up towards the cypresses.

If there was a plane in among those trees I still couldn't see it. I didn't notice a thing until I was within twenty yards of the first tree. Then, suddenly, it was there; an outline among the columns of the trees. It was one of the weirdest sights I ever saw.

It was a Dakota, lying flat on its belly with its wings along the ground. It was pointed away from us, up the gentle slope, and turned slightly left, just as it had come to rest ten years before. In that time, the trees had grown up close around it, so that you could never see it from the air save by flying directly overhead, and then only by the faint outline defined by the trees themselves.

Aeroplanes are my business, and Dakotas are my speciality – but not this one. When I stepped in among the trees the sounds of the sea and the light and warmth of the sun were cut off as if a door had closed behind me. I felt very much alone. The trees were so thick that almost no sun would ever reach the ground in here, but the shadows had the same lucid quality as the light outside. And it was very still. There is nothing as still as a grove of thin, straight trees, and no trees as still as these.

In ten years the Dakota had taken on a green-grey, shadowy colour that made it belong there. It didn't look as if it had crashed. It had come there, and it had meant to come there, and when it had come the trees grew up around it as part of it, and it had turned into something natural. It looked a thousand years old. It made me think of other groves where men were half goats and that this aeroplane belonged more to them than to me. It looked like a shrine. I began to get a prickly feeling in my hair.

I walked a few paces and found I was walking on tiptoe. I cleared my throat loudly, but it didn't sound loud. I looked around; Miss Brown and the Nawab were standing just outside the shadow of the trees, staring. Irrationally, I wanted to heave them out.

Then I made more noises in my throat and turned back to the Dakota, and it was almost just a crashed aircraft in a wood. Almost.

The door was gone, and some of the glass from the windows. The fabric of the control surfaces had rotted or been eaten away, leaving just the metal frameworks. Both props were missing, and when I peered into the nacelles, parts had been taken from the rusted engines. But somebody had put the cowlings carefully back in place. And the fuselage and wings seemed intact.

I walked on around. The right side of the nose was nuzzling up against a large, flat boulder. It was blurred on to it with lichens, so that now there was no sign and no sense of the wallop when they had first met, ten years before. I went right around and in through the doorway.

It was very dark inside. When my eyes got used to it, I started up towards the cockpit, and walking with the floor almost level was a strange feeling. The main cabin was empty, the seats were all gone – if there had been any there – but the plyboard floor panels were still in place, curling at the edges and buckled with damp.

In the cockpit the emergency roof escape panel had vanished, but the pilots' seats, less their padding, were still in place. So was the control wheel and the pedestal of engine controls. The instruments were all gone, leaving the panels agape with empty sockets.

I've been in crashed aircraft before, and I've been in aircraft that have been partly dismantled – cannibalized – to feed parts into other planes. This didn't have the look of either. Somebody had done a careful, unhurried job of looting on this one, but they had left it still, basically, an aircraft. It was the details that were missing. For a moment I thought of the men with horns on their foreheads, and then I thought of the island children.

I went outside. The Nawab and Miss Brown were standing by the doorway, peering timidly in. I grunted at them, and walked back a distance, trying to imagine what had happened in the crash.

The pilot must have seen the little valley from very low down, too low for him to have seen the wide, flat area on Saxos, a couple of miles farther on. And he must have been in bad trouble to have tried such a landing – one engine dead, perhaps, and the other coughing on its last drops of fuel. He would have turned straight in, put down the flaps – they were still part-down – skidded across the beach and the grass and come to a stop where the valley turned upwards and the boulder stuck out of the slope. And then? I didn't know. There was no way of knowing.

I walked back to the tail and peered closely at the metal skin. It was covered in a thin, furry film of lichen. I scratched at it and it peeled off, and under it a few flakes of old paint came away too. I took out a handkerchief and began to scrub across the fin, about as high as I could reach. I felt like a grave robber.

Finally I found what I was looking for, and gently rubbed it more or less clean. It had faded and I had knocked off a few flakes, but it was still clear what it was: a square of green with a yellow crescent moon and, between the horns of the moon, a single yellow star. The sign of Islam. The emblem of Pakistan.

I stood back and looked at the Nawab. He stared at the emblem for a long time, then he looked slowly along the length

55

of the whole plane. I balled up the handkerchief and made to put it in my pocket, then to throw it away and finally put it in my pocket anyhow.

The Nawab moved towards the doorway.

'There's nothing left in there,' I said. I don't think he heard me. He was moving as if he knew exactly where he was going, his eyes fixed on the dark hollow of the doorway. He climbed in.

I glanced at Miss Brown. She was standing with an unnatural tensity, as if she were waiting for something but didn't know quite what. She jerked her eyes away from the doorway long enough to give me a quick, nervous glance. I bent the muscles of my face at her. I wanted a cigarette, but for some reason I didn't want to light one there.

We heard the Nawab walk slowly up inside the plane and back again, into the tail, and then back to the door, and step down.

His face was frozen in a taut, expressionless look. He looked at me suddenly.

'What happened to the pilot?'

'He could have walked away from this one.' I shrugged. 'Or he could have broken his neck.'

'Can't you tell?' he snapped.

'You saw what it was like inside. All I can tell is that he could be still alive.'

'But the cargo? What would have happened to – to what was on board?'

'How would I know that?' I said, very calmly. His eyes bulged out at me.

'Don't the villagers always loot a crash?' he demanded. 'Isn't that what usually happens?'

'I'm here because I'm a pilot and because I've seen crashed planes before. How the hell would I know what the villagers would do?'

'Isn't that what happens?' he squawked.

I've got no firm prejudices against clouting Nawabs, but the least I could do was wait until this one had paid me for the trip. I turned around to get out of the grove.

Miss Brown stepped forward.

'The Captain's telling you all he can,' she told him. 'There's no reason why he would conceal anything. How could anybody tell what happened ten years ago?' She sounded very calm. He

56

jerked his head round at her and they stared at each other for a long time.

I stared, too. This wasn't the Miss Brown who had wanted to get out of the boat because it bounced too much. This was a cool, competent girl telling the Nawab not to be a damn fool and making him listen to it.

He got the message and grunted and dropped his stare. She turned to me.

'Perhaps you'll go on looking around here, Captain, while we go up to the village.'

I said: 'Yes, Ma'am.' I didn't even feel a fool saying it. It was the only thing to say. I watched them go out of the grove and back along the path and then turn up towards the village.

I walked out to the edge of the grove and lit a cigarette. Then I took off my uniform cap and scratched my scalp where it had felt prickly and put it back on again. The sun was warm and bright and the outer branches rustled slightly in the wind.

I couldn't blame the Nawab too much for his blow-up. He had tried to pick the moon out of the sea and it had trickled away between his fingers. But he shouldn't have hoped to find the moon so easily. Wherever his lost loot was, it certainly wouldn't be aboard a plane which had crashed ten years before within a quarter of a mile of a village. And anyhow, he knew already that some of it had wandered as far as Beirut.

I finished my cigarette, trod it out carefully and started looking for another path up to the village. The Dakota couldn't tell me any more. Not after ten years.

I found my path: first a harsh, stone-and-dust trail leading up in wide zigzags, then becoming wide, worn stone steps. A few chickens squawked at me from the first house, but I reached the village proper without seeing a person.

PART TWO

9

I WALKED UP into what I supposed was the main street, a crazy-paved alleyway only a couple of yards wide, running between the rough white walls of the houses. Every now and then an arch of wood or stonework spanned the alley, so that folk could walk across into each other's first floors. The sun was low now, and the alley was mostly in shadow, but the white walls made it very light. They were freshly painted: somebody had even painted the cracks between the paving stones.

As a village, as a place to live, it was almost completely pointless; the little island couldn't hope to support as many people as the houses suggested. But I guessed it had started out life as a corsairs' hideout: the island was almost impregnable, and, stuck out on the end of the island chain, it would be nicely placed away from authority but near the shipping routes. Now, half the population was probably retired Athenians.

I wandered along, seeing a small black cat and a small girl in a white frock. Neither of them wanted anything to do with me. A strange man in a uniform probably didn't mean anything good to them.

Then I got a hefty middle-aged woman and after a bit of misunderstanding she directed me to the village bar.

It was an empty doorway bare of any tables, and very dark. I stuck in my head, nearly fell down two steps and arrived in a small dark room with a wooden floor, a couple of old dark tables, a few chairs and a short bar. Behind the bar was a shelf of bottles. This looked like home.

The proprietor came out to see what the commotion was about. I asked for beer and got a lukewarm bottle for six drachma. I drank it down and ordered another.

Then I remembered Nissis' friend, the one that spoke English. I asked for 'Nikolas Dimitri' in a friendly inquiring way. The proprietor nodded, hauled a small boy out of the back room and dispatched him out of the front door pronto.

As I was finishing my second beer the boy came back with Nikolas. He was something of a surprise: big – nearly my height and broader – and fair-haired. He stood a moment in the doorway, then came slowly down to meet me.

'You speak English?' I asked.

He nodded, then said slowly: 'How are you? My name is Nikolas Dimitri.' His voice had a faint guttural. He had a deep tan and, from what I could see in the dim light, he was about my age.

'Jack Clay.' We shook hands. Then he asked:

'Will you have something to drink?'

I thought of saying Let Me, Old Boy, or something like that – but you don't say that to a Greek in his home town.

'Do you like *ouzo*?' he asked.

Not much, I don't. 'Yes, please,' I said. It would be a bit hard sticking him for the price of a beer. The *ouzo* here would cost no more than a drachma a shot.

He brought two small glasses to a corner table and we looked each other in the eye and sipped.

'Where did you learn to speak English so well?' I asked, just as a starter.

He put his glass down carefully. 'In Germany. I am German. I came here during the war, and then after the war I came back to live here. I like it here very much.'

That wasn't as odd as it might have been. The Greek islanders are a pretty tolerant, hospitable bunch, and they didn't have the rough time during the war that some of the mainlanders got.

We sipped our *ouzo*. I said: 'I am interested in the crashed aeroplane down by the sea.'

He nodded gravely. 'It has been there a long time. The trees have grown up round it.'

'How long has it been there?'

'Before I came back here. I came back in' – he seemed to have trouble translating the date – 'in 1950.'

'Would the proprietor' – I waggled a finger at the bar in case he didn't get the word – 'would he know?'

Nikolas turned to the bar and asked a long question. The proprietor shrugged, then gave a long answer, ending by pointing off through the shelf of bottles, northwards. Nikolas turned back to me.

'He says he was not badly hurt and went away soon.'

'He was English?'

'I think so.' He threw another question at the bar. They decided he was probably English.

'Did the aeroplane have any cargo on it?' I kept my face dead straight and my voice normal. I think I did, anyhow.

The proprietor was quite emphatic about this: no.

Did the pilot have any luggage?

Well, perhaps. The proprietor thought he took something away with him to Athens. He wasn't sure. It was, after all, ten years ago.

It was my turn to buy the *ouzo*. Nikolas thanked me. Then he asked:

'This man was a friend of yours?'

'No.' I shook my head. 'I have brought a man from Athens to Saxos to find this aeroplane. It was his aeroplane.' I wasn't sure that this was quite true, but it was as near as I was going to get. 'He comes from Pakistan.'

Nikolas nodded slowly. 'The aeroplane came from Pakistan?'

'Yes. I looked at it in the grove. It had the Pakistani sign on it.'

He frowned at me. There were small scars up on one side of his forehead that showed lighter than his tan, now that I was getting used to the dimness in the little bar.

I guessed how he – probably the whole village – felt about the old Dakota. If they'd felt any other way it would have been taken apart and chucked into the sea. And here came the big boy in a uniform and started scratching about at it. But he didn't say anything.

Then he asked: 'Your friend – the man you brought here – where is he?'

I said I didn't know. Nikolas shouted up the boy again and gave him instructions. Then he said:

'I will go and look for him also. You wait here.'

He and the boy went off. I wanted another beer, but the take-off from Saxos was going to be difficult enough as it was, so I settled for a bottle of *limonade*. It came out warm and very sweet. Almost every drink you can find in that tough, harsh country comes very sweet. The only places you can find tough, harsh drinks are in the American bars like the King George.

I added this poetic thought to the body of poetic thought which has been worked up about Greece over the past two centuries and lit a cigarette. The bar was growing darker. Outside, more people were coming and going as the street cooled. A couple of donkeys ambled past and I wondered why the Nawab hadn't commandeered them.

I looked at my watch. It was about half past five. The boat would just about be reaching the area of the oil stain. If they weren't back here in under a couple of hours, we were going to spend the night on Saxos. That was all right with me; I could slap a hire fee on the Nawab that would leave blisters on his wallet. No, not his wallet, Herter's. Herter would carry the money. Herter carried everything. Herter carried Miss Brown. I bet I could carry Miss Brown better than Herter could. No, I couldn't. Herter was broader than I was. But I bet I could do everything else about Miss Brown better than Herter could.

On this happy thought, I went to sleep. Slumped in a rickety wooden chair, with a half-glass of *limonade* and a smouldering cigarette on the table, I just dozed away.

I woke up to find the barman and Nikolas and the little boy all grinning at me, the Nawab scowling and Miss Brown simply looking. I had been asleep for just long enough to let the sap drain out of my muscles and leave my mouth like a dried-up duckpond.

'I hear you've been asking questions,' the Nawab snapped at me.

I mumbled 'Yes' or something like it.

'I'll ask the questions. I hired you to fly the aircraft and I told you to stay down there.'

'No, you didn't,' I told him. 'Herter hired me and Miss Brown told me to stay down there.' My fee was getting smaller all the time.

He glared at me, then turned away and motioned Nikolas away to the other corner. Miss Brown gave me a long, cool look, then went with them. I lit another cigarette, and tried to wash away the taste of sleep with the rest of the *limonade*. It took time.

In the far corner – about eight feet away – the Nawab was asking the same questions that I had, and was getting the same answers, rather less politely. Being a Nawab isn't good training for asking questions that the other party doesn't need to answer if he doesn't want to. Miss Brown dropped in a question or a smile every now and then, and that seemed to keep Nikolas going.

Finally they established that, as far as anybody knew, the pilot of the crashed Dak had gone to Athens and that he'd taken something with him. That might have been the truth, might

64

even have been the whole truth. There probably wasn't any way of being sure; it was *their* Dakota on *their* island. We were strictly outsiders. City folk. At that point I got up and walked out into the air.

The alleyway main street was cool now, without the fierce reflections from the white walls. People were standing around gossiping in doorways and they all turned to look at me as I came out. The uniform again. I scratched myself here and there to show I was human underneath, but they stayed cool. I sat down at the foot of somebody's steps and watched a small kitten chasing its imagination around a doorstep.

The Nawab and Nikolas came out of the doorway and headed down the street and started talking with the first group of people. I watched for a while. The Nawab was obviously taking a census of opinion on what had happened ten years ago.

Then Miss Brown came out and looked around and came over to me. I stood up. The kitten stopped and watched her for a moment, then went back to chasing around.

She smiled at me.

'Sit down,' she suggested. She sat on the steps and wound her long legs underneath her. I sat down beside her. She was holding an unlit cigarette. I nearly broke a wrist getting at the matches.

'Thank you.' She blew smoke away from me. 'You made His Excellency angry, you know.'

I nodded.

'You shouldn't, you know,' she told me gently. 'He is paying your fee.'

'Nobody told me to leave my brains at home.'

She smiled again. 'Well, he just doesn't like having his business discussed everywhere.'

'He's a lousy interrogator,' I said. 'He's been in the money too long. He doesn't know how to handle people.'

'You do, I suppose?' She looked slightly amused.

'I'm people. He isn't.'

'Could you handle me?'

I looked at her. Her mouth was slightly open in a small, almost expectant smile. Her eyes were wide and calm.

. My mouth was open, too, and my eyes were wide. But not calm. I was close enough to get the warm, womanish scent from her, and I wanted to grab. It would have been the island's biggest

65

event since the Dak crashed, and ten years later nobody would have been in any doubt about the details of what had happened. But I didn't grab.

'I could try,' I said slowly. 'For my usual fee, of course.'

She chuckled, a rich, warm sound down in her throat.

'We'll have to see, some time,' she said calmly. She drew slowly on the cigarette. I watched the kitten. It was sitting up now, trying to remember how cats washed behind their ears.

'Do you spend your whole life hiring out as a pilot?' she asked.

'That's what I am: a pilot.' I got out a cigarette myself and lit it. My hands were fairly steady.

'You knew Ken during the war, didn't you?'

'That's right. Transport Command.'

'He was a good pilot, wasn't he?'

'One of the best. One of just a handful.'

'Then what was he doing, flying off like that and crashing?'

I glanced at her. She seemed honestly worried.

'Maybe he just ran out of luck,' I said slowly. 'We all do, sooner or later. And some of us get killed doing it.'

'But what made him do it?'

I shrugged. 'He was your pilot. I hadn't seen him in ten years before yesterday.'

'He didn't tell you of any troubles or anything?'

'Last night? No. No troubles.'

'You didn't see him before he flew off this morning?'

I shook my head. A shake of the head presents no moral problems. 'I saw him take off. And the engine conk out.'

She frowned slightly to herself, dropped the cigarette butt and flattened it with her toe.

'You're worried about him,' I said.

'Yes.' Her dark eyes looked full and sad. 'Aren't you?'

'I gave up worrying about other pilots a long time ago. If he's dead he's dead.' I flicked my cigarette across the street. It burst into sparks on a house wall and the kitten whipped around like a Wild West gunfighter hearing a footstep in the sagebrush.

I could feel her eyes on me.

'You're a hard man,' she said gently. She put a hand on my wrist. 'Don't be too hard. You could be very easy to like very much.' She pressed my wrist softly and smiled. 'I'm going to see where Aly's got to.' She stood up and went off down the street.

I watched her go, long and easy and lovely, turning her head to smile as she passed the little gossiping groups. I watched her out of sight round a bend in the alleyway.

I said: 'Fzzzzt!' to the kitten. It went into its gunfighter stance again and watched me warily. 'Reach for your guns,' I dared it. It went on watching me. I spread my hands wide.

'No guns,' I confessed. Poor Jack Clay. Mikklos has a gun, and Ken had a gun, but not hard Captain Clay. Shot down by a tough kitten. Poor Jack Clay.

I wasn't hard. I was as soft as a flat tyre. She'd interrogated me, tempted me and left me feeling as if I'd spat on my grandmother's grave, all in the space of one cigarette. I nodded to the kitten, man to man, and walked down from the village and up on to the other point and stayed there until the boat came back, watching the sun slide down towards the sea.

10

I MET MISS BROWN and the Nawab as the boat drove on to the beach again. Herter splashed out. He looked pale and a bit rumpled, but he was still on parade.

'What did you find?' the Nawab asked.

Herter stuck a hand towards the boat.

'I found a life-jacket and a tyre and a seat cushion, Your Excellency,' he said stiffly.

'From the Piaggio?' the Nawab asked.

'Yes, Your Excellency.'

The Nawab looked at me. 'Well, Captain?'

'Let's have a look at them,' I suggested. Herter offered his arms to Miss Brown. The Nawab and I got our feet wet again. The boat reversed off and swung out towards the sea. Shirley Burt was sitting aft, near the old boatman, looking cold and pale and staring hard at nothing. She didn't seem to want to notice me.

The things Herter had picked up were still slick with oil. The life-jacket didn't tell me anything. The seat cushion had a rip along one side, as it might have got from being thrown about in a crash, or floating out through a broken window. The tyre was badly worn.

'Well,' the Nawab said. 'What do you think, Captain?'

I tried to think of anything else I might ask Herter. I couldn't think of a thing. Aircraft can go straight into the sea and never leave a trace. Or they can spread themselves far and wide and leave debris and oil that you couldn't miss with your eyes shut.

'It looks as if he went in hard,' I said.

'Mr Kitson couldn't have escaped?'

'I think I'd expect more debris if he escaped,' I said. 'And if he did, where is he?'

'But you can't be sure?'

'No, Your Excellency,' I said slowly. 'I can't be sure.'

The Nawab smiled nastily. 'Thank you for your expert opinion, Captain.' Herter looked at me sharply. He'd hear the full story of my irreverence later.

Then we hit the open sea and nobody said a word until we reached Saxos again.

The island taxi was waiting for us on the quay, the owner having guessed that folks who come in their own aeroplanes are folks who prefer riding to walking. It was an old Ford V-8 Pilot with springs like marshmallows and the driver didn't try to save anything but time on the ride back to the plane.

We got there just as the sun went down, and I reckoned we had ten minutes to get clear. Mediterranean twilights don't last long. I got everybody on board and strapped down, asked our schoolmaster friend to keep the mob clear of the road, and started the engines. They liked the cool air. I got a good hundred more revs out of her than I'd seen since we left Berne.

In the desert, the difference between a noon take-off and a night take-off, fully loaded, can be as much as three hundred yards of runway. I wasn't fully loaded, but I hadn't got three hundred yards of runway to spare either. As it turned out, I had about fifty feet. We staggered off the ground just before the road took a left turn a lot sharper than I could have taken it, blared across the harbour village and out over the sea. I set course for Athens.

'Did you see the oil?' Rogers asked me.

I told him what Herter had found, then what we'd found on Kira. He listened quietly. Then he said:

'So it really happened? The jewels, I mean.'

'Looks like it,' I said.

'Could he have flown all the way from India?'

'I've been thinking about that. No, he couldn't. He'd have done it in two jumps, about 1,500 miles each. Landed in Arabia somewhere to refuel. The next 1,500 miles would bring him just about to here. He cut it very fine, too fine. My guess is that he hit Kira on his last drop of fuel.'

He was quiet for a while. I didn't think we'd have His Excellency up in the cockpit this trip, and I was right.

Then Rogers said: 'And Ken Kitson did the same thing, same place. Only he didn't reach an island.'

'Looks like it,' I said. I left it at that, and, for once, so did he.

The jittery, bad-taste feeling was with me again. I wanted to bust something or barrel-roll the plane or get drunk or just get to hell *out*. A Dakota cockpit was a bad place right then. I'd spent too much of my life in Daks and flown them with too many men who were dead now, and until I got away from Dakotas I'd still be flying with them.

But I wasn't going to get away from Dakotas. We were growing old and obsolete together and when they brought in a Dakota replacement they'd bring in a Jack Clay replacement, too. And I could go and spend the rest of my life in a quiet place among the trees.

You were wrong, Miss Brown. Not hard – not me. Nothing as noble and resolute as that. Just old and obsolete and frayed at the edges. You should learn to tell the difference, Miss Brown. It could be important, some day.

Just bitter, Miss Brown, just bitter.

I called Athens tower and told them what we'd seen by way of oil and wreckage, positively identified as from the Piaggio, and recommended the search called off. They wanted to debate what I'd been doing in landing on Saxos and endangering whatever I had been endangering, but I told them my receiver was fading badly and they gave up. They'd get me in person later.

I was in a bad mood for a night landing, but it was easy enough. Everything seemed easy enough; the hard thing was finding a reason for going on doing it.

Shirley Burt vanished as soon as we got parked. I felt bad about her, but there didn't seem anything I could do. The Nawab and Miss Brown climbed into the big Mercedes that materialized under the hangar lights when Herter willed it to. Then he turned to me.

'I understand that you insulted His Excellency,' he told me.

I shrugged. I thought 'insult' was pitching it a bit strong, but he could be right. My experience of how to speak to Nawabs is limited.

He frowned at me. 'This,' he said weightily, 'will be taken account of in the payment.'

'The cost is £400,' I told him. 'Cash – in any hard currency you like.'

'His Excellency can be generous. Also he can show his displeasure.'

'£400,' I said. 'Here and now.'

'You do not tell me what to pay!' he trumpeted. 'For this I report you!'

I sneered at him. 'Who to? International Air Transport Association? The Swiss Chamber of Trade? We don't belong. We don't belong to anything. Pay up and go to hell.'

He got six inches taller at a jerk. I'd dropped my sabre on parade.

I said: 'If you don't pay, I'll put the story of that crashed aircraft on to every front page in Europe. In twenty-four hours you'll be knee-deep in foreign correspondents, and they'll be hot men who know how to ask questions and dig for information. In two days they'll either have found the jewels or driven them so far underground that you won't find them in another ten years. My co-pilot will give you a receipt.'

He was either going to burst or hit me. Either would have been fine with me; I was in just the mood to be picked up for brawling on the parking apron to the inconvenience of the law-abiding citizens. But he was going to pay, whatever else he did. And he knew it.

Very slowly, he reached inside his jacket and turned one of its bulges into a roll of currency that would have choked a jet engine. He peeled several off the top, counted them again and passed them over. He made it seem like handing over his sword.

They were U.S. dollars: ten hundreds, two fifties and two tens. Fair enough. I turned to Rogers.

'Write a receipt,' I said. 'To His Excellency the Nawab of Tungabhadra. For 1,120 dollars. With thanks. Sign it and give it to Mr Herter.'

I turned around and walked away, towards the Mercedes.

The back window was rolled down and as I came up to it the Nawab stuck his sharp little face forward out of the shadows of the back seat.

I smiled at him and leant down with my hand on the window. Miss Brown was just a dim white blur on the far side – that and a tingle of scent in the quiet air.

'I hope you enjoyed the flight, Your Excellency.' I smiled some more. Me? Insult a Nawab?

He grunted.

'And I hope you find the jewels,' I added. I straightened up.

'Wait.' He frowned out at me. I waited. He asked: 'Mr Kitson did tell you, then?'

'Something.'

'You haven't heard of them?'

I shrugged. 'Not so far. But I get around quite a bit. Of course' – I leered at him – 'I might not know whose they were even if I met them.'

'There would be a reward,' he said.

'Really? How much?' I sounded interested.

He looked me over carefully, then his mouth twisted. I was just another beggar with just another wooden bowl outstretched. He shrugged carelessly. 'I might offer a small percentage. They are worth over a quarter of a million sterling.'

Herter came up behind me, gave me a raking glance and climbed into the driving seat. 'I had heard,' I said to the Nawab, 'that they were a million and more.'

That shook him. But he recovered quickly. 'Captain – do you know much about jewellery?'

'I knew a girl with moonstone ear-rings, once.'

From the shadows in the back seat Miss Brown gave a little diamond-studded chuckle. The Nawab frowned at me, then leant back and said something to Herter.

The big car zipped away, nearly taking my arm with it.

I stood and watched them wind past the refuelling bowsers and out of the apron lights and away. Rogers came up under my elbow.

'You didn't even kiss her goodbye,' he pointed out.

'Why should I say goodbye? How d'you know she isn't expecting me to come climbing up to her window with a guitar between my teeth?'

'Don't stub your toe on the Nawab,' he said nastily.

'He can always play the guitar.' I stared around the empty,

lighted apron. 'Get the tanks filled; we're flying tomorrow. I'll see you back at the hotel.'

I walked over to the tower ready to be pleasant to anybody – which was as well, when they started asking about the Saxos landing. I pleaded alternate excuses of Aircargo carburettors and Nawab's orders and got away with a warning. I paid off for the maintenance we'd had that morning and the fuel we were getting now. Then I started telephoning.

I'd lost some of my spare good humour by the time I'd fought my way through the Athens exchange. But I was lucky: it was one of Mikklos's rare evenings away from the nightspots, and an even rarer one away from climbing walls with roses in his teeth.

We said how nice it was to hear each other. Then I said: 'Mikky, old friend. I've been thinking things over. Maybe I was a bit hasty yesterday. I'll take that cargo to Tripoli.'

11

BY NINE O'CLOCK the next morning we were ready to take on cargo. On the phone, the night before, Mikklos hadn't sounded at all happy. He was suspicious of my change of mind, and he didn't trust me farther than he could see me – and in Tripoli I was going to be 650 miles out of sight. But he sounded in a state to mistrust his own signature. He was jumpy, badly jumpy.

Contraband cargo is bad stuff to have lying around for long. It starts whispering behind your back.

But he told me that the cargo would be there on the dot of nine. He himself wouldn't be. I could come and collect the documents from him at ten, in his office. There was no more mention of 350 dollars.

Bang on nine the yellow Dodge coupé swept around the corner of the hangar, trailing the same old lorry. Driving the Dodge was a lithe Arab youth, about twenty years old, wearing a pair of fancy mirror-glass sun spectacles that looked like two fat pools of black oil. He also had on a pair of cream cotton slacks and a bright blue denim jacket.

He climbed out and showed me his big white teeth.

'I am Yussuf. You are Captain Clay?'

'I'm Clay.'

'You ready for the cargo, okay? I come with you to Tripoli.'

'Who says?' I asked him.

'Mikklos says. I fix it all at Tripoli.'

'Got a visa?'

He swept off the sunglasses with a flourish and gave me a sideways grin that was supposed to tell me he knew the price of everything and where he could get it for half of that.

'I'm Arab.'

'That doesn't mean a damn thing. Either you've got a visa, or you're a Libyan, or you don't come.'

He gave a quick, nasty look and admitted: 'I'm Libyan Arab.' He reached into his hip pocket and stuck a passport into my open hand. He was Libyan all right.

'I tell you where to go, okay?' he said briskly, trying for a come-back.

'I know where to go,' I said. 'Tripoli.'

He gave me his I've-been-around look again.

'After Tripoli,' he said, grinning.

'I'll talk that over with Mikklos. Start getting the cargo on board.'

I wasn't much surprised at the suggestion that we'd be going farther than Tripoli. Mikklos wouldn't want his stuff to hang around in the city if he could send it on south, into the desert, while he still had an aircraft on charter. The oil-drilling equipment story was a good excuse for this; most of the drilling rigs have their own airstrips by now.

Yussuf stuck his glasses back on and shouted to the men on the lorry. They backed up and started unloading.

I let Rogers handle the arrangement of the boxes but I was keeping his signature off any of the documents for this flight. The night before, I'd suggested he develop a bilious attack and stay in Athens. He'd just looked at me and said: 'I'm second pilot on this plane. I'll fly if you're flying.'

I left it at that. I could always off-load him somewhere if the going seemed likely to get rough.

It took us twenty-five minutes to get everything arranged on board and tied down, and then it was time for me to start into Athens to pick up the documents from Mikklos. I left Rogers sitting on the doorway steps keeping a sharp eye on Yussuf to see that he didn't try to sell the propellers off the plane before we could get airborne.

I reached Mikklos's office by ten, climbed the dim stone steps and beat on the outer office door and got no answer. Miss Fluff was having her daily hair-set. I shoved in, past the piles of dusty files and cluttered desk, and banged on the inner office. Still no answer.

I was getting jumpy myself by this time. The cargo was now on my plane and I'd have to answer any questions about it if they got asked. I wanted to be on my way. Things might be fixed but the fix can wear thin when a man has had time to spend the money. I opened the door.

Mikklos was behind the desk, flopped forward on to it, his head on his arms. I thought for a moment he'd been coshed, then I sniffed a new tang among the dust and cigarette smoke. The smell of wartime, and a few times since the war. The smell of gunfire.

Something crunched under my foot. I looked down and could count five bright little copper tubes: ·22 cartridge cases. I went very carefully back to the outer door. I wanted to scream for the police, but I wanted to find that Customs document even more. I locked the door and went back and very gently lifted Mikklos off the desk.

There were five neat little holes punched in the chest of his shirt, spread no farther than I could cover with the palm of my hand. Some blood, just a little, had leaked from two of the holes and formed a cross pattern along the weave of the shirt. Still very gently, I let him lean forward again.

The top of his desk was a mess of papers, but no more messy than he could have got them by himself. The office bottle of *ouzo* was on display, along with two small glasses, each with a dreg at the bottom. The top right-hand drawer was a fraction open. I wrapped a handkerchief round my hand and pulled it right open. The Beretta was still there. I took it out and sniffed it for no reason at all. I knew it hadn't been fired. Perhaps, at the last second, he had reached for the drawer, but it had been too late by then. Whoever it was had stood up from the chair in front of the desk and put five well-grouped, unhurried shots into his chest and Mikklos had shoved his nose down into his paperwork and died.

Some of the paper had spilled off on to the floor. I shuffled them with my foot, and picked out a long white envelope with what looked like a cargo manifest sticking out.

I opened it gingerly and took out a bunch of consignment notes, manifests and a Customs clearance document. I saw the word *Tripoli* and that was enough for me. I shoved the whole lot into the front of my shirt.

I had been there too long for an honest man. Miss Fluff was due back from the hairdresser. The coppers were due back from coffee break. I was due far, far away – and fast.

I went back around the desk to replace the Beretta, then didn't. Instead, I took a box of 7·65 mm. cartridges out of the drawer, closed it and pocketed the gun. At the door I stopped and looked back. Mikklos looked uncomfortable, unsettled, as he had when I had last seen him alive. He looked like a small crook in a small office. Not one of nature's gentlemen, but probably not deserving of five holes in the chest, either. I nodded to him and tiptoed on my way, wiping doorknobs as I passed.

12

BACK AT the airport I presented the clearance, and took across the Customs man to check the cargo. He gave the seals the quick one-two and signed me out. Then I herded Rogers and Yussuf across to the Customs office and got the three of us cleared. Then I practically ran back to the plane.

Rogers was amused at my jitters. He'd had me marked down as a cool, shady gun-runner from long ago – but Rogers didn't know what I knew now. And I didn't tell him, either. He'd make a better job of looking innocent if he had no guilty knowledge.

I showed Yussuf a seat, told him to get in it and stay in it. He gave me a knowing leer and as he reached down for the seat-belt I got a glimpse of the gun-butt under his left arm. It didn't surprise me. This season, everyone was wearing them. Even me, nearly. By now the Beretta was under a bunch of manuals in the locker behind the cockpit door.

We turned on to the runway at five to eleven. At eleven o'clock we were outside the three-mile limit and not at home to any radio calls. I plotted a course that took us south for about a hundred miles and then turned south-west between the Peloponnese and Crete. Knowing my feelings about flying over more sea than I had to, Rogers thought the termites had got at my head, but he also knew my feelings about being argued with. And I was sticking to the wide open spaces beyond the three-mile limit. Mikklos probably hadn't been fool enough to have any documents mentioning me and the cargo lying around, but I wasn't prepared to bet my liberty on it.

We turned after three-quarters of an hour and Rogers put in the autopilot and started collecting bearings off the radio-compass. After he had plotted what he could get and made the necessary alterations to course, he said:

'You haven't told me what made you take this cargo, Jack.'

'Money.'

'Did you get the dollars?'

'No.'

He looked at me, then at the instruments, then at the wind-screen.

'Of course, it's only a suggestion,' he said thoughtfully, 'but you wouldn't be going off your nut, would you?'

'I'll see a psychiatrist when we get back to Berne.'

He nodded. 'What I was thinking was that you'd be seeing Hauser.'

'I'll convince Hauser.'

He may have believed that; I didn't. The only thing that would convince Hauser would be Mikklos's cheque, and I didn't think Mikklos would have posted it. But Hauser was a long way off.

Time and the Mediterranean passed steadily by. The Med is a good sea to fly over – if any sea is good on Aircargo standards of maintenance. Most of the time the winds are fairly steady and fairly light. But it can also blow up some vicious storms without too much warning.

Today the sea was calm and glossy 6,000 feet below and Miss Brown was calm and glossy half an inch below the surface of my conscious mind. Already the three of them, and Athens itself, were becoming unreal in my mind, glamorous, remote film-screen figures. It happens. To a professional pilot 'up here' can eventually become 'up here', and the world where he lands is episodic, fragmentary. It happens to some earlier than others. Then, perhaps, he does something damnfool in the half-real world down below and he finds that being able to fly doesn't make him one of the gods.

It isn't new. It's been happening to birds ever since cats.

Getting on for one o'clock we met a couple of U.S. Sixth Fleet jets who came and sniffed us over in case we were Moscow's latest secret weapon. When they decided we weren't, and had shown us how well they could fly on their backs, and gone away when I didn't waggle the wings to show how marvellous I thought that was, I announced lunch. Tinned stuffed vine leaves, bread, cheese and a thermos of coffee.

Yussuf hadn't brought any lunch. After a while he came and stood behind our seats and looked at things, especially at the lunch. I didn't offer any conversation or any food. As far as I was concerned he could eat his pistol, and if he tried to be a smart guy in my aircraft I'd help stuff it down his throat. He went back again.

Three hundred miles before Tripoli we got a radio-compass bearing on Luqa, Malta, and found we were more or less in the right place and heading in the right direction.

I took control. I opened the gills a fraction, switched the feeds on the tanks, fiddled with the trimmers for a while and then turned on the autopilot. I'd been putting things off long enough. It was time to talk to friend Yussuf.

He was sitting on one of the boxes, smoking. I dropped into one of the seats and asked him:

'Where are we supposed to go after Tripoli?'

He grinned. 'I tell you at Tripoli, okay?'

'No.' I shook my head. 'I want to know now.'

He grinned even wider and shook his head. He was the boss.

'I want to know how far we've got to go,' I told him. 'We may be short of fuel. If so, I want to refuel at Tripoli.'

That worried him.

'No. Not refuel,' he said firmly. 'No time to refuel.'

'You may want to crash in the desert. I don't. Tell me where we're going.'

'I tell you at Tripoli.'

'Okay,' I said. 'At Tripoli I shall give the cargo to the Customs and tell them to open it. I won't carry it any farther.'

He stood up swiftly and made a wriggling, groping movement. A big black automatic was pointing at my chest.

I got up, slowly and carefully, and stood close to him.

77

I said: 'Put that thing away or I'll stuff it down your throat and drop you out into the sea.'

He smiled. The gun made him ten feet tall. 'I kill you easy, yes?'

'Wait till you're safe down on the ground.'

That thought – that he was 6,000 feet up in the air and not used to it – got through to him. We stood and stared at each other, the gun about a foot from my chest.

He wasn't going to shoot me – not unless I asked him to. Pulling that gun had been just a gesture of self-assertion; he wouldn't fire it unless I dared him to.

I shrugged and sat down again.

He watched me carefully, then smiled and put the pistol carefully away under his jacket.

'You don't give the orders, see?' he said.

I lit a cigarette and looked away from him. He wouldn't pull the gun again if there was a risk I wouldn't notice.

I said: 'The flight ends at Tripoli.'

'I tell you where to go, then.'

'You can walk it.'

He sat down slowly, still watching me.

'I have a map,' he said.

'I've got dozens.'

He dug inside his jacket with his left hand and brought out the map and opened it on his knees. It was an RAF sheet, printed in shades of purple for reading under cockpit lighting. He tapped it with his finger.

'Mehari,' he said.

'Never heard of it.'

He practically shoved the map in my face. 'Look. You see – Mehari.'

I looked. It was about two hundred miles south-south-east of Tripoli, just below the Hamada el Hamra, the big stony desert escarpment north of the Sahara proper. It didn't show any airstrip there. What it did show was that Mehari stood on one of the camel train routes that run up through the Sahara from West Africa and then east, skirting the patches of sand desert, through southern Egypt to the Nile.

I hoped Mikklos had had enough sense not to send me somewhere where there wasn't a landing strip; he had picked a place where, as far as I knew, there wasn't an oil rig. I looked around the map until I found a place that had both a strip and a rig:

Edri, about 150 miles farther west. I might need it both as an excuse and as a panic landing ground.

Then I needed to know just one thing more: 'Does Mehari have a radio?'

He shook his head.

I stood up and smiled at him. He'd told me everything I wanted to know – perhaps more than he knew himself. We'd settle the business of him pulling a gun on me in my own plane some time later.

I went back to the cockpit.

An hour from Tripoli we got a radio-compass bearing from the Wheelus U.S. Air Force base a few miles out of the city. Not long before we sighted the coast we contacted Idris Tower and I identified myself. They gave me the runway, wind and altimeter setting and didn't say anything about the Athens police having requested an exclusive interview with me. We rolled down on to the big dusty, parched field at ten minutes past four.

Yussuf stuck his head over my shoulder as we taxied round to the civil hangars.

'You need to refuel?' he demanded.

'Some,' I said, pointing to the fuel gauge. He scowled at it. It meant no more to him than the theory of relativity did, but he didn't argue. In fact, I reckoned I could have made it with a good margin – but there might be a time coming when it would be inopportune to stop for fuel.

I let Yussuf do the talking to the Customs. They poked and peered at the boxes and studied the bunch of consignment notes and I stood in the shade of the wing looking bored. They asked me if I had any whisky or yellow fever on board and took my word for it when I said no. They didn't ask about the Beretta and they didn't find it. I sent Rogers over to the airport building to rake up what food he could and got them started on refuelling.

I had them put a hundred gallons in each of the front tanks and the refuelling supervisor sneered at my meanness. We were ready to go again at half past four.

We started up and rolled to the end of the runway, a good half-mile from the tower. There was nobody else in the circuit and nobody taxiing either. I called the tower and told them my tail-wheel appeared to be jamming and that I was getting out to look at it. They okayed this without being very interested. They'd met Aircargo planes before.

Rogers was staring at me. I winked back.

'Go down and open the door,' I said. 'Look worried.'

He looked worried already, but he went. I checked the cockpit for take-off, tightened the throttle nut, set the brakes and got out of my seat. I took the Beretta out of the locker and stuffed it down the back of my trousers.

Rogers had the door open; Yussuf was looking at me suspiciously. I went down within two seats of him and bent to peer out of the side window, putting the seat-back between him and me. When I got up I had the Beretta in my hand.

I pointed it at him.

'Take your gun out with your left hand,' I said. 'Do it very slowly.'

He stared at the Beretta with a look of sick surprise. Then he looked up at me and slowly his face twisted into something very vicious.

'I kill you,' he said softly.

'Not today you won't,' I said. 'Your gun.'

He took it out, slowly, and dropped it on to the seat. It was a big Colt army ·45 automatic, a good sort of gun for fighting wars and frightening old ladies but not much use for fast, accurate work in a confined space. He'd probably try to kill me all right, some day, but he wouldn't make much progress unless he got himself a gun that matched his build better.

'Now get out,' I said.

He got up, tensely, his eyes flicking around, looking for something brave to do. There wasn't anything. He went slowly down to the back and jumped out. There he turned and stood in the wash of the port engine, his hair blowing, and went on glaring at me.

'I hope to hell you know what you're doing, Jack,' Rogers said beside me.

'Me too,' I said. 'Now you get out.'

His mouth sagged open. I pointed the gun at him.

'In the hackneyed phrase,' I said, 'this is for your own good. I'm going on to Edri. Edri – spread that around. And I'll be back. The aircrew hotel's the Uaddan. Wait for me.'

'Now, Jack —' he began. I waved the gun. He shut his mouth, shook his head and jumped down. I reached out, slammed the door and ran for the cockpit. I had the brakes off and the throttles against the stops before I was properly in the seat.

Ten minutes later I hadn't climbed higher than a thousand feet and was still belting along at nearly take-off power. I flew south-east. Already the indignant orders from Idris Tower, telling me to come back and explain what the hell I was doing, had faded out. But I wasn't worried about Idris. It was Wheelus base which might pick me up on the radar.

Below me, the countryside died quickly once I was out of sight of Tripoli. The Greek landscape looks harsh, but it looks worn, too, as if the harshness were partly the muscles showing through. Libya looks dead, untouched, as if nobody had yet found a use for it. You don't see much greenery beyond a few miles south from the coast.

The desert proper isn't supposed to begin for about three hundred miles, but I'd hate to try and make a living in those miles. Some have tried it. You can find occasional clumps of stone and plaster huts, with the doors, windows and roofs missing, and around them straggling rows of brown, brittle vegetation.

Twenty-five years ago those were the outposts of the new Roman Empire, and the desert was going to blossom like the rose in Mussolini's button-hole. It didn't.

Nobody lives there now except in the oases, and the rest is shallow gullies and low, flat-topped mesas and drifts of sand. The oil companies have divided the whole place into neat little patches and erected a few rigs, but it looks a lot more on the map than it does on the ground. There's still a hell of a lot of plain simple nothing.

I kept the engines pounding in rich mixture to keep them cool, and watched the sky for contrails. Idris probably wouldn't get the USAF interested in hunting for me, but they just might. After three-quarters of an hour I hadn't seen anything. I turned south and climbed gently.

At five thousand feet I had got about 200 miles from Tripoli. I set the autopilot and went back and fiddled the W/T set alive and tried to find Wheelus on it. I was lucky. I put it on the radio-compass and weaved about until I had pulled the compass around to give me Wheelus at 335 degrees. I reckoned that if I kept it there and flew the reciprocal of that, 155, I'd reach Mehari in about three-quarters of an hour. If I didn't think again. Meanwhile I had other things to do.

I set the autopilot at cruising speed, with a slight nose-down tendency. I hoped that would balance up when I went aft. Then

I dug out my tool kit and took a pair of pliers and a screwdriver and went back to look at the cargo.

I cut off all the Customs wire and took it back to the cockpit and slung it out of the window before I forgot. Then, without shoving things around too much, I opened the first box.

They were guns all right. But they weren't going to shoot anybody; they hadn't shot anybody in a long, long time. There were a few nineteenth-century Mauser rifles, a few Martini-Henrys and some even older and weirder pieces. The rest was German stock left over from the last war. Every single one was rusted or jammed or had a bent barrel or some part missing. You couldn't have started a revolution in an old folks' home with that lot.

I screwed it down and opened the second box. It had the same sort of junk in it. I closed it up and started looking at the boxes to see if there were any markings to make one stand out. There didn't seem to be. I opened the third and got another helping of scrap iron.

The whole idea was very much a Mikklos idea. It was the sort of double bluff that would appeal to a man who would rather steal the Chief of Police's lighter than simply ask the man on the corner for a light. I grinned and started on the fourth box.

It was there, right at the bottom; a flat box about eighteen inches long and a few inches deep, and labelled *9 mm. Luger*. I got a screwdriver under the lid and wrenched and was a rich man.

13

I T W A S some time before I got around to counting the pieces, and then there were twelve.

Three of them were rings or thumb rings: great wide bands of gold with a single diamond or ruby sunk into them.

There were a pair of ear ornaments, made up of complicated flowers of gold wire and small diamonds strung on rows of pearls and ending in fat gold bells with ruby clappers.

There were two pairs of forehead ornaments, wads of strung

pearls, set wherever there was room with more gold wire and small stones.

And there were three necklaces, and they were what I looked at longest. Each was built in a broad half-moon swathe across the chest; two of them sheer mats of small pearls traced with patterns of diamonds and rubies and ending in fringes of larger stones.

The third was different – and it was the star of the show. No pearls, just a glittering slab, almost a waistcoat, of gems, and not a zircon or spinel among them. A glowing mass of diamonds, rubies, sapphires tangled on a framework of gold wire, ending in a ragged fringe of diamonds and sapphires, none of them going under fifteen carats, and the biggest, a sapphire, reaching over twenty-five. The diamonds were pure ice-blue Golcondas.

But at first I didn't count the pieces, stones or carats. I gloated. I picked pieces up and breathed on them for the joy of watching the brilliance develop again, slowly. Then I snatched up other pieces for fear they'd scuttle away from me if I didn't hang on to them. Then I loaded the lot into my two hands and just sat there on the floor of the Dak, surrounded by junkshop rifles, and looked at the glitter in my hands and listened to the blood in my ears, louder than the engines.

I was God in a twin-engined heaven and I was rich. *Rich, damn you down there, rich!*

Suddenly I was on my feet, panicked and running for the cockpit. The Dak was in a 45-degree dive and only five hundred feet from the ground and —

The ground was steady, far below. The instruments showed 5,000 feet, straight and level at just under 130 knots.

I sat down, limp, and put on my sunglasses against the glare and let sweat dribble down from my forehead to blur them over. My hands trembled against my thighs. I waited what seemed to be a long, peaceful time, then lit a cigarette.

Probably Morrison, the man who'd first flown the jewels out of India, had gone down the back as soon as he was alone, and had lifted them out of the boxes and gloated over them. He'd had a lot more to gloat over. I'd got only a small part of the load he'd swiped.

But they had ended up flying the aircraft for him, flying it down to the last gasp of fuel, a thing he'd never have done himself.

I looked at my watch and the map and reckoned I should reach Mehari – if I was going to reach Mehari – in about fifteen minutes. I checked the autopilot, and jacked up the under-carriage, which was trying its old trick of flopping down in flight, and adjusted things here and there.

By the time I went down the back again I was a pilot once more. A rich pilot, perhaps, or just a pilot with a natty new line in stolen goods, but a pilot first.

I scooped the rifles back into the box, screwed it down and tied the whole load back in place. Then I took the small box and the jewellery back to the cockpit and threw the box out of the window. I switched on the cross-feed to drain fuel from the port auxiliary tank and settled down to examine the loot.

Looked at soberly, which is how you seldom look at jewellery worth, I guessed, about £300,000, they looked like things off a Christmas tree. They had the over-elaboration of a doodle and the too-obvious symmetry of a Rohrschach test ink-blot. An elephant would have looked overdressed wearing a quarter of this lot.

But, with Indian jewellery, that wasn't the point. Forty years before, an Indian Prince wouldn't have gone out to tea wearing less than twice as much, and for a very simple reason: what he left at home, nobody knew about. An Indian gem cutter could do more with a gem than anyone else in the world, but he never shaved a carat more off a stone than he had to. He cut it to look like what it was – a solid, clearly visible chunk of personal wealth.

I could see a lot in his point of view.

My watch made it five minutes to my estimated-time-of-arrival at Mehari. I tried to tune in to Wheelus again but couldn't get anything. The ground below told me nothing. There were definite gullies and mesas and patches of sand but I had nothing to relate them to.

I flew and looked. Suddenly I saw what might have been a track: a long winding scratch across the landscape that didn't look quite natural. It led away left of my course and ended in a dark smudge half-way to the horizon.

I leaned the Dak towards it. After a few minutes the smudge began to turn a dark green. I made a positive turn. Gradually it grew into a single fat clump of tall palm trees, laced with dusty yellow-white little houses. To the west of it there was a short north–south strip showing slightly lighter than the rest of the desert. At the north end was a faint white M.

I landed northwards, with the wind, so that I would end up as far from the village as I could. There wasn't enough wind to make much difference, anyway. My arrival so close to the estimated time proved that.

I swung right at the end of the strip, showing the starboard side of the plane to the village, set the brakes and dived out with two pocketfuls of £300,000.

Even in the wash of the engine it took me no longer than ten seconds to get the cap off the port auxiliary tank, and not much more again to stuff the jewellery inside. In just over half a minute I was back on board pulling the door shut and working up an expression of unfallen innocence.

And all the time Yussuf's big Colt was sitting on the seat in plain view.

I gave a moment or two to deep thought and then chucked it out of the window. It was unlikely anybody would start scouring the airstrip for any reason. That still left the Beretta, by now back in the locker, but I thought I could pass that off lightly. Arabs appreciate the desire to have a gun around as something normal. Two guns might have struck them as greedy.

I taxied up into the lee of the oasis, swung into what wind there was and shut down the engines. It was suddenly very still. The tall palms leant out over the village and waved gently above me.

The oasis was about a third of a mile long and nearly as broad and it looked very much like an oasis; desert oases always do. Outside the walls it was sand and grit, without a leaf to make a lizard's breakfast; inside, the palms stood up thick and green and lush like a giant flowerpot. In a way, it was just that: the wall did as much of its work keeping the soil in as the faithless out.

I made a long, leisurely job of getting down and lighting a cigarette.

Then a couple of characters in long dusty yellow *burnouses*, hooded desert cloaks, came around the corner and strolled towards me.

I smiled and offered a '*la-bas*', hoping there was no ill upon them, and the first of them intimated, as politely as he could without taking the cigarette out of his face, that no ill was upon him. Then he jerked his head, suggesting I followed them and no please about it. I followed.

The main gate to the village faced south, a twenty-foot arch showing me a sandy street with one-storey shops and houses spaced among the walled groves of palms and orange trees. My new friend indicated that I was to wait there with his mate. He went on ahead, not into the village but out along a track leading west. We waited.

Opposite the arch, on the outside, was a small new-looking building of mud bricks, unplastered, with barred windows and a heavy plank door. As we waited a short tubby man, wearing a rumpled blue serge uniform and a red fez, came out. He saw me, nearly went straight back in again, then hurried past into the village without giving us another glance. His face was more negroid than Arab, and more worried than either.

My second new friend gave him a swift sneer, then turned to me to make sure I got the point. I got it, all right. The one in uniform was the village cop, and he'd been paid not to notice me, the Dakota or its cargo. The sneer was a bonus from the side which did the paying.

We waited. I finished the cigarette and ground it carefully out so that it wouldn't set the rocky track on fire, and began to feel thirsty. Finally I asked: *'Dove albergo?'* and hoisted an imaginary glass so that he'd follow my Italian. He followed, but he didn't approve. He shook his head several times and pointed off where first friend had gone.

I was too thirsty to care. I did a little mime to indicate that he could do the waiting while I did some drinking, and ploughed off through the arch myself, leaving him shouting at me angrily and wondering whether to chase me, chase his pal or just wait.

There was hardly anybody about. A donkey standing peacefully by a doorway, one or two solid-looking citizens standing watching me go past, and returning a *'la-bas'* when I offered it.

The street curved gently downhill to the right. After about a hundred and fifty yards it broadened into a sandy plaza, with one lone palm in a small circular wall in the middle. Facing east was the long, low, decorative façade of the *albergo*.

It was a nice place in any setting, and a remarkable one in Mehari, until you remembered that the only people who came down the camel track outside the gate were rich merchants and army officers with months of desert pay in their pockets.

The frontage was mainly arches and windows filled with stone grillwork, so that behind it there was a long cool patio which the sun never touched. From the patio a bead curtain opened through another arch into the bar itself, a deep, dim room which seemed entirely monochrome after the glare of the sun. I had it to myself.

The bar was topped in aluminium. I coughed and shifted a few empty Cola bottles around until I produced some service: a thin middle-aged Frenchwoman as colourless as the room itself.

I asked for a Cola and she handed it out, in the bottle, and gave me Libyan change for one of Herter's ten-dollar notes without comment. I thanked her and took the bottle out on to the patio.

The sun was low and most of the plaza was in shadow. It was very quiet. An Arab village is always very quiet. The bazaars near the coast are for the tourists and the people who live in towns because they like the noise. In the villages there isn't anything to make a noise about.

I waited a long, quiet ten minutes and then had company. Six of them; four in long white robes and complicated *tarbooshes*, and my two from the reception committee. Two of the white-robed ones carried long rifles with ornamental butts.

They stopped in front of the hotel and I went out to meet them. The leader was a tall man with a thin, strong face, a big nose and a small moustache. Without the robes, he would have been gaunt; with them, he looked like a Roman statue – except for the green turban, the badge of a Mecca pilgrimage. He looked a little much for Mehari. I should have guessed who he was, of course – but I didn't.

He bowed very slightly, and murmured: '*Allah i-sad msa-k*,' which I recognized as a hope that God should make my evening a happy one.

I dredged my memory and managed to give him the same wish redoubled in spades, and wondered where we went from here.

He solved that by saying: 'I am very glad to meet you,' in almost perfect English. I gave that back, too, and he went on to apologize for his servants having tried to keep me standing in the sun when I was obviously desperately tired and thirsty after my long journey. It was nicely phrased, and it managed to suggest that I should have stood in the sun none the less.

Then we went back on to the patio and sat down at one of the bleached, sand-blasted metal tables. One of his boys went inside to order coffee.

'You have brought a cargo from Athens, have you not?' he asked.

'That's right.'

'I am deeply grateful. My caravan has waited several days for it.'

This shook me. I hadn't expected to find myself dealing direct with the master of a camel train. I'd known there had to be a camel train sooner or later – this was Mikklos's idea of a cunning back alley route to Beirut – but I'd expected to find myself dealing first with another agent. And I'd have preferred it. The desert Arab is a tough breed. The rifles his two lieutenants were carrying began to look a lot less ornamental than their butts suggested.

'I will help you unload as soon as you wish it,' I said solemnly, hoping it wouldn't be too soon. If this was the man who was going to carry the jewellery off, the first thing he'd do would be to rip open the boxes and dump the junk rifles. He wouldn't waste good camel space on scrap iron.

'Please do not trouble yourself.' He held up a hand. 'My servants have already started. They are familiar with Dakotas.'

I managed some sort of a smile. This was no fool, this one. No fool at all. I was beginning to feel a long way from home.

Small cups of a thick, sweet Turkish coffee were brought out and we sipped. He asked if I had had a pleasant journey, and I assured him I had. He asked after my family and I explained I didn't have any, and he hoped I would collect some soon. It was all very polite and delicate, and I was beginning to feel sticky under my shirt. The wise thing to do was to be aboard that Dak and heading north. There might be trouble with the authorities in Tripoli, but I could weather that. Authority in Mehari right now was a rifle with an ornamental butt.

We sipped and smiled at each other.

Two more characters in long white robes and *tarbooshes* came down the road, not quite hurrying, but covering plenty of ground. They salaamed the boss and dived into explanations without giving me a glance. He listened, nodded, once or twice, and dismissed them.

He gave me a long, steady, raking look. Then he said something that sounded like an order.

Something smashed on to the back of my head. I pitched across the patio with lights exploding behind my eyes. When I got my face up off the stones and my eyeballs rolled into place, I saw one of the lieutenants grinning and fingering the ornamental butt of his rifle.

The train master stood up. 'We will talk more privately. I think you have been very foolish.'

The two boys in *burnouses* hauled me up and started lumping me along the road. My feet weren't helping them much, and bits of my brain seemed to be rattling around in my head.

We went to the police post. There was a long delay there while somebody raked up the policeman. He came up looking more worried than ever, but not offering any arguments. We went in.

Most of the building was an office. The furniture was simply a trestle table, a bench in the far corner, a couple of chairs and a cupboard. And something else. Something I should have guessed at, something I shouldn't have taken Yussuf's word for.

Standing on the bench was a shiny grey W/T set three feet high. You could have tuned it on the penguins at the South Pole. Getting a message from Yussuf in Tripoli would have been no bother at all.

Somebody lit a paraffin pressure lamp hanging from a ceiling beam, and found a semi-respectable rug for the master to sit on; I got the concrete floor.

He sat on the far end of the rug and his boys squatted back against the wall behind him; somehow, they managed to look very much like a tribunal.

I giggled nervously.

That surprised me. A reaction to being slugged hard and unexpectedly was starting in my head and stomach. The lamp fizzed softly, throwing a harsh yellow light with very black shadows. I leant my head against the wall and then took it away quickly. It was too hard. Anything was too hard for my head right then. The sudden movement made my stomach surge.

I shut my eyes. I had to think. Think quickly. This man was no fool.

'What have you done with my cargo?' he asked gravely.

'I brought your cargo in,' I said. My voice sounded thick, as if it were only speaking inside my head.

'Why did you open it?'

'Didn't open it,' I lied.

'Who took off the Customs wire? There is always Customs wire.'

'They took – took it off at Tripoli.'

'Why did you leave Yussuf and your friend at Tripoli?'

I had to think that one out. Carefully. It was like trying to memorize an encyclopedia. I bent my head, away from the lamp. Any light was too bright. But when I closed my eyes it was much brighter.

'I left my – co-pilot because I didn't want him mixed up in this. He hasn't touched guns before. Didn't want him to. Left – left Yussuf because he threaten' me. In m'own plane. With gun. Nobody threatens me – in m'own plane. Never.'

I had made it. My speech. Impeccable diction throughout. I was elected. I grinned at my feet, stretched out in front of me. They stretched a long way, as far as I could see. Almost as far as the voice.

The voice was speaking. I couldn't understand it. I could have repeated the words, but I couldn't get the meaning. It was just a drone from the mist beyond the lamplight.

'There was something else besides the guns. Where is it? Where is it?'

I tried to smile at the voice, to show that I was trying. But my head flopped forward and my body followed it. There was a moment of wonderful clear painlessness as I fell. The floor spoiled that. But after the floor there was nothing.

14

I HAD CRASHED.

Why? Must have been engine failure on take-off. Nothing else could smash me up. I'm too good.

There was a faint crackling sound. On take-off I'd have full fuel tanks. Fire!

I tried to lift my head. That hurt. Pain went down through my whole body. But when it faded I was awake, and I knew I wasn't in the Dakota. Then why the fire? I saw my hand stretched out in front of me, my fingernails crackling on the rough concrete floor as I groped for the controls that weren't there.

It took time, but I managed to drag an arm back and lift myself, very cautiously, on one elbow. Without trying, I began to absorb the room.

It was about eight feet square, seven feet high and made of mud bricks, with a rough concrete floor. Light filtered in through a small barred opening in one wall. Opposite that wall was a door, a thick plank door, with a small peephole panel. The door had no catch or handle on my side.

I was in the police post jail.

More time passed and I managed to sit up against the wall, being very careful not to let the back of my head touch it. The head throbbed, but it was a diminishing throb, like the note of an aircraft which has passed overhead. My mouth felt dry and very full of tongue.

Apart from myself, the cell had just a worn mat the size and thickness of a bath towel, and a clay jug. I crawled across to the jug and found water. I used some to wash out my mouth and some more on my face and head. I didn't drink any. That would come later. As the pain in my head faded I was becoming aware that my stomach wasn't in full working order. And at some time in the night I had been sick down my shirt.

My watch said it was eleven, and the light from the grill said that meant eleven in the morning. I went through my pockets and found I had everything still on me, right down to Herter's wad of dollars. I had cigarettes. I lit one. It was almost a bad mistake, but having something to concentrate on helped.

I rinsed my mouth again, and sipped. If it was full of microbes I ate them alive. I couldn't feel much worse.

Time went past. The cell was cool – the walls were thick, and the air didn't have a chance to move around much – and very quiet. I hadn't heard a sound from the office outside, so I guessed the village bobby was staying well clear of the place. He wouldn't be happy about me. I was locked up for being crooked to some bigger crooks, and they were going to pass judgement and sentence on me. Even to a copper with his hand out for dirty money, that was an irregular situation.

Perhaps I was being hard on him. He couldn't argue with the master of the camel train. The most he could hope for would be that they'd bury me quietly and dispose of the Dakota somewhere and not leave any bloodstains on his concrete. *Allah i-jalu hadd el-bas.* God grant nothing worse. I went on thinking hardly of him.

My watch said four o'clock and I was down to my last cigarette when I heard him come in. I went and beat on the door. He stopped shuffling around and came near to the door and grunted.

'You speak English?' I asked. I got another grunt.

'*Vous parlez Français?*' I got a grunt that could have been *oui*.

I thought of demanding a few civil rights, then thought better of it. First things first, and I didn't want to frighten him off.

'*J'ai des dollars,*' I trumpeted. '*Et je desire des Colas. Beaucoup des Colas. Et des cigarettes. Je vous donnerai cinq dollars. Okay?*'

He mulled this over. I wasn't too worried about him coming in and just taking the *dollars* without giving any room service in exchange. He'd be too wary of me for that. He probably didn't know who or what I was, but if I was significant enough for the camel train to want me locked up, then I was too significant for him.

On the other hand, if they were going to bury me they certainly weren't going to bury the dollars along with me. This might be his last chance at them.

'*C'est impossible,*' he growled reluctantly.

'*Fut! Vous êtes timide!*'

'*Dix dollairs,*' he compromised.

I was home and dry. It was going to be an expensive smoke and sip, but this was no time to argue. I hadn't got any dollar notes smaller than tens, anyway.

'*Okay. Deux paquets des cigarettes and trois Colas, Bien?*'

The peephole in the door slid open and an eye peered at me.

'*Les dollairs, s'il vous plait, Monsieur,*' he suggested.

I took out Herter's wad and waved it at him, then put it back. He'd get the ten when I got my cigarettes and Colas. He peered at me a while longer, then went away.

A quarter of an hour later he opened the peephole again, found I wasn't trying to hide behind the door, and came in carrying three bottles of Cola, two packets of cigarettes and his pistol. He kept both eyes and the pistol on me while he put the rest down inside the door, then ducked out and demanded the ten dollars through the peephole.

I told him he was very brave and shoved the note through.

The Colas cleared my throat without making me worry about microbes and the cigarettes kept me ticking over until I felt like food. I sat down on the mat and started worrying about my speech for the defence.

They would search the Dak thoroughly, but I didn't think they'd get the jewellery out of the petrol tank. I wasn't at all sure how I was going to get it out myself, but I was prepared to take a tin-opener to it if necessary. The stuff was worth ten times what the plane was worth and it was Hauser's plane anyway.

They'd come and ask me what I'd done with it. That's where things would get tricky. The desert Arab has used knives, fire and boiling water as more or less normal business methods for a thousand years and more.

But before they got to that stage I had two good (I thought) arguments to put up. One was in the hope that they didn't know too much about autopilots, so I might argue that I couldn't have opened things in the air, and anyway, what could I have done with the gems?

The second was why the hell I'd bothered to come on here if I'd pulled a fast one across them.

The Customs wire was a shaky point, of course. But it might take a little time to contact Yussuf in Tripoli and verify that the boxes had been wired up when last seen.

Towards sunset I heard a car, probably a jeep, come up from the west and turn into the village. I wondered if it could be an official visit – the departmental chief of police, perhaps. If he wanted to inspect the jail it might be an interesting development.

Or it might be friend Yussuf.

After I heard my true believer of a cop come in from prayers, I started beating on the door and demanding food. Spaghetti, or some such, and Cola.

I got spaghetti and meat balls and two Colas at the standard rate of ten dollars, and it tasted worth it. My stomach was firing on all cylinders again and it hadn't seen hot food in two days. I had a dull ache in the back of my head that became a sharp ache whenever I moved too suddenly, but I was mending fast.

Later, at about ten o'clock, I thought I heard the growl of another vehicle. It didn't come past the police post. They came for me after that.

The cop let them in, then vanished. Three of them – two in rough *burnouses* and one in more elegant robes plus a rifle. They hoisted me out and we started off westwards, past the village and into the desert.

The night was clear, as it usually is, and the stars were brighter than you ever see them anywhere north of the Mediterranean except when you're flying. There was no moon.

I let them do most of the work, half-carrying me; there was no point in seeming too fit. We went up a slight mound, the ground turned to almost pure sand, and we turned off to the left, south.

The camel train was camped in a hollow among the dunes: one large tent built of carpets, several smaller lean-to affairs, and behind them a pack of about thirty camels or more. The stars and sand were bright enough for me to see all that. I could also see a lorry. Cooking fires burnt beyond that, and there were lamps alight in the big tent. It stood about five feet high, open all along one side, and with carpets spread out in front of it.

My helpers brought me up to the edge of the carpet, and stopped. They pointed at my feet. I kicked off my shoes into the pile of boots, sandals and worked-leather slippers, and stepped in on to soft, thick rugs.

Three oil lamps stood in the middle of the tent in a litter of small coffee cups. Five men were stretched around them, leaning up on one elbow. Some of them were smoking. Four of them were dressed in long white robes. The fifth was in jeans and a bright blue cotton windcheater. Yussuf.

He half got up as I came in and his eyes glittered in the lamplight. The caravan master said something sharp and Yussuf spread himself out again, but there was nothing relaxed in the way he did it.

The master greeted me politely and told me to sit down. I sat with my back to the desert. I shivered slightly. The night was getting cold.

'I hope you are recovered?' the master asked solemnly.

'Thank you, not quite.'

'I think you will notice that Yussuf has now joined us. I shall ask you again – what did you do with what was in the boxes with the guns? You are delaying my caravan.'

'I didn't touch the boxes. How the hell could I? I had an aircraft to fly at the same time.'

'I believe,' said the caravan master solemnly, 'that it is possible to set the aeroplane to fly itself.'

I gave him a wide grin with a hint of wryness in it. I hoped the lamplight was good enough for him to get all of it.

'In the big, expensive jobs, yes,' I told him. 'Not in an old crate like the Dakota. My boss can hardly afford human pilots, let alone automatic ones.'

This wasn't as stupid as it might have been. Telling if a plane has an autopilot isn't as simple as sticking your head into the cockpit and looking. All you can see are a lot of knobs and a layman probably couldn't pick one from the other. And there weren't any labels left on anything in our Dak.

The caravan master had a few quick words with Yussuf. Yussuf shrugged, and added some sort of suggestion. The master turned back to me.

'There is still the matter of the Customs wire. When was it taken off?'

'Tripoli.'

'It was not!' Yussuf spat. The caravan master turned his head warningly.

'Yussuf said it was not,' he repeated, making it clear who was running the interrogation.

'He was too sick to notice,' I sneered. 'He was drunk when he came on board and sick all the way across. He didn't know if we'd landed in Tripoli or Timbuctoo.'

Yussuf was crouched, shouting for somebody to give him a weapon and let him get at me. The caravan master was shouting him down.

I raised my voice.

'Mikklos probably stole whatever-it-was from under his drunken eyes. Next time send a grown man and not some young girl.'

Probably there are worse things to call a devout Moslem tough guy than a drunken untrustworthy girl, and – given time – I could probably have thought of them. As it was, I seemed to have managed. Yussuf snatched at the belt of the man next to him and plunged at me with a long knife in his hand.

I rolled back and sideways, on to the carpet outside the tent. As I went I saw something white move at the corner of my vision. The tent was full of shouting and scuffling.

I came up on one knee with my hands open, ready to grapple. There was no need. Yussuf was stretched out flat and still, the knife by his open hand. Standing beside him, just outside the tent, was one of the tall white-robed birds, holding his ornamental rifle loose in his two hands.

I was happy to see somebody else's head getting practice with that butt.

95

I climbed cautiously to my feet, not wanting to excite anybody. The caravan master got up slowly and stepped outside. He gave orders and Yussuf was dragged off-stage. Then he turned to me.

'Captain,' he said calmly, 'you have been very lucky. Twice you have escaped my questions. Yussuf is a dog; I do not yet know what you are. Tomorrow we will find out.'

He gave me a long look, then bent down and picked up the knife. He said something and two men held me, tight. The knife came very close to my left cheek.

'*Allah y-a'fu,*' he said simply. God forgive. Then he drew the tip slowly down my cheek.

It didn't hurt more than a sting. It was too sharp. I felt the skin part and the warm blood start down my face. The muscles in my cheek jerked.

He turned back to the tent. I reached for a handkerchief as they hustled me away.

15

THE NIGHT died slowly in the cell. I didn't sleep. I leaned back stiff against the wall and felt the cold in the air burning my cheek, and the deeper burn inside at having had to stand still and take it.

In the office I heard the cop blunder around for a while and then flop down on his mat. The whistle of his breathing seeped in under the door. I sat and smoked and listened.

It was a bad mood for thinking up something clever to say in the morning. I didn't want to think up clever things. I wanted to get my hands on a gun and start shooting. I wanted to end the whole damned silly business.

I had come here on a guess and it had been a bad guess. I had been a fool and a crook and a lot too much of either. I had got slugged and cut and slung in jail and when I got out in the morning I would get slugged and cut some more.

I was going to die nastily on a patch of sand at the backside of nowhere and for no good reason.

I heard movement against the wall outside. I flipped my cigarette butt quickly into a corner. If it was Yussuf wanting to try a little assassination, he wasn't going to have a glowing bull's-eye to shoot at.

Something scraped at the barred ventilator. Something moved against the small bars of starlit sky. I went quietly under it, then reached up gingerly.

I had a gun.

I listened hard, and something moved outside and went away. I backed into a corner and struck a match and looked at the gun in my hand. It was a 9 mm. Walther P38 with a fat, comfortable butt of ridged plastic. A nice gun. I broke out the magazine and it was fully loaded. Nicer yet.

My watch gave it as after four, less than two hours before dawn, and prayers, and what was planned for after prayers.

I beat on the door.

'*Monsieur!*' I screamed piteously. '*Monsieur le gendarme!*'

He didn't like being woken. He called me several things I couldn't follow and one or two I could.

'*J'ai mal,*' I pleaded. '*J'ai beaucoup de mal. Je desire de l'eau. J'ai des dollars. Dix, vingt dollars.*'

The dollars woke him. He shoved aside the peephole cover and poked around with the torch beam until he had a good view of me sitting in the middle of the floor, my face covered in dried blood, holding my middle and rocking with pain.

He got no view of the Walther at all.

'*Des dollars,*' he growled.

I fumbled the wad out of my pocket and threw it towards the door. He shut the peephole, struck a match to the lamp in the office and came in with the water-jug in one hand and his pistol in the other.

I was crouching with the Walther aimed at his middle.

He could have fired and I would have let him have the first shot. I was ready to risk that to save waking the caravan. But he wasn't expecting to fire, and I looked as if I were. His pistol clattered on the floor – loudly, but not nearly as loud as it would have been going off.

I told him that if he started screaming for help before he heard the Dakota's engines, I would come back and put a hole in his head. He appeared to believe me. I picked up the pistol and the dollars, shut the cell door on him and stepped out into the cold night, Two-Gun Clay, ready to take on the world and hoping the first two would be the caravan master and Yussuf.

I must have spent nearly a minute just standing there, in the middle of the track, breathing the night air and feeling the solid power of the two guns. It was a very sweet feeling.

Then I woke up. The desert was as quiet as the tomb, but a damn sight lighter. I ducked quickly through the archway into the village and went cat-footed down the sandy street towards the hotel. There was no light, no sound, nothing.

In the plaza in front of the hotel was a jeep, one of the de-militarized types with a box bodywork of plywood and scratched perspex, and the name of an American oil company painted on one door. I walked softly around it and on to the patio.

It was very dark there. I stood just under the roof until I could see a dark shape at one of the tables. I walked towards it.

He didn't get up. He said: 'They don't seem to have caught on to the idea of old-fashioneds down here yet, but there's a bottle of fine old fifth-rate cognac here, if you're interested.'

I said: 'You were a hell of a time getting here, weren't you?' and sat down and took the glass he passed me.

16

FIFTH-RATE WAS a just estimate, but it was still alcohol. He passed me a cigarette and lit it. In the flare of the lighter I could see he was still dressed as he had been almost three days ago, on the tarmac at Athens. Suède jacket, cavalry slacks, white shirt. He looked a lot cleaner than I felt.

He stared at my face across the flame.

'They cut you up a bit,' he said softly. 'I'm sorry about that. I was watching, but I didn't think I'd get too far butting in right then.

'You did all right, down there,' he added.

'Thanks.'

We sat and smoked and sipped. The plaza was bright in the starlight, with very dark shadows, and very still. My swallowing sounded like slamming a door.

He said: 'You said I'd been a long time getting here; you wouldn't have been expecting me, would you?'

'I can make an engine go bang, too: cut out the switches, keep the throttle up to build up a bit of vapour, then switch on again. And you wouldn't have swung as badly as that if you'd really lost an engine.'

'I suppose I hammed it up a bit,' he said. 'Did anyone else spot it?'

'You fooled everybody,' I assured him. He had fooled Shirley Burt, anyway. 'How did you get here?' I asked.

He had come across the coast near Benghazi, picking his landfall carefully and coming in high so that nobody could identify him if they saw him at all. Then well south into the desert, before turning west to follow the camel trail and spotting the train itself parked at Mehari (he was brighter than I was, there: I could have spotted it, too). Then fifty miles farther on to an oil-rig airstrip where he'd borrowed a jeep on some pretext and a handful of dollars. And driven back.

He didn't say why.

We had another glass of fine old fifth-rate. I pulled the Walther out of my belt and slid it across to him.

'Your gun, I think. Thanks.'

'You got another off the guard at the jail?'

'Yes.' I hauled it out of my pocket and ran my fingers over it. It was a heavy revolver with a breakback loading action, probably a service Webley and Scott ·38. Loaded in all six.

'How d'you feel about a take-off in the dark?' he asked.

'Later. I've got something to attend to.'

'Hold on, Jack,' he said. 'No point in stirring things up.'

'No,' I said, 'no point. But a damn good reason.' I reached up and touched my cut cheek with the tips of my fingers. It felt hot under the hard crust of blood. A nerve jumped erratically.

'Don't try it,' he said gently.

'God damn it – I was the one they cut up! You've never had to stand still and just take it!'

My voice sounded very loud in the dark patio. The silence after it seemed very silent.

'Sorry,' I said quietly. 'You have, too.'

After a while he said:

'Will you try the take-off in the dark?'

'Yes – if the plane isn't guarded. I'll try anything in the dark if it means I don't meet those rifles in the daylight.'

'Fair enough.' He looked at the luminous dial of his wristwatch. 'It'll be light in about half an hour. Better get moving.'

'Yes. Over the wall, I think. Just in case there are guards.'

He stood up.

'Want to take the cognac?' he asked.

'Aren't you coming?'

'As far as the plane. I've still got business here. And there's nothing to connect me with your escape.'

I doubted that. There were plenty of people to guess that the escape of one foreigner had had something to do with the only other foreigner in the place – and I'd experience of how far they'd go on guesswork. But I had something to think out.

We went quietly across the bright plaza and into a zigzag of narrow sandy alleys leading between the groves and small houses towards the east wall.

He asked, 'Did anybody find the oil and junk I dumped in the sea?'

'Yes me.' I told him about the trip with the Nawab and company.

'Well, well, well,' he said softly. 'And all the time little you knew I wasn't dead.'

'It wasn't my business,' I said. 'I think the Dak's just over there.'

We had reached the wall. Outside, it stood about fifteen feet high; inside, with the sand that had drifted or been piled against it, it was no more than seven feet. A lower wall, meeting it at right angles made an easy step up.

'You haven't yet told me why you changed your mind on this cargo,' he said.

'Nor I have.'

'It wouldn't be —' then there was gunfire. Three quick flat-sounding shots too faint to come from the police post. We froze against the wall.

Then there were two more shots, with the same flat quality, and the distant roar of an engine starting up. Then another shot, with more crash to it. The engine roar faded gradually, broken by more crashing shots.

'Pistol, then rifle,' said Ken softly. 'And that truck from over by the caravan camp. What d'you make of it?'

I had a theory, but all I did was grunt and start on the wall. I went up slowly and cautiously. It was dry-stone, without cement, but it had been there a long time and the stones had worn to a close fit. I lifted my head above the village wall.

The Dakota was about twenty yards to my right, facing directly away from me, just as I had left it. There was somebody standing under its starboard wing-tip, watching the end of the village, his back to me. I saw the long robes and I thought I saw the long line of a rifle.

I bent down.

'One guard,' I whispered. 'I think I need help. If it interests you at all, the contents of the port auxiliary tank should value out at over a quarter of a million.'

He stared at me.

'Well, well, well,' he said. 'My old friend Jack Clay. Who'd have thought it?'

'Coming to Tripoli?'

'I might do just that. Now.'

'Get on the wall. We'd better go over together.'

I hoisted myself on to the wide top of the main wall and edged along a few feet. The starlight was bright enough for me to do it quietly. Ken came up alongside me. He pulled the Walther from under his jacket.

'Petrol tank,' he said, 'I love you.'

We jumped. Fifteen feet is a long way in bad light, but we hit sand at the bottom. I went on to my knees and came up with the revolver in my hand. The guard whirled around. He was about thirty yards away.

Ken and I fired together, and with the same idea. Two spouts of sand jumped up around the man's toes. Then his rifle went off.

He had fired too hastily; there was a large *crunch* in the wall above me, then we were running at him, swinging to take him from either side. He pulled down the rifle and started jerking the bolt, but he was still too jittery. We were less than ten yards away by the time he swung the rifle back into his shoulder.

I yelled at him, then slid to a stop and raised the gun.

Ken fired on the run. The guard went down as if somebody had jerked the rug from under him. The rifle didn't fire.

Ken picked the rifle up and slung it from his shoulder. Then he turned the man on his back and gave him a quick once-over for other weapons. The guard suddenly started groaning. There was a dark patch spreading in the coarse robe over his left knee. He'd carry a limp to his grave – but he was lucky there was still time and distance to go.

'Nice shooting,' I said. In that light, running, it was very nice shooting.

'Get her started,' Ken said. He stood up and heaved aside a curved dagger. I went around and climbed in and stumbled up to the cockpit.

The Beretta was gone from the locker, but they had left me a torch. I sat down and started a hasty cockpit check.

Everything seemed to be all right. I looked out of the window. There was a hint – no more – of light in the east. In twenty minutes I'd have a clear run. But I didn't have twenty minutes. Right then, I could only guess at where the strip lay. I wished I had taken a compass bearing when I landed. The landing lights would help, but with an accurate compass bearing of the strip I could have taken off without any light at all.

'Ready to start,' I yelled, and reached for the port starter switch. The flywheel wound up slowly. I meshed in the engine. It ground reluctantly, fired, missed, fired and missed again, then practically jumped out of its mountings catching on. Blue flame flickered on the desert floor. I switched on the starboard engine.

It was more reluctant still, but I now could feed it power from the port engine and skip the batteries – which I didn't trust after two days in the sun. It started.

Ken was tying up the guard's knee.

'All aboard!' I yelled.

He stood up, then stiffened. Three figures were coming round the end of the village. I snapped off the parking brake, shoved up the port throttle, swung the plane to point at them and braked again. Now, if it came to shooting I could switch on the landing light and perhaps dazzle them while I gave Ken a clear target.

Two of the figures seemed to stop. One came on. I took the revolver from my belt and laid it on the seat beside me.

Twenty yards away, he stopped and spread his hands to show he was unarmed. I throttled back, took the revolver and scrambled down the back and out of the door.

He was one of the caravan master's lieutenants. I kept him between me and his friends at the end of the village and yelled at him across the blare of twenty-eight cylinders.

'Don't try to stop us!'

'Meester Clay?'

'Yes?'

'The caravan master,' he called. 'He is dead.'

That had been my theory.

'I did not kill him,' I yelled.

'No. I know who killed him.'

'Yussuf?'

'Yes. He kill the master.'

'Yussuf is not my friend.' I shook my head emphatically. 'He killed the master because the master wouldn't let him kill me.'

He absorbed this, translated it and nodded.

'That is true. Yes. But the cargo you have not given to us?'

'It is not yours.'

There was a pause.

'I have men.' A simple flat statement.

Beside me, I felt Ken make a quick movement, turning to see we weren't being outflanked from the other end of the village.

'We have guns,' I said loudly. If it was going to come to shooting, it was going to come to it now. I was tense and jumpy, but the roar of the engines behind my back was friendly. It was my kind of noise, in a place which wasn't my kind of a place.

It was getting light fast, and time and light were on his side.

I said: 'We are going to Tripoli. I will not report to the police.'

He nodded slowly. It was probably the best bargain he could make. He might try for a better one, but he would get several ·38-sized holes in the belly trying for it. There would be other days, other bargains. As God wills.

'Triq es-slama,' he said gravely. May the road lead to salvation – a pretty fair wish, in the circumstances.

'Amin.'

He made a quick, stiff gesture, turned around and strode off, the long white robe flicking at his heels.

Ken looked at me.

'Get on board,' I said. 'He's newly elected; he may not have them all under control.'

We ducked under the port wing and I climbed in. Ken stepped back and patted the wing root and came away grinning.

'A quarter of a million,' he called.

It seemed less, somehow, than it had two days before. I went forward to the cockpit.

The strip was beginning to show now, a faint flatness in the harsh surface. I felt the door slam; I eased on power, turned left of the dawn and pushed the throttles full forwards.

PART THREE

17

AT THREE thousand feet we climbed into sunlight. I let Ken take over and went aft to see what the searchers from the caravan had pinched or broken.

They seemed to have been thorough – they'd even had up some of the floor panels – but pretty careful. Apart from the Beretta, they'd taken a couple of maps and some of the simpler tools, spanners and screwdrivers and such. I found three rounds of Beretta 7·65 ammunition left at the back of the locker.

My clothes were rumpled, but all there, including my leather jacket. Not suède; just a simple truck-driver's leather zip jacket. I changed uniforms, put the jacket on, then went back to the lavatory and squeezed the last drops of water out of the hand-basin tank and started picking the dried blood off my face.

The cut seemed clean enough, and not very deep. It had been intended to mark me, and it had. Even with stitches, I would have a thin white line down my cheek, about three and a half inches long, for the rest of my life. But I still had my life; the caravan master didn't.

I went up to the cockpit tired, hungry and with a beard like a prophet, but at least a bit cleaner. I sat down and just relaxed in Ken's flying. It was ten years and more since we'd sat in the same plane.

He seemed asleep, except for his eyes glancing over the instruments and his hands making small clenching and unclenching movements on the wheel. The air around us seemed as still as a frosty night: no bumps, no beam gusts, no up- or down-draughts. That was normal – with Ken's flying.

After a while he said: 'What's your story when we get back to Tripoli?'

'Shouldn't be too much trouble,' I said. 'I'll say I dumped my cargo at Edri, stayed overnight, started back the next day and had engine trouble. I put down somewhere in the desert to fix it and lost another night.'

'Suppose they go down to Edri to ask questions?'

'I don't think they will. On the record, I was carrying oil-drilling parts. Anybody who suspects they weren't drill parts thinks they were guns for Algeria. Officially, Libya's in favour of the Algerian rebels, so all they'll want is to make sure the whole business doesn't come out in the open and get the French accusing them of allowing gun-running. So I think that as long as I stick to my story, they'll back me up.'

'What about the caravan master and the lad I clipped in the knee?'

'Same answer. The odds are they aren't even citizens of Libya – those caravans don't believe in belonging in one place: it hinders trade. I don't think anybody will know anything, officially. And the cop certainly won't talk.

'You know, probably the most serious thing we did was my pinching his gun. That belongs to the state.'

'Got it all worked out,' said Ken dryly.

I looked at him. 'This is my parish, chum, remember? I've been flying around these parts for ten years. I know what makes the clocks tick.'

He nodded. 'Sorry.'

'What about your story?' I asked.

'I'm clean and clear except for one thing: I've got a Libyan visa in my passport, but no entry stamp. So if you landed about the same time as some airliner, I might squeeze through with passengers.'

He could do it, too. Even after three days in the desert, his clothes still screamed money. Nobody would ask him too many questions.

'We might do that,' I said. 'What about the Walther?'

'I'll try and hang on to it. I like it.'

I took the policeman's revolver out of my belt and weighed it in my hand. There was a number, not the maker's number, stamped crudely in the frame below the cylinder.

'I've got a feeling this is too obviously government property,' I said. I slid up the window and flipped it away, clear of the propeller. 'I'm getting careless about guns: that's the third I've lost in three days. Ah well, maybe they'll keep coming.'

Ken was looking at me curiously, his long face set and frowning slightly. Then he nodded and bent forward to fiddle with the radio compass. I took over soon after. The air felt as if it had rocks in it.

I had about four hours' fuel for a two-hour flight, and I used most of it hanging around until we picked up radio messages between Idris and an Alitalia flight. I timed my arrival for just after Alitalia, identified myself to the tower and came down on the airfield at about eight in the morning.

Ken hopped out as soon as we had the engines stopped and just drifted away; I waited for whatever was coming. It turned out to be another cop, with a fine white belt and holster, but obviously no gun in it. I felt mean about losing them that pistol.

Would I come and see Signor somebody? Signor somebody – if it would help me make up my mind – was of the police.

I would be honoured to go. We went.

He was a small, brown man in a white shirt and grey flannel trousers, sitting in a small office in the airport building. He stayed leaning forward on his arms on the table and stared at my stomach and asked:

'Your passport, please.'

I gave it him. He looked to see that I was here legally, then started flicking back to see where else I'd been. The simple answer to that was everywhere. He gave up and put it on one side.

'You have been to Edri?'

'Yes.'

'You have delivered your cargo safely?'

'Yes.'

'Perhaps I could see the receipts?'

I took out a handful of papers and gave him one. It was signed by a Mr Patterson. Good old Mr P. His name had appeared on a lot of useful papers for me in the past ten years.

The Signor studied it, and nodded.

'The cargo was what it says it was?'

'I don't know. I didn't look.'

For the first time he looked up at my face. He gave me a long, steady look, then smiled, very slightly. The game was going according to the rules. The prescribed questions, the required answers. Nothing probing, nothing incriminating and all straight out of the textbook.

'There is just one thing, Captain Clay —'

'Yes?'

'When you landed here first, two days ago, two men got off your aeroplane unexpectedly. Perhaps you can —'

'Of course. One was a young Libyan boy. He hadn't flown much before, and he got very frightened. At the last minute he didn't want to take off again, and he jumped out. My co-pilot went after him – to see that he was all right. It seemed he was unwell, so I suggested to my co-pilot that he should stay and look after him. I didn't need another pilot on so short a trip.'

He nodded and smiled again. 'I see. Of course.'

'You don't know what happened to him, do you?' I asked.

'Your co-pilot, Rogers? I believe he is at a hotel.'

'No, the Libyan boy.'

'I am afraid I do not know, Captain. Boys are sometimes impetuous, undependable. I know how it is.'

He looked up at me again, his face blank. Quite, quite blank. Then he handed me my passport and made a few quick marks in a notebook.

Investigation satisfactory. Explanations adequate. No further action recommended. The game was over. No runs, no wickets, no result. We had both been on the same team.

He stood up.

'Thank you for sparing me this time, Captain. I am sorry you had a delay, and you are tired. But there is one thing more – I believe a gentleman from the Athens police wishes to speak with you for just one minute. I think he is here by now —'

This wasn't in the game.

He went to the door, opened it and called down the corridor. Then he stood aside and let in the gentleman from Athens.

'Captain Clay, I introduce Signor Anarchos.' Then he stepped out and closed the door behind him.

Anarchos was shorter than I, but wider, and collecting a slight stomach. I put him at about forty-five: he could hardly be younger and be the man they trusted with overseas jobs. He had a flat, square face made flatter and squarer by his sleeked-back, dark hair and rimless glasses. He was wearing a rumpled coffee linen suit, a cream shirt and a square-ended tie striped like a Neapolitan ice-cream.

We shook hands and he gave me a small smile, then waved at a chair, and went round and sat behind the desk. I sat down and watched him.

First he shuffled his chair around until it was in just the right position. Then he took a notebook, a pen, a pack of Chesterfields and a big, flat chromium lighter out of his pockets and placed them as precisely as if he were arranging a chessboard.

110

Then he looked around until he had a tin-lid ashtray and added it to the collection.

It was all very neat, in more than one sense. In a few moves he had made the desk very definitely his, and me very definitely a visitor.

'Captain – I wonder if I might examine your passport?' He had a soft, unhurried voice with a slight hiss in it.

I gave him the passport. He studied the last few pages, then put it aside, in formation with the ashtray.

'You know Mr Mikklos?' he asked.

'The agent? Yes – he gave me the cargo I brought across here.'

'What was the cargo?'

'Oil-drilling parts.'

'You examined them yourself?'

'No – the boxes seemed the right shape, and they had Customs seals on them already – Greek Customs seals.'

That didn't seem to embarrass him. But suddenly he seemed to remember something. He grabbed at the Chesterfields.

'I'm very sorry, Captain. My manners are not very good. You smoke?'

I shook my head. I wanted a cigarette badly, but I didn't want to seem like a man who wanted a cigarette badly.

'Too dry right now,' I said. 'Now, what's this all about? Was there something wrong with that cargo?'

He put the cigarettes delicately back on the table.

'It is possible, Captain.'

'If Mikklos gave me an illegal cargo, I'll go back to Athens and kick his teeth in.'

He smiled, just a little sadly, and said: 'I'm afraid Mr Mikklos has been murdered.'

I froze. When I thought I had frozen long enough, I leant forward stiffly and asked: 'When was this?'

'The day you left Athens. Perhaps just before you left.'

I stared at an oily mark on my knee and tried to look as if I were thinking.

'I took off at about eleven o'clock that morning. I went to see Mikklos at his office just before. About ten o'clock. He wasn't in.'

He probably knew I'd been there; volunteering information wouldn't do any harm and it just might help – if I needed help.

'You went into his office?'

111

'Not his inner office. I knocked on the door and got no answer, so I assumed he was out somewhere.'

'Did you see anybody else there?'

'No. Not his secretary, not anybody.'

'Nobody coming or going outside?'

'Nobody.'

He made several precise marks in his notebook.

'About this cargo I brought here,' I said slowly. 'Is there any connexion?'

He smiled and spread his hands. 'Since we do not know what the cargo was – if it was not oil-drilling parts – we do not know what its connexions are.'

He waited for me to offer more information. When I didn't, he asked: 'Where did the cargo come from?'

'Mikklos said it had been stored in Athens since it came out of Iraq.'

'It did not come from the islands, the Cyclades?'

I wanted a cigarette very much now.

'Not that I know of. Why should it?'

'But Mikklos did a lot of trade with the Cyclades, did he not?'

'I don't know.' I hadn't known, either.

'And you landed on Saxos the day before?'

'Yes, but not for Mikklos. I was hired by somebody else for that trip.'

'And Mr Kitson, did he know Mr Mikklos?'

'I don't know. I shouldn't think so.'

He made several more neat little marks. Then he wanted to know just why I'd gone to see Mikklos before leaving Athens. Answer: because Mikklos was going to up-date the cargo manifest he'd given me two days before. As I hadn't found him, I'd used the outdated one anyway.

Then he inquired about my cut cheek. I turned so he could get a good look at it – and see that I must have come by it since Athens – and explained it had happened in the desert, when I was repairing the engine. I'd slipped and hit a sharp cowling edge.

He took it all without batting an eyelid and probably without believing a word, but it all went down in the notebook. He was a good cop, probably a very good cop, but he wasn't in his own country. He could disbelieve what he chose, but if he started investigating what I'd been up to in Libya, he'd walk straight into a wall. Thank you very much but that has already been investigated; we see no reason to doubt Captain Clay's word. *Triq es-slama* and don't bang the door as you depart.

He thanked me for my time, advised me to see a doctor about the cut and showed me the door. As he opened it he said: 'I believe I travelled with some friends of yours on the flight from Rome. The Nawab of – Tungabhadra, is it? – and his two charming secretaries.'

The 'charming' was a nice touch – applied to Herter.

'It's getting to be old home week in Tripoli, isn't it?' I said, and then wished I hadn't.

18

TRIPOLI IS probably the best-built town in North Africa, and certainly the dullest. The wide main streets and the tall, spacious public buildings look, and are, Italian. Behind them now are the big, square blocks of flats for American families off Wheelus air base. And west is the Arab quarter, the Medina, with its correctly narrow alleys and dark doorways and its properly gnarled old men bashing hell out of bits of brass. But they don't look as if they believe in it. They look as if they've been hired to sit there because somebody once saw something like it in Morocco and reckoned it would add a bit of local colour for the tourists.

In town, you ride in a one-horse garry. From the airfield you ride in the latest model Chrysler taxi and sit there wondering at the sanity of Washington and Whitehall politicians who shell out eight million sterling a year to keep the Libyans solvent and then let them spend it on Chryslers.

I booked in at a seafront hotel, dumped my bag in the lobby and asked the address of a European doctor. He turned out to be a fussy little Frenchman with delicate fingers and suspicious eyes. He didn't believe my story of falling against a cowling – he'd seen knife wounds before – but he put eight stitches in it, a piece of lint on top and gave me a shot of cognac to get me on my way.

The stitches had taken away any idea I had about breakfast, so I walked back to the hotel and up to my room. There were one hundred rooms in the hotel, all identical. All giving you space to undress in and space to lie down in and if you were rich enough to want to do anything else in a hotel room, you were rich enough to book in at the Uaddan down the road. But right then, all I wanted was space to lie down and the hell with undressing.

It was a sunny-side room and the heat bred dreams like little white grubs. I woke at two o'clock trying to tear the pillow apart as I dreamt back that knife, slicing down my cheek. I staggered into the cubbyhole of a bathroom I shared with the room next door, washed the sweat off my face, shaved cautiously and went down to the bar. Two large Scotches later I was back on the bed; this time I slept without dreaming.

Ken woke me at five o'clock. I staggered off the bed, opened the door to him, lit a cigarette and flopped back again.

He wrinkled his nose at the room.

'For an international jewel thief you seem to spend a lot of your time lying on your back,' he said. He had been shopping: new lightweight grey flannels, blue-and-white striped Italian jacket shirt and a silver silk choker. They weren't quite Brioni's of Rome, but they were the nearest Tripoli could get. He sat down on the foot of the bed and lit his own cigarette.

'His Excellency's in town,' he said.

'I know.'

'And, for some reason, a Greek policeman.'

'I know. Our Athens agent got killed.'

'So? Well, for a man who spends his time lying on his back, you certainly get to know things. Did you kill this Athens bird?'

'Pass me my diary and I'll tell you. Actually, no.'

'But the Greek police think you did? Does that complicate matters?'

'They ruddy well don't think I did. At least, they haven't got any reason to.'

'I so much hope you're right. Personally, when you arrived in town with a four-inch knife-slash and a three-inch beard, I'd have arrested you for every crime on the unsolved list. But that's just my opinion.'

'Damn it all,' I said, 'for a man who's officially dead and who's walking around in daylight with a Walther under his shirt, *you* can talk.'

He patted his stomach. 'No gun at the moment. And I can go down to the beach tomorrow and say I've just swum in from Greece. That'll clear me.'

'Really?' I swung my feet on to the floor. 'Incidentally, how did His Excellency feel about you carting around an offensive weapon – or didn't he know?'

'Nawab, him like having people with guns around him – as long as they're on his payroll. He don't carry one himself, but he feels safer if his employees do.'

I nodded and went through into the bathroom. The bright crosstalk had cleared my brain a little; I cleared a little more of it with tepid water. Ken came and leant on the doorway.

'You haven't seen my co-pilot?' I asked.

'Now, there's a good question. This is something you clearly don't know. Your bright boy – Rogers, I think? – flew off with friend Herter this morning in a hired plane. For Edri, as I heard. To see where you had got to.'

I took the towel away from my face. 'Well, I'm damned.'

'When they find you haven't been to Edri, that may cock up your story with the authorities, no?'

I lit another cigarette.

'I don't think so; not necessarily. The cops liked my story and I think they'll stick to it as long as I do.'

'The Nawab's a big man.'

'Not in this town. Not yet. Beirut and Athens he was expecting to go to. He'd had time to buy sources of information and influence there. But he wasn't expecting to come to Tripoli. He's on his own here.'

He looked dubious. 'He's a Muslim.'

'That won't get him anywhere with the Arabs. He's the wrong sort of Muslim. They hate them worse than Christians and Jews.'

'I so much hope you're right,' he said again. 'Well, what now?'

'I was thinking of eating – for the first time in twenty-four hours.'

'Too early.' He looked at his watch. 'In fact, I make it the old-fashioned hour. Get your shoes on while I ring for a one-horse sleigh.'

'I'm eating first,' I said firmly.

'You sadden me,' he said, looking saddened. 'I'll drop in

after dinner. Don't get preoccupied: there are some important repairs to be done on that port petrol tank, remember.'

I just nodded.

They didn't start serving dinner for another half-hour and I didn't feel like going out to look for other places to eat, so I ended up in the bar anyhow. It was a bigger place than the bedrooms, but it was built on the same principles. There was room to buy a drink and room to drink it and the overheads stopped there.

Sitting at one of the tables doing a crystal-gazing act with a glass of beer was young Rogers. I bought two large Scotches at the bar and took them across.

He jumped up and nearly knocked over the table.

'My God,' he said, 'I thought you must be lost.'

'And here you are, organizing a search for me.' I sat down and handed him one of the glasses.

'What happened to your face?' he asked.

I told the cowling story again and he was the first to believe it. But he had other things on his mind. He hauled out a wad of cable forms and waved them at me.

'We're in trouble, Jack.' He handed over the cables; there were five of them, all from Hauser, and all asking the same thing: where were we, what were we doing and were we making any profit at it?

'I didn't dare answer them,' he said. His eyes looked worried. 'I didn't know what to say. And there's a Greek policeman looking for you. Mikklos has been murdered.'

'I heard about Mikklos. We'd better send a cable to friend Hauser.'

'Saying what?'

'Got delayed in the desert with a faulty magneto. We patched it up and got back to Tripoli. Now doing further repairs. Love and kisses.'

'Is that what happened?'

'More or less. You send it, over my name.'

He stared moodily at the table.

'I don't like this, Jack. I don't like saying so, but I wish to hell I knew what you were doing.'

I took a deep breath of Scotch.

'Look, Tony,' I said, 'why don't you do what I suggested in Athens? – get the galloping bellyache and take a few days off.

116

I want to spend the next couple of days in Tripoli and I want the Dak with me. So why don't you just get sick and not know what's going on?'

He was still staring at the table top.

'I just can't do it, Jack,' he said in a small, strained voice. 'After all, we're both drawing our pay from Hauser and we can't just . . .' he waved his hands and looked up at me miserably.

He was right, but if I was wrong I was too far wrong to start admitting it now. I finished off my Scotch and semaphored a barman.

'Okay,' I said. 'It's too late to fly out today anyhow. And we can't fly out anyway until I've checked the engines, because you don't know how. So just lie back and enjoy it. Have another Scotch.'

He shook his head. 'I'll send that cable.'

He hurried out and didn't come back for dinner.

I had been dreaming of steak, but I had forgotten where I was. In Tripoli you eat veal; if you don't eat veal, you don't eat. But they had a no-complaints customer; I would have eaten the chef with the head waiter grated on top.

I had soup, caneloni, escalope *Milanese*, an ice, cheese and coffee. The waiter was just suggesting a cognac and I was turning it down on the basis of my recent experience with Libyan cognac when the dining-room door whanged open and Herter was giving the diners a sifting glare. He popped his eyes at me and marched across.

I said: '*Strega, per favore,*' to the waiter and smiled pleasantly at Herter.

He said: 'Where have you been?' He said it so that everybody in the room heard.

I held up a hand. 'Don't discuss your employer's business so loudly. Sit down and have a drink and tell me what you're doing in Tripoli.'

He sat down, leant at me and whispered harshly: 'We have been looking for you?'

'That's very thoughtful of you. But why?'

'Because you have some of His Excellency's private property. What have you done with it?'

'You've got proof of this?' I asked sweetly.

The waiter brought my Strega and Herter boiled silently

When the waiter had gone he said: 'We know you had it. Now tell me —'

'If I've got any of the Nawab's property,' I said, 'I'll return it. If, that is, I'm convinced it is his. Possibly you'll be kind enough to tell the Nawab that.'

He hadn't expected that. He glared at me suspiciously, then said:

'I will tell His Excellency what you say. Stay here at the hotel and I will call you.' He marched off. The head waiter gave him a little mock bow, then grabbed for the door just too late to stop it whanging closed.

I swallowed the Strega, signed the bill and walked slowly out to the bar. Herter's visit meant I was slap back in the social whirl: I'd hoped for one good quiet night before I started being rude to people again. I had things to think out.

The jewellery was probably safer in the petrol tank than anywhere out of it. Two handfuls of gems don't take up much room in a 170-gallon tank; you'd need to be pretty sure they were in there before you got down with your little piece of bent wire and started fishing for them. And anyhow, the airport staff wouldn't let anybody but me start fiddling with that plane.

Neither Ken nor Rogers was in the bar. Rogers I wasn't worried about: he could sit around and brood about the need for engineering licences as well as scruples. But I needed to see Ken if I could, before I talked to the Nawab.

He wasn't signed in at the hotel, so I asked the desk to find me a taxi. They found me another Chrysler. One of the few overheads the place allowed itself was a front garden, thirty yards of palms and bushes with a crescent driveway to the front steps. But they'd built the drive before they'd thought of the problem of having a twenty-foot Chrysler turn into it. So if you took a Chrysler, you took a short walk first.

We tried the Uaddan, where the Nawab and party were staying, and the Grand, and two other places before I found where Ken had signed in. But we didn't find him. We started a round of the bars. That isn't as hopeless as it sounds – Tripoli has a strictly limited list of places where they serve respectable liquor. Ken would probably stay clear of the upper-crust places, to stay clear of the Nawab, but he wouldn't sacrifice his taste in booze.

We tried four places I knew and three more the driver suggested, and we didn't find him. That left the airport bar and the English and American officers' clubs. It takes a few days to get yourself invited to the clubs, so that left the airport. A telephone call would be quicker than the ride out there; we went back to the hotel. It was getting on for nine, and dark.

The driver had inflationary ideas about how much I owed him, so we stood in the road and wrangled. I beat him down to twice what it would have cost in Paris, paid, and started back up the driveway.

Something cracked in the bushes and something tore the air by my head; I slammed on to the drive and rolled right, away from the crack, into the bushes. Whoever it was fired twice more, then ran. I heard him go. I lay where I was, wishing to hell I'd hung on to one or two of the guns I'd acquired and lost so lightly over the past three days.

Nobody came a-running. It had been a small-calibre gun fired in the open, and that doesn't collect crowds. There might have been some subtle reasoning behind that – if the gunman hadn't also chosen to fire when I was on the darkest patch of the drive and then at my head. If he'd waited ten seconds until I was on the lighted porch, he'd have had me on toast.

I went on hands and knees through the bushes to the steps, whizzed through into the lobby and headed for the bar and the Scotch bottle. I don't perturb easily, but I don't get shot at much either.

The Scotch got me up the stairs and into my room. I had a gravel burn on my left palm, a cut on my right knee that was staining my good lightweight suit and a bruise on the thigh from having flopped on to a pocketful of coins and keys. I washed, changed into my uniform and went down to the telephones in the lobby, watching shadows all the way.

I established that Ken wasn't at the airport bar. The desk clerk couldn't think of any respectable bars which I hadn't tried already, but he had a message for me: the Nawab would find it convenient if I called on him at ten o'clock.

That left me half an hour. I thought about another Scotch, then thought about somebody still waiting for me with a gun, and made it a Cola. Then I suggested to the clerk that he found me a taxi that drove right up to the door. He looked at me oddly, but phoned here and there and ten minutes later I had a Renault at the bottom of the steps. If anybody took another shot, he missed even the car on that trip.

19

THE NAWAB had a three-room suite on the first floor. A uniformed flunkey announced me by phone and showed me up. Herter let me in.

The lounge was a big, tall room, with a lot of plaster doodling up in the stratosphere, deep red drapes across the windows and a good crop of orange-shaded reading lamps. It was a Herter's sort of room; put a sabre at his belt and you could have opened the window and watched the lights of 1914 Europe going out one by one.

He didn't have a sabre, but he had something heavy in his right-hand jacket pocket. I let my hand swing against it as I went in. He recoiled, then gave me a quick up-and-down look. In my uniform shirt and trousers anybody who could see my hip pocket could see I hadn't got a gun in easy reach.

Neither the Nawab nor Miss Brown was in sight, but there was a tray of bottles on one of the small tables. I mixed myself a long Scotch and soda without being invited. Herter watched.

'Well,' I said, 'is His Excellency going to be here, or are you handling all his business calls?'

'His Excellency will be here when he is ready. Please sit down.'

I drank some of my drink and didn't sit.

'You wouldn't try and kill me, would you?' I asked him. 'I'd say it was in your interest to keep me alive – or am I wrong?'

'You are frightened?' he asked, puzzled.

'Up to a point. Anybody can be frightened up to a point.' A new thought came to me. 'You wouldn't even want me to think you wanted to kill me – just to get me frightened?'

He looked more puzzled.

'Never mind,' I said, 'it's too complicated.' It probably was, for Herter. I drank more of my drink, and lit a cigarette. After a while the Nawab came in.

He was wearing the same sort of rig as last time: a short-sleeve shirt, grey flannels and a pair of thin Moroccan slippers. He gave me one sharp look, then glanced at the drinks. Herter jumped for them and whipped up a quick brandy and soda.

The Nawab took it and said: 'Thank you,' then, to me: 'It's very kind of you to come here, Captain. Please be seated.'

We sat down in ornate silk-covered armchairs. Herter moved around and stood at the Nawab's elbow.

The Nawab said: 'I believe you've found some of the jewels we were looking for, Captain. I hope that your coming here tonight means you are going to return them to us.'

I said: 'Let's put it this way: I might know something about where some of them are. But I don't know, of course, whether or not these are the ones you're looking for. And even if they are, I've been to some trouble and expense to locate them.'

Herter said: 'Of course they are His Excellency's.'

I smiled politely at him: 'Well, perhaps you'd describe the ones you're looking for and I'll tell you if I recognize them?'

That had them. Apart from not wanting to give me any more information than I'd already got, they'd need to describe well over fifty pieces if Ken had been right about the 'two ammunition boxes full'. Still, they must somehow be able to do it; it wouldn't have been worth coming to look for them if they couldn't.

The Nawab said: 'I feel sure we'll be able to satisfy you that these are the pieces we're looking for, Captain. How many were there?'

I thought about answering that, then didn't see why not. 'About ten or so.'

He nodded gravely. 'Now, you mentioned "trouble and expense", I think, Captain. Would you estimate that?'

'It isn't easy. The expenses weren't all that high: the trouble was considerable. I nearly got killed – and that's difficult to price. But I seem to remember – in Athens – that you mentioned a reward. A small percentage. How would you estimate that?'

He didn't want to estimate it: he would rather I'd forgotten all about that conversation.

He said slowly: 'That would depend on the value of the jewels. That, we do not know yet.'

'I could give you my estimate,' I said helpfully. 'At a conservative price, I'd put them at £200,000.'

There was a long, fragile hush.

Then the Nawab said sarcastically: 'You are an expert, Captain?'

'By no means. But I've had – some experience. And I was talking, of course, of the full open market price. The only really fair way we could judge that would be for me to dispose of

121

them elsewhere and you to buy them back on the open market. Then you'd know exactly what they're worth.'

There was another hush. Herter leant slowly forward, his eyes glinting behind his glasses and hard furrows across his forehead.

The Nawab looked up at him and shook his head, then held out his empty glass. Herter relaxed slightly, took the glass and started refilling it.

The Nawab said, to me: 'Just what were you thinking of, as a reward?'

'A small percentage? I would say five is small enough. That's £10,000.'

Herter held out the filled glass. The Nawab took it and they glanced briefly at each other and he said: 'Perhaps you would ask our guest to come in?'

Herter very nearly smiled. He nodded and went out into the corridor, closing the door behind him. The Nawab sipped and said pleasantly: 'How do you find Tripoli, Captain?'

'Same as last time.'

'Of course, your work must bring you here often.'

'Yes. How's Miss Brown?'

He frowned at his brandy. 'Very well.'

The door opened and Yussuf came in.

He was wearing the same cotton jeans, blue cowboy jacket and knowledgeable sneer that he had worn since we'd met. The jacket and trousers were smudged by now; the sneer looked fresh and new.

I kept my face calm, dead calm. Or at least, I tried.

Herter shut the door behind him and came up to the Nawab's elbow again.

The Nawab said pleasantly: 'I think you have met before?' He looked happy; Herter looked happy; Yussuf looked happy. It was a great big wonderful world and me on the outside looking in.

'We've met,' I said. 'Now what?'

'We found Mr – er, Yussuf, at Edri this afternoon. He was able to tell us something of your adventures at Mehari – and it was very interesting. He was also able to tell us something of your adventures in Athens just before you left there. That was very interesting, too – especially after what the gentleman from the Greek police told us on the aeroplane from Rome.'

He paused and I got another chorus of mutual happiness. They had a big Christmassy surprise all wrapped up for me, and they loved the business of unwrapping it.

'It seems,' the Nawab said, 'that the man who was handling the jewels in Athens got killed before you left. *Just* before you left. I understand, from what Yussuf tells me, that you went to see this man before leaving. And that, when you arrived at Mehari, you were carrying this man's pistol; Yussuf recognized it.'

That was the surprise: I was a murderer.

They leant forward, waiting for me to go pale and start babbling for mercy, I swear it had been an accident, the gun went off in a struggle, I'll never do it again, and please take these jewels, free, as proof of my sincerity.

I gulped the last of my drink and stood up. Yussuf put his hand quickly inside his jacket, but did nothing more.

'I need a drink,' I said thickly. I trudged across to the drinks table. That put me within arm's-length of Yussuf. He stood where he was, leering happily at me. I splashed whisky into the glass, shot soda on top if it and dumped the syphon down again, knocking over the whisky bottle.

Yussuf looked down at it – and I had him.

By the time Herter had got his hand into his jacket pocket and out again with a big, black Luger, I was holding Yussuf's right arm up his back and had him in between Herter and me.

'Hold it,' I said quickly, 'I'm not trying to kill anybody.'

It was a close thing, though. They had me marked down as a murderer already, and Herter would have been quite ready to blast me through Yussuf if he thought I planned any harm to the Nawab. With that gun, he'd have reached me, too.

I stuck my left hand over Yussuf's shoulder and slipped the gun out from his waistband. It was a small, silvery automatic, ·22 calibre, engraved with gold wire patterns and with ivory inlays on the butt. I sniffed the barrel and threw it down into the chair near Herter.

I let Yussuf go and stepped back.

'I was shot at earlier this evening,' I said. 'By my hotel, a couple of hours after I saw you. Three shots from a small-calibre gun. Smell the barrel of that one.'

Herter bent down cautiously, took the little automatic, sniffed it and looked sharply at Yussuf.

I said: 'Yussuf once said he'd kill me. He'll try again. Just remember that wherever those jewels are, nobody can find them but me. If I'm dead, they're gone – for good. Keep your little lad under better control if you want to do business with me.'

Herter slipped his own gun back into his pocket, broke the magazine out of the small automatic and emptied two cartridges into his palm.

He stared at Yussuf. 'Three shots have been fired from this gun. You tried to kill Captain Clay.'

I said: 'Yussuf's a dangerous pet to have around the house. One of the things I bet he didn't tell you about Mehari was that he killed his last boss down there. And he'd have had me tonight, if he'd known enough not to try a head shot in the dark.'

Yussuf stuck his face forward. 'Next time I do it better! Next time I kill you good!'

I hit him. I put twelve stone and a lot of sincerity into it, and caught him on the side of the jaw. His head whipped around, twisting his body after it, and he went down. After that, he was just a new pattern on the carpet.

Herter was reaching in his pocket again.

'Relax,' I said. 'It just happened to be my turn to hit somebody. People have been picking on me for days. Where were we? Ah, yes – I was getting myself a drink.'

Most of the Scotch was on the carpet by now. I took a fresh glass and mixed a weak brandy and soda and went back to my chair. Nobody said anything. The Christmas spirit had faded badly.

'Well,' I said, 'I believe we were discussing a deal. Part of your side of it seemed to be that I had killed Mikklos. I don't admit I did, of course, but let's hear what you were going to offer on that basis.'

The Nawab pulled himself together, took a deep breath and said: 'I didn't intend Yussuf to try and kill you – I am sorry that happened.'

'It didn't happen, not quite. I should try and see that it doesn't – at least until this deal's complete.'

'Yes. Yes, of course.' He took another breath. 'Nevertheless, Captain – I think you'd probably prefer me not to hand over Mr Mikklos's gun to the Greek detective who is here in Tripoli. Nor tell him how we came by it. It is, after all, evidence that puts you very much under suspicion. So, since we're talking of a bargain, I suggest we give you the gun – in return for the jewels, of course.'

'Of course,' I said. I looked at Herter. 'Does this strike you as a good idea?'

They both went stiff. Herter was a hired man; it wasn't for him to have ideas about his employer's ideas.

'That doesn't enter into it,' the Nawab pointed out.

'But you don't advise against it?' I asked Herter.

'Of course not.'

I nodded. 'Okay. I just like deals to be unanimous. Well, now – there's still this question of my time and trouble. In fact, if I actually did kill Mikklos, it must have been so I could get at the jewels – so that really adds to the trouble I've taken. Still, if you prefer to see it another way, I won't argue. Let's just say £5,000, for reward, time and trouble. And the gun.'

The Nawab frowned slightly. 'I wonder if you realize that I'm serious about this, Captain. If we give the gun to this Greek policeman —'

'I know. I know you're serious – and I know exactly how serious the gun and me and the Greek copper are. But however serious, he can't do anything in Libya. He'd have to get me extradited – and at the moment I'm on good terms with the Libyan police. So let's just say £5,000. In effect I'm offering you £5,000 for that gun, and I don't think you'll get any better offer elsewhere. I should settle.'

The Nawab went on frowning to himself. Then he said: 'I will think this over.'

'Good.' I smiled at them. 'Heard any more of Ken Kitson?'

They both went stiff again; Ken was a dirty word in that company.

'We did not hear of any more wreckage being found,' the Nawab told me.

I shook my head sadly. 'A business, that. He was an old friend of mine. I don't like to see him go out that way – on an unauthorized flight. Almost like a criminal. I'd like to do something to clear his name.'

The Nawab looked pained. Herter took the cue.

'His Excellency does not wish to speak of Mr Kitson.'

'But I do,' I said, 'I'll complete my side of the deal. I want two letters, back-dated to the day before Ken flew out of Athens. One releasing him from his contract, nothing owing on either side, from the end of the following day. The second authorizing him to make that last flight. Let's say you sent him to' – I put on a face of deep thought – 'to Tripoli, here, to make arrangements for your visit. And I'd like both letters signed by you.'

The Nawab was frowning at his feet; Herter was frowning at me.

'Just a bit of foolish sentiment,' I said, 'but they'll clear him for whoever's interested. Friends, relatives, so on. Put them in the deal and we're doing business.' I stood up. 'All right?'

'You forget,' Herter snapped, 'we can give the gun to the Greek policeman.'

'And you forget we're in Tripoli, not Athens.'

The Nawab said: 'You need to go to Athens for your job, I believe, Captain.'

'Very true. That's very shrewd of you. But the letters won't cost you anything. I still think we can do business on the terms I suggested.' I put my glass down on the table and nodded to them. 'Goodnight, Your Excellency. Thank you for the drinks.'

Yussuf was squirming around making heavy breathing noises: I stepped over him. They let me find the door for myself.

20

I WALKED BACK to my hotel. I wasn't going to get shot at again – not just yet, anyway. I didn't trust Herter keeping an eye on Yussuf – this was Yussuf's home town. But he wasn't going to be shooting at anybody else tonight.

I asked at the desk if there were any messages. The clerk shook his head and gave me a big juicy leer. I couldn't interpret that, so I said goodnight.

I had got my hand on the door handle before I saw the light under the door. Without thinking about it, I was flat against the wall at one side, holding my breath. Being shot at makes you sensitive about surprises.

Thinking about it didn't do much good – except for the thought that anybody waiting to take a shot could just as well have waited in the dark and got me outlined against the corridor lights. Probably Rogers. I went in.

It wasn't Rogers. It was Miss Brown. She was curled up on my bed reading a magazine. She smiled up at me.

'Hello,' she said, 'I've been waiting for you.'

'Yes,' I said slowly, 'so you have.'

'Come in and shut the door. Would you like a drink?'

'Yes,' I said, 'I'd like a drink.' Good, sparkling conversationalist, our Jack Clay. I shut the door. When I turned back she had uncurled and was pouring Scotch from a half-bottle into a tooth-glass. She was wearing a white mohair jumper over an emerald shirt and a slim emerald skirt.

'I see why the desk clerk gave me the big smile,' I said. I went across to take the drink. She smiled again, then saw the lint and plaster on my face.

'What happened?' she asked, big brown eyes wide.

'I fell against an engine —' I started, but the hell with that. 'A man with a knife,' I growled.

She stood up, close, and put long, cool fingers on my face.

'It looks dirty,' she said softly. It probably did. I had rolled on it ducking Yussuf's second shot. 'Wait a moment.'

She picked a big, square, white handbag off the dressing table and went into the bathroom. I sipped the Scotch. When she came back she had a wisp of damp handkerchief in her hand. She stood close again and started peeling the lint off the cut.

It hurt, a bit, but I had other sensations to occupy my mind.

'You should curl up on beds more often,' I said. 'It suits your legs.'

She paused and looked at me, from about eighteen inches away. Her face was lovely; even at that distance it was flawless. Big, dark brown eyes in a perfect honey-coloured skin, and a touch of a smile on her mouth.

She turned back to the cut on my cheek. She knew her job there. She wiped it gently, put something cooling on it and finally another lint dressing – all from the junk in her handbag. Then she stepped back.

'It's a bit cleaner now.'

'Feels wonderful.'

She went quickly back into the bathroom again. I sat down on the edge of the bed and sipped more Scotch.

She came back in and closed the door gently behind her and stood looking at me.

'It's very nice finding you here,' I said, 'but I don't quite see why. Usually the only things I find in hotel rooms are hotel bills.'

She came quickly across and sat on the floor beside me, her arm on my knee and her head on her arm. Just like that.

'I just wanted someone to talk to.'

I ran my hand slowly through her long, black hair and she moved gently against my hand.

'I don't have to go on calling you Miss Brown, do I?' I asked.

'Dahira.'

'Dahira.'

'Did you see Aly – the Nawab?' she asked.

'I saw him.'

'Are you going to give him the jewels?'

'I may do a deal with him.'

She lifted her face and her eyes were wide and anguished.

'He'll cheat you. He's sure to cheat you.'

'He may try,' I said. 'He won't necessarily succeed.'

She shook her head slowly. 'He will. Him and that big Gestapo thug of his.' That made us unanimous on Herter; I smiled.

She said: 'I think you're the only man I've seen stand up to them. But they'll still cheat you. Jack – don't have any more to do with them than you have to. Go away – go away with the jewels.'

'Should you be saying this – to me?'

She put her head down, cheek against my hand.

'What do you think he is to me, Jack?' she said in a soft, throaty voice. But she wasn't asking any question. 'A job – that's all. I need him; I need a job. I'm Eurasian – half-caste, if you like; I've been called that before – but not since I became the Nawab's girl.

'Do you know what it's like for a Eurasian girl, Jack? My father was an English major in the Indian Army. My mother was a Muslim girl. What would they think of me in England, Jack? I can guess. I know what they think of me in decent, respectable Muslim families.'

She said it without rancour, almost without feeling, but when she moved her cheek against my hand it was like fire on my skin. My other hand was clenched tight in her hair; I seemed to be listening without breathing.

She lifted her face.

'I'm a rich man's girl,' she said simply. 'I'm that – or I'm nothing. I'm a luxury. What happens to a luxury when she gets old and ugly?'

I reached for her and she came. Her hands raked through my hair and her lips whispered on my face and then on my mouth. I opened my mouth wide against her and breathed her and tasted her and knew only that, that and her soft breasts crushed and yet moving against me. And desire; desire pure and clear as spring water.

She dragged her lips away and whispered urgently; 'Take me with you, Jack. Wherever, wherever – take me with you.'

If I could have opened the door and stepped out into a plane, I would have started for wherever right then. But wherever is a long way. It's just off the map, and just over the horizon, and just farther than the fuel in the tanks. It's the little valley on Kira island.

The mood was blurred, and she sensed it. She lowered her head against my chest and clung to me and I moved my hand through her hair. She was still the most beautiful thing I'd ever seen, but I was still a tired Dakota pilot in a second-rate Tripoli hotel with unfinished crooked business for the morning.

'Jack,' she said softly, without lifting her head. 'What is it you want – out of life?'

I said: 'I'm going to sound mundane. I'm an airline pilot – that's what I want to be. Except with a better airline than right now.'

'No far-away places with strange-sounding names? No champagne and quail's eggs?'

'The bubbles tickle my nose. And the far-away places are full of men with big knives.'

She looked up at me. 'What happened to him – the one who cut you?'

'Somebody else killed him.'

'Before you could?'

'I was running away at the time.'

She sat back on her heels. 'Give me a drink. I want something to throw in your face.'

'Aim at the mouth.' I poured more Scotch into the glass and she sipped at it and watched me over the rim.

I gave her a cigarette and lit it and mine. We didn't say anything for a long time. The mood died gently around us and we looked at each other and smiled, the way you do when you both know something that hasn't been said and isn't going to be said.

'You're a complicated man, Jack,' she said.

'Muddled. Just muddled. Too many people and too many places.'

'But no far-away places?'

'Are there any?'

'Don't tell me about the aeroplane making the world smaller. There must be far-away places still.'

'For some people. It depends on the people. It depends on how you get there, too.'

She stood up slowly, a lovely, long movement, and dropped her cigarette in the ashtray. 'If you find an aeroplane that will get you there . . .'

I got up. 'Yes.'

She smiled quickly and brushed my good cheek with her lips and was gone, leaving me with the smell of her in the air and a voice inside that shouted for me to go after her and bring her back. The voice was going to last a lot longer than the perfume.

21

I WAS AT the airport by nine o'clock. I changed into overalls and started to give the Dak a proper check over. A few mechanics wandered up to see if I wanted any paid help, then wandered away again.

After an hour and a half I was pretty sure the plane was in as good shape as she was likely to be, and I had established myself as part of the landscape.

I got a long piece of heavy-gauge wire, bent a hook at one end and started to fish in the port auxiliary tank.

It was a long job. The petrol fumes made me giddy and the heat made me angry, but the jewels made me go on. By half past eleven I had all nine major pieces and two of the rings spread out to dry on a piece of oily rag along the top of the wing. The petrol didn't seem to have harmed them at all; it had made the pearls look a lot fresher.

I changed back into uniform, stuffed the jewellery in my pockets and hauled myself across to the airport bar. I was getting my head down into the second glass of beer when somebody stopped beside me and asked if I minded sharing my table.

It was Anarchos, the Greek cop.

'Sit down,' I invited. 'Drink?'

'Beer, if you please.' He smiled pleasantly at me. The loot in my pockets suddenly seemed to be bulging; I had to remind myself he was working far from home and without judicial authority. I reminded myself while I waved at the barman.

When I turned back to Anarchos, he had his little chess line-up of Chesterfields, lighter, pen and notebook set out across the table. He smiled again.

'I hope your night's sleep restored you, Captain.'

'I'm fine, thanks. You off back to Athens?'

'Not just yet.' He didn't tell me why he was at the airport, though.

'How's it going, the investigation?'

He opened the notebook. 'One or two points, Captain, I'd like to clear up. You don't mind?'

'Not at all. Go ahead.'

He waited while the barman brought our beers and took my money.

'Three days ago,' he said, 'you flew from Athens to Tripoli and then on to Mehari, yes?'

'Edri,' I said stiffly.

'Edri? Ah yes,' and he made a mark in his notebook. 'And you handed over the cargo and got a receipt.'

'I showed you the receipt.'

'You did, yes. Who were the guns for?'

Outside, an Alitalia Viscount swished down on to the runway, silver and blue and sprightly, like a well-tailored society lady.

'I don't carry guns,' I said harshly.

'Come, Captain.' He smiled confidentially. 'What is there to be ashamed of? Carrying guns is no great crime. If it were, many of my countrymen would be far greater criminals than yourself. Guns go from Greece to – to many places. We know. Guns are an international currency, perhaps more so than dollars, I think. So, you carried a few guns – what of it? Mr Mikklos was certainly not murdered over a few guns.'

And there it was: admit to carrying a few rifles – and clear up the mystery of my flight. Admit to a bit of gun-running and be cleared of suspicion of murder.

Only it wouldn't be like that. What he wanted was a lever into my story. Once he had that, just that one admission, he could use it to prise away until he had the rest. He was a good cop – and he didn't think I'd been carrying guns, anyway.

'I don't carry guns,' I said again.

He stared at me with a gentle, puzzled look, and went on without any apparent change of step: 'What I don't understand about you, Captain, is why you should be flying for a small, down-and-out airline like Aircargo.'

I jerked my head up. *I* call Aircargo down-and-out but nobody else does, not while I'm around.

He held up his hand to stop me. 'I know what sort of an airline it is, Captain. Do not feel insulted – the mystery is that *you* work for them. I have asked questions about you, at Athens, at the airport here. Those people, they know the pilots; they watch them come down through bad weather, they watch them land with failed engines. Year after year, they watch you. And they all say the same thing: you are one of the best, the safest, pilots they have ever seen.'

'There are better.'

'Perhaps. But if so, they are all working for the big air companies – BOAC, BEA, Air France. So – why not you, with all you have to offer them?'

'I have unstable morals. I get drunk on Saturday nights.'

He nodded. 'Perhaps you have unstable morals, Captain, but it is not that you get drunk on Saturdays. I have written to London about you, through Interpol. I must wait for the reply.'

'London hasn't heard of me in years.'

He nodded again. 'Possibly, Captain. Now I ask myself, why not?'

'What kind of a reply do you get?' I snarled.

He smiled. 'I must wait for that, too.'

The doors of the bar swung open and about half a dozen people came in, carrying luggage.

Among them was Shirley Burt.

Anarchos turned around casually – except that I knew by now that he didn't do anything casually. I suddenly guessed this might be why he was at the airport: he had connexions with me, and his department in Athens would have tipped him off that she'd bought a Tripoli ticket.

She stared around the bar, saw me and I waved her across. She was wearing a straight-cut navy blue linen suit with a white collar, carrying a blue suitcase and with a battered pigskin camera bag slung from her shoulder.

She dropped into a chair and grinned wearily at me. 'Beer. Cold, cold beer,' she said.

Anarchos had half got up. It occurred to me that it might be embarrassing for him to meet her, face to face, straight away.

'Shirley,' I said, 'meet Mr Anarchos. Mr Anarchos, Miss Shirley Burt.' Anarchos bowed his head gracefully. I said: 'Mr Anarchos is from the Athens police department. He's out here investigating a murder he thinks I know something about.'

Anarchos gave me a slow, cool look.

Shirley looked him over carefully. 'You wouldn't be something to do with the little men who were running to hell and gone all over Saxos and Kira the other day?'

'You have just been to Saxos?' Anarchos asked politely. He knew already exactly where she'd been.

Shirley said, to me: 'I went back to photograph that plane you found on Kira. The place was lousy with Athens cops, asking questions everywhere. So now I know: you bumped a guy in Athens, did you? Have you confessed yet? Why did you do it?'

I spread my hands. 'He claimed to be more devoted to you than I am. Could I ignore that?'

Anarchos looked a little troubled. After the grilling he'd given me, that suited me perfectly.

Then he scooped his bits and pieces off the table. 'I must go now.' He offered his hand to Shirley. 'I am very happy to have met you.'

'Aren't you arresting him?' she asked. 'Aren't you going to lug him screaming back to Athens?'

He looked at me sadly, as if that was exactly what he'd like to do. 'I fear I have no powers.'

'I'll be back in Athens,' I told him. 'In my own good time and my own good way.'

He looked at me again. '*Good* way, Captain?' Then he went away. I watched him: he went to the bar and pointed us out to the barman as in need of care and attention; then to the door. He looked back and I raised my hand and he nodded.

It was a nice touch, telling the barman about us, after what I'd been trying to do to him.

Shirley stared at me. 'Did someone really get killed?'

'Yes: a man called Mikklos, an agent we dealt with.'

'Was it anything to do with you?'

'The killing? For heaven's sake – we just took cargo from him. Why he got killed ...' I shrugged.

The barman came across and I ordered two more beers.

Shirley waited until he was gone, then asked: 'Was this Mikklos a crook?'

'You don't have to be a crook to get killed, not in this world, and if you are a crook, you don't necessarily get bumped off. The injustice of life is frightening sometimes.'

She nodded, then asked: 'What happened to your face?'

Here we went again. 'Slipped against a cowling. Down in the desert.'

'What were you doing in the desert?'

And again. 'Delivering parts to an American oil-drilling rig. Was there anything more in Athens about Ken's crash?'

It was a brutal way of changing the subject, but it worked. Her face sagged and she shook her head. 'Nothing more. They had a Greek Navy boat out there when I was on Kira, but they didn't find anything.'

The beers arrived and we devoted a pause to them.

I asked: 'Did you get good pictures on Kira?'

She nodded. 'The old Dakota under the trees – I got it in colour. It took a hell of an exposure, but it should make a two-page spread in *Life* magazine.'

'Did you meet that German, Nikolas?'

'Yes – a sweet man. He showed me around. It says something about the islanders – the way they'll take to a man who was their enemy fifteen years ago.'

'That's pretty good. Good story, then?'

'With those pictures it'll make a story whether the Nawab finds any of his jewels or not. Where's he staying, d'you know?'

I laid my hand against the Nawab's jewellery in my pocket and said: 'The Uaddan. Big place down towards the harbour. Any taxi'll take you.'

'Thanks.' She finished her beer, shook her head at the idea of another, then asked: 'Why did he come here, do you know?'

I shrugged. 'It's a pretty free-and-easy place. Some stuff goes through Libya on the way to Tangier. Maybe that's why.'

She nodded vaguely and collected up her bag. 'I'll run along and book in.'

'You'll be sticking close to the Nawab?'

'Sure. At this Uaddan place, if they'll take me.'

'I'll drop in if I may.' The closer she stuck to the Nawab the better chance she had of not meeting Ken.

'Do that.' She got up and I got up after her. There wasn't anything to keep me around the airport. I picked up her case and opened the door for her. The white sunlight sizzled down at us. I led the way to the taxi stand.

Ken walked around the corner.

I took a long breath and held on to it. Shirley stood quite dead still. Ken reached up slowly and pushed his hair back out of his eyes and said: 'Hi! What're you doing in these parts?'

She said softly: 'You're alive.'

He ran his hand through his hair again. 'Yes – I'm okay, thanks.' He looked a bit worried.

'Did you crash?'

'Well, no. The whole thing, it was – I wanted to break my contract with the Nawab. It seemed the easiest thing. Then.'

'Why didn't you tell me?'

He smiled a very small smile. 'Look, honey, it was between me and the Nawab. It was ... why should I have told you?'

She stiffened. Then she spun around, her face set hard, and grabbed the suitcase out of my hand and stamped around the corner.

Ken looked at me and made a broad, helpless gesture. 'I need a drink.'

'Me too.'

We turned back into the bar and lined up at the counter. Ken tapped a wad of bills on the counter and the barman zoomed up. Ken ordered two double Scotches. The barman rushed them across, then looked at me and said brightly: 'You were in here now, yes? With a lady?'

'Yes. Now I'm back again, with a gentleman. If that's the right word.'

The barman looked puzzled. Ken gave me a sideways look, then said: 'Make out a separate bill for my friend. If *that's* the right word.'

The barman looked even more puzzled. I asked him: 'Will you take it in diamonds or rubies?'

Ken said: 'Oh hell and corruption,' and threw a Libyan pound note across the counter. The barman smiled, relieved, and whisked it away.

Ken reduced the double to a single, and stared across the bar. 'All right, all right. What would you have done?'

'Me? Nothing different. I just like seeing you suffer.'

'Forgive me. I thought you were taking a moral stand.'

'You're thinking of two other people.'

He grinned suddenly, then went serious on me again. 'I just don't know what I should have done, Jack.'

'Nothing. Skip it. What are you doing out here?'

He nodded at the door. 'I've hitched a ride on a plane going down to the oil strip where I left the Piaggio. I'll fly it back: should be here by the end of the afternoon.'

'I'll be here.' I thought about telling him about last night's talk with the Nawab, then thought not. Last night was just talk. I didn't know how far the Nawab would follow it through.

He emptied his glass, and glanced at his watch. 'See you, then.'

'Ken – has the Nawab got a list of the jewels he lost?'

He looked at me. 'Yes, I think so. He must have.'

'You haven't seen it?'

'No. It isn't the sort of thing he'd flash around. I was a hired man there; I got told what I got told because he needed my help.'

'So you don't know what the jewels were like? What sort? Gold? Jade? Just plain necklaces and rings?'

He spread his hands. 'I just don't know. But I know they weren't plain – not if they were worth a clear million-and-a-half. Anyway, you've seen some of them – you should know.'

I nodded. 'Just wondering about the rest. That's all. See you this evening.'

He turned away, then turned back. 'Jack, if you see Shirley treat her, well, gently. Buy her a drink from me. Except don't say it came from me.'

'Will do.'

He looked at his feet. 'In the long run, it's better I'm a live bastard than a dead hero.'

'Worry about staying alive; you'll stay a bastard.'

He grinned quickly and went away.

I finished off my Scotch. The barman came back with Ken's change, carefully too late. I told him to keep it.

He felt moved to say something to mark the occasion. 'The gentleman – he is your friend?'

'That's right,' I nodded emphatically. 'He's one of the great men of his profession. And he'd be recognized as such, except that he once ran into a little trouble. Do you know what happens to a little trouble when it wraps itself around a great man?'

I fixed him with my steely glare and he shook his head hastily.

I said: 'It becomes big trouble. That's what.'

Then, turning neatly through 180 degrees and banking no more than seemed necessary, I set course for the door, wondering what had got into me besides no breakfast, a long stint in the sun, four beers and a double Scotch.

The sunlight was like a wall: I just stood there, squeezing white light out of my eyes, until I could make out a Rapide, standing about two hundred yards away, its propellers turning over. Ken was climbing in. I turned away and nearly rammed Anarchos.

He smiled and nodded towards the Rapide. 'A friend of yours?'

Suddenly I was sober again. 'Met him once before, somewhere.'

Anarchos nodded absently. 'I feel I, too, know him.' He was a damn liar. 'Now what was his name?'

'Kilroy, I think. He sells motor parts.' *Careful, Jack, careful.*

'Yes, I believe I remember.' He beamed. 'Perhaps I can offer you a lift back to Tripoli. I fear Miss Burt took the only taxi left.'

'That's very kind of you.'

We climbed into a small, hired Renault that had been standing around long enough for the inside to get up to oven heat, wound down the windows and rolled off down the concrete drive.

I lit a cigarette; he refused one. As we turned off the drive on to the Tripoli road, he said: 'I believe you have met many policemen, many times, in many places, Captain.'

'That's inevitable, if you travel around.'

'Not quite in the way I mean, Captain. A man who is used to business with policemen can hide what he knows. He can never hide that he is hiding something.'

'Everybody has something to hide. That's why we wear clothes.'

He laughed gaily. 'And yet, what could you have to hide, Captain? You say you did not kill Mikklos. But, perhaps you know something about why he was killed.'

137

'I know his reputation as an agent; I also know his reputation with women. There must be a number of husbands around Athens who'd like to stick a knife or bullet or something into him. How *was* he killed?'

He hunched his shoulders and the back wheels jerked in the ruts. 'Ah – they did not tell me. I wish they would.'

I grinned. 'I've met a lot of cops in a lot of places – as you said. They differ: a British cop is different from a Swiss one, a Swiss from a Greek, a Greek from a Libyan. But there's something about a good cop that's the same everywhere. One of the things you know about a good cop is that he's hiding something. Always.'

'Always,' he agreed happily. 'As you say – we all have something to hide. But always there must come the day when we shall tell all.'

'Please, not Judgement Day. Don't try that on me.'

'My apologies. It is my English phrasing. I mean, when you come back to Athens. You are a pilot; to do your job you must be able to go everywhere. Some time you must return to Athens. Then we shall tell all.'

I flipped my cigarette at a goat standing on the bank. 'Blackmail? That's a pretty crude weapon, for you.'

He smiled. 'The good policeman does not use every weapon. He uses just the right one. I could talk about God or your mother, if it would be the right weapon. But for you, this is the right one: blackmail. Where do you wish me to drop you?'

'At my hotel. I'm sure you know which it is.'

He nodded and we went the rest of the way in silence.

I was told there had been a cable from Hauser, but Rogers had opened it. He wasn't around. There was also a message from Herter. They would like to see me in the Nawab's room at two o'clock.

It was just one now. I got on the phone and demanded to speak to the Nawab's private secretary. If it meant dragging him off his feeding trough, go ahead and drag him off. He'd want to speak to me.

Eventually Herter came on the line.

'You have the message?' he asked.

'Yes. But I'm not coming up to anybody's room. I'll meet you in the bar at two.'

'We cannot discuss this in public,' he informed me.

'And I'm not discussing it in private. If you'd rather do a deal out on the pavement, that's all right with me. I thought you'd prefer the bar.'

He gnashed his teeth on this for a while, then decided: 'I will meet you in the bar at two o'clock. I cannot say whether any discussion will take place.'

'That's okay, too. You boys make up your own minds on that. Only I shall take a good look around before I come in and if I spot you or Yussuf or anybody outside, I'm not coming in.'

He rang off.

Too much can happen in a private room when you've got something to lose. In the bar, they'd hardly be likely to start pointing guns or jump on me and tear the jewels out of my pocket.

I went up to my room and washed and then spread the jewels out on the bed and looked them over for the last time and said goodbye to them in my own personal, private way.

Then I went down and had lunch. Veal, of course.

22

I TOOK A taxi down to the Uaddan. My expenses were getting to be something fierce, but if I was a target, I wanted to be a moving one.

The front entrance of the Uaddan is a modest street door on an almost blank wall. Nobody could have been hiding within easy range. I paid off, hurried through and arrived in the bar at five to two.

It was a tall, quiet, square room between the lobby and the dining-room. The bar stood on one side of the main fairway, up on a small stage, with small tables and chairs and dark leather wall benches along the other side. There were no windows and the place had a sober club atmosphere that muffled even an American oilman in a tartan shirt and Davy Crockett jacket sitting under a personal cloud of whisky in one corner. In the other were the Nawab, Herter and Miss Brown.

I had been braced for her – but not enough. She looked up as I came in and suddenly there was nobody else in the room.

She was Dahira, the tall and lovely, with her long, black hair and her golden skin – and all of it the biggest mistake of my life.

Then she looked down and she was Miss Brown again. Still tall, still lovely – but not for me.

I went across and sat down on the bench seat, getting my back against the wall.

Herter looked at me, his watch and turned to the Nawab. 'Would your Excellency like to go up to the room now?'

His Excellency nodded.

'Goodbye all,' I said. Herter looked at me sharply. Miss Brown turned her head slowly and I thought there was a touch of amusement in her eyes. She was wearing white again, a full-skirted dress cut as simple and plain as a piece of typing paper. I looked away again.

The barman was hovering near, waiting to have his eye caught. I caught it, and ordered a Strega. Herter waited until he was gone, then said in a sharp, low voice: 'We do not do any business here, in public.'

I said: 'We don't do any business anywhere else. I've got the jewels and this is the first and last chance you'll get at them. I'm too old to start playing games behind locked doors.'

Herter glared. The Nawab made a sharp hissing noise. I looked around, and we had Anarchos on the strength.

He beamed at us, and sat down before anybody could invite him not to. 'How delightful to find you here. Tripoli these days is so full of uncultured oilmen. Will you drink with me?'

The barman came across with my Strega. I asked Anarchos: 'What will you have?'

'It is my turn, I believe, Captain, after your hospitality of this morning.'

He ordered beer.

Nobody said anything. The Nawab stared down at his brandy; Miss Brown looked at nothing in particular; Herter fiddled with his glass and looked as if he was having trouble staying below boiling point.

Anarchos just smiled.

The beer came and he lifted it in a small gesture, sipped and said: 'I believe another old friend of yours has arrived in Tripoli, Your Excellency. Captain Clay was kind enough to introduce me to her this morning. Miss Burt, a charming lady.'

The Nawab looked up briefly, but without expression.

Miss Brown said: 'With her cameras?'

'So I believe.' He sipped again, pulled out his Chesterfields and stuck one in his mouth. Then he remembered his manners and offered them to Miss Brown. She took one. Nobody else did.

Anarchos said: 'Miss Burt must be honoured to have so distinguished a subject for a photographic story. I believe she got some very good photographs on Kira, of the crashed aeroplane there.' Herter glared at him. Anarchos snapped his big, chrome lighter several times without getting a light, then offered it apologetically to Miss Brown and started searching his pockets.

She took the lighter, lit it first go, lit her cigarette and tossed the lighter contemptuously back on the table. I thought Anarchos looked a little shamefaced; he found his matches and lit his own cigarette.

Then he asked: 'Have you known Captain Clay long, Your Excellency?'

The Nawab looked a little startled. 'Not long.'

'Ah.' Anarchos shook his head sadly. 'Then you cannot know much about him. Strange – I would not have thought he was a confidant of yours. A man of mystery.' He shook his head again. The Nawab was beginning to look worried.

I said: 'Perhaps you hadn't heard – His Excellency lost his personal pilot and plane recently. Naturally he's interested in hiring personal transport during the rest of his trip.'

Miss Brown smiled. The Nawab looked relieved. Anarchos swung round to look at me.

'Of course,' he said. 'I'm sure you'll find Captain Clay quite satisfactory. Alas' – he swung back to the Nawab – 'the Captain is getting short of places where he can fly. I trust your Excellency will not wish to return to Athens?'

The Nawab didn't say anything. I couldn't see where Anarchos was leading, unless he was just spreading dissension in the ranks – and dissension wasn't something we were short of already.

Herter said stiffly: 'His Excellency's travel arrangements are confidential.'

'Of course,' Anarchos spread his hands. 'His Excellency is free to go wherever he wishes. I only felt it was my duty to inform him of something about Captain Clay which he might not know.' He gave me a swift sideways grin.

Then he stood up and beamed calmly all round. 'You must

141

excuse me. It has been very delightful.' He picked up his lighter off the table, smiled at Miss Brown from short range and walked away.

There was a long pause, filled with breathing noises from Herter. I sipped my Strega and lit a cigarette and waited for the shop to open for business.

Then Miss Brown stood up, mashed her cigarette out and said: 'I think I'll go and lie down for a while, Aly.'

Herter and I jerked ourselves into jack-knifed efforts of politeness; the Nawab stayed where he was. I watched her go. The bar had been still and quiet before; as she drifted through, it became breathless. The barman stopped polishing his glass. The oilman in the corner froze with his whisky half raised. Then she was gone and it was just still and quiet again.

I swallowed the rest of my Strega and leant back. Herter looked at me, then at the Nawab. The Nawab looked at me: my move.

I took one of the rings out of my pocket and slid it across the table. Herter slammed a big paw over it as if it were a runaway beetle, looked quickly all around, then half-opened his hand and peered into it.

'That's my credentials,' I said. 'I'm ready to start dealing.'

Herter slid the ring off the table and on to the seat beside him with the casual innocence of a man pocketing a ten-ton truck.

The Nawab glanced across the corner of the table at it.

Herter asked: 'Where are the others?'

'They're here,' I said, 'but I've still got to be convinced that they're the Nawab's.'

Herter said stiffly: 'I think you do not doubt they are His Excellency's.'

I shrugged. 'He lost some jewellery ten years ago in Tunga-bhadra. I found these this week – in a Mediterranean port. What reason have I got to connect them with you?'

'You know the man Mikklos sent you to here with these. You know it was because we had to come to Athens to find them!' His voice was beginning to get the parade-ground blare; the Nawab looked at him warningly.

Herter spread his hands slowly apart and gripped the edges of the table. For a moment I thought he was going to heave it in my face. But he just needed something to grip.

The Nawab said quietly: 'I'm sure we can convince you that

the jewellery you found belongs to me, Captain.' He looked at Herter. 'Perhaps you would show the Captain the list?'

Herter relaxed slowly, still watching me, then reached into his inside pocket and pulled out a folded typescript. The Nawab took it, glanced at it and pushed it across the table to me.

'Perhaps you can identify the pieces, Captain.'

It ran to two closely-typed foolscap pages. At a quick glance it listed about sixty items, devoting about three lines to each. I turned back to the beginning and read it carefully through.

It made good reading. A lot of it was mutton-fat jade set with gems: cosmetic jars, dagger handles and sheaths, turban ornaments. There were about a dozen pieces of trellis-work gold jars and things, decorated with rubies, that sounded Burmese in origin. That left fifteen other items: rings, thumb rings, ear ornaments and necklaces; three of them, two rings and a pair of ear ornaments, were marked with ticks. I had just about all the others in my pockets.

I asked about the ticks.

The Nawab said: 'We have recovered those already.' So they must have been the pieces that turned up in Beirut and started off the whole hunt.

I put the list down. Herter was still glaring at me and breathing heavily; he hated me having my hot little hands on that list. By now, he hated me anyhow and anywhere, but most of all he hated the idea that I had something to sell.

I said carefully: 'Apart from that ring I have another ring and nine other pieces. I'm prepared to hand them over on the terms we discussed last night.'

They looked at each other.

I said: 'First, the gun.'

The Nawab nodded gently. Herter slid a Beretta out of his pocket and pushed it around the corner of the wall seat to me. I picked it up and examined it under cover of the table. It looked like Mikklos's; I hadn't taken the number originally, but why shouldn't it be Mikklos's?

I broke out the magazine and worked the slide. It was empty. I had expected that; I took the three 7·65 mm. rounds that had been left in the Dak's locker out of my shirt pocket, pushed them into the magazine, worked the slide again and slipped the gun into my right trouser pocket.

The world and I were on equal terms again.

I took a handful of jewellery and slid it around the corner of

143

the seat back to Herter. He sorted it quickly and said: 'They are not all here.'

'I haven't got the money or the letters discharging Ken, yet.'

The Nawab nodded again and Herter took more paper from his pocket and passed it over. I read them over while he examined the jewellery.

The letters said what I wanted them to. With those in Ken's hands it would be too much trouble for the Nawab to start trying to slap charges on him.

I slid across the rest of the jewellery.

Herter brought his head up sharply and said: 'I think these are not in perfect condition!'

I shrugged. 'They've been ten years away from home. I only got them a few days ago. Why blame me?'

Because he liked blaming me, that was why. But all he did was glare and ram the lot into his pockets.

He had never set eyes on the pieces before and probably the Nawab himself couldn't remember them too well. All they had was a typewritten list, and to describe a valuable Indian necklace properly, you need to spend a page on it. Anybody could have clipped off every third gem and, if it had been done neatly, all Herter would have got was a general feeling the mice had been around. Wouldn't have hurt the design much, either.

'Now, the cash,' I said. 'I think we agreed a price.'

Herter let a very small smile creep on to his face. 'We have reconsidered the matter. The price seems too high. Perhaps we will pay expenses – a few gallons of petrol – but no more.'

He had me. He had the jewels, and all they had cost was two letters and a second-hand Beretta. A fine business sense.

I had been expecting something like this. I stood up. 'Okay, I'll sell the rest of the jewels elsewhere.' I eased my way out from the table.

They swapped a gabble of startled glances, then Herter said: 'Wait.

I waited.

He asked: 'You have more of the jewels?'

I gave him a nice, easy smile. 'Of course. I brought these in as a try-out. Now I see you boys don't honour your debts, I'll try elsewhere.'

The Nawab opened his mouth to take over the conversation himself, then shut it again and went back to staring at his brandy.

Herter said grimly: 'There is Yussuf —'

I leant down and grinned at him. 'Send him along.' I slapped the pocket with the Beretta in it. 'I'll send him back to you in a bucket. And everybody will be asking themselves how could such a thing happen to a nice little Libyan boy who happened to get mixed up with a Nawab.'

The Nawab winced. Then he waved his hand impatiently and said: 'Sit down. We will talk about this.'

'Not before I get paid, we won't.'

'We'll pay you.'

I waited.

He nodded to Herter: Herter reached into another pocket and came up with the usual slab of currency. He peeled off several notes without shrinking the wad visibly, stuffed it away and handed over the cash. I sat down and counted it.

It came out at 9,000 dollars and 22,000 Swiss francs, near enough to £5,000 in all. I put it away.

The two of them were watching me suspiciously.

I leant back and stuck my hands in my pockets. 'Do you boys always do business this way?' Neither of them said anything. I said: 'I'd like to give you a bit of advice.'

Herter said: 'His Excellency does not wish for your advice.'

I said: 'But I have qualifications you don't know about. I'm the bird who's just bluffed you out of £5,000. And if you've got any ideas about taking it back' – Herter had: he was rising out of his seat like a genie out of a bottle – 'remember you also sold me a gun. I've got my hand on it.'

I had, too.

Herter said: 'The gun is empty —' Then he remembered it wasn't. He sat down again, very slowly, his eyes tearing me apart and stamping on the pieces.

I said: 'Thank you. Here comes the advice. Handling stolen goods – which is what these jewels are – is a professional business. You boys are strictly amateurs: you've proved that. Had it occurred to you that if you got within spitting distance of whoever has the rest of the stuff, he'd probably blow your heads off before even saying hello? Had it occurred to you that if you tried that last piece of double-cross on almost anybody else around Tripoli, he'd knife you?

'As for that nonsense of trying to bargain with me about this gun: don't you know *anything* about the laws of evidence? Don't you know that if it *had* been incriminating evidence, the last thing I'd have done was buy it off you and risk having it found on me?'

'You bought it,' the Nawab pointed out.

'I wanted a gun, and I didn't want to attract attention stumping around the Medina trying to buy one. Don't think I'm now going to chuck it away: it's just a gun. It isn't evidence of anything.' Nor was it. Mikklos would have spent too much trouble making sure the Beretta couldn't be traced to him for it to be evidence of who killed him. He hadn't been too bright – he'd got himself shot, for one thing – but he'd been far too much of a professional ever to handle a gun that was registered to his name.

I said: 'You boys have got just one thing on your side. You *haven't* got experience, or contacts, or even a working knowledge of the law – but you've got money. So if anybody ever offers to sell you the rest of the jewels, just buy them. Don't argue and don't try to double-cross anybody and don't try to swap them for guns. Just buy them. You can afford it.'

I stood up. 'Though where your profit is, I don't know. If you were so careless as to lose them in the first place, you must have so much more at home that coming chasing after these just couldn't be worth the risk.'

The Nawab suddenly smiled and went all Oxford on me. 'It's just that I like to have what I own, Captain. And this – well, it breaks the routine, you know.'

'Well – that's your business. I'd thought there were other ways.'

He said softly: 'And a week ago, you were just an airline pilot.'

I just nodded and went away, leaving Herter staring after me with fifty-seven different violent thoughts showing behind his glasses.

23

I GOT BACK to the hotel about half past three. For the moment, I didn't have anything to do. I took the Beretta to pieces and checked it, then counted my money again, then found the trousers of my lightweight suit and looked at the knee, where I'd hit the drive ducking Yussuf the night before. The cloth seemed all right, but there was a dark bloodstain. I scrubbed it off and hung the trousers over the window sill to dry.

Then I looked at the money and the gun. I couldn't go stuffing them into any petrol tank, not if they were going to be any use to me. Finally, I sorted them into various pockets and went down to the bar.

Rogers was there, still trying to foretell the future in a glass of beer and not liking what he could see of it.

I took a beer across, and sat down at his table. He looked up without enthusiasm.

'Here I am,' I said, 'rushing about like a mad thing on the firm's business and all you do is look at me as if I'd gone and pawned the propellers.'

'Haven't you?' he asked sourly.

'So young and yet so bitter! Never mind, you'll learn. Commercial flying isn't all leaping about the sky; sometimes there are negotiations, deals, arrangements – in a word, business. Now, don't you worry about a thing. Jack Clay has control.'

'We're going to get fired.'

'Nonsense. We're going to get promoted. Hauser will buy us new braid for our caps.'

He hunched his shoulders. 'How's the Dakota?'

'Never better. Gave her a going-over this morning. Drink up and have another.'

'Have you spent all the money we got for the trip to Saxos with the Nawab?'

'If I have, I've got it back tenfold.' I thought of throwing the latest wad down in front of him, then thought perhaps the bar wasn't the place.

He gave me a long, sad look, then kicked back his chair and mooched out. From his point of view, I had fallen a long way in the last few days, and was still going down.

I'd have liked to explain what I was doing – except that he wouldn't have thought it any better than what he already thought I was doing.

I sat and sipped my beer and tried to think out what the Nawab might do now. He would probably do something: in his mind – and Herter's – I had somehow cheated them by tricking them into keeping their word. That would probably call for revenge.

They might send Yussuf after me, or Herter might come himself. Or they might even take the jewels to the police and complain that I must have the rest of them somewhere about. I hoped they'd work out the logic of that before they tried it on. If they created too much fuss and got too much publicity, they'd simply drive the rest of the jewels underground for another ten years.

If only they'd been just crooks, I'd have felt much better. A crook – a successful one – is a businessman. He may blow your head off, but only if it's good for business. He does things for reasons – and knowing that, you can usually avoid giving him reasons for blowing your head off. With amateurs, anything can happen.

I finished the beer, found a taxi and drove out to the airport.

I got there just before five, changed some dollars and ordered the Dakota refuelled. Then I scrounged around and managed to buy some tools to replace those that had been swiped at Mehari. I was out running up the Dak's engines and making sure I hadn't been short-changed on fuel, when the Piaggio came into the circuit.

He was flying her. She drifted down on to the ground like a gull, turned off the runway and ran away behind the far hangars. I shut down the engines and walked across.

When I got there, Ken was negotiating about refuelling. We nodded to each other and I left him to it and wandered over to look at the Piaggio.

She was much smaller than the Dak, and the high wing and tricycle undercarriage, keeping her low and level, made her look smaller still. But the fuselage had the fat sleekness of a well-fed cat.

She had pusher engines, the propellers at the back of the wings, a point you'd need to remember in the dark. I walked around to the left-hand side and opened the cabin door just in front of the wing.

I had been right about the Nawab still having plenty of capital untouched at home.

The cabin would have taken eight easily, but was fitted to take four. Each was a big armchair, two facing forward, two aft, covered in grained, cream leather; each had little silver ashtrays and fitments to take drinks attached to the arm rests. The ceiling and the walls down as far as the windows were covered in light, embroidered silk; below that, they were polished wooden panels. The windows themselves had little green velvet curtains held back with gold-shot ropes.

I put an impious foot inside and nearly lost it in the dull, golden carpet. To my right – aft – a small door opened between the two seats. I peered in: galley on one side, cupboard and counter straight ahead, toilet on the left. All in slightly darker veneered panelling.

I turned up front. The two pilots' seats weren't cut off from the rest except by a velvet curtain which could be pulled across to keep the cabin lights from dazzling the pilot. The seats themselves were slightly slimmer, and more business-like, but finished in the same cream leather. The instrument panel was covered in a darker leather with a big soft crash pad across the top to bounce your head on. Each of the dials had its own little silver eyebrow and light. The controls had ivory knobs.

The whole effect of the spaciousness and the trimmings had an odd unreality for me: it belonged more to the way they used to doll up the old touring Rolls than to a modern aircraft. But that could be just unfamiliarity. I had been brought up in aircraft where they built space for the passengers, space for the controls and instruments, and only then started to think of somewhere for the hired hand to sit.

I was reaching out to try the control column – a half-wheel coming out on an elbow column from the wall, when Ken opened a second door alongside the co-pilot's seat.

'Don't monkey about with the controls, sonny,' he said. 'We flying men are particular about these things.'

'No colour television,' I said. 'I just positively won't fly in an aeroplane without colour television.'

He grinned and climbed in. 'We've got a refrigerator. Will you settle for Scotch-on-the-rocks?'

'I'll take it as an attempt to please.' I stepped back to the cabin and he went past and into the galley. I dropped into one of the aft-facing passenger seats and watched him at work. There *was* a refrigerator – a small square door under the counter that I'd missed.

'Does this regency boudoir really fly?' I called.

He came back out of the galley with two chunky glasses. 'You've seen it in the air, what d'you think?'

He gave me a glass and sat down in the forward-facing seat

149

on the other side. 'Don't fool yourself – bleached leather and embroidered silk and veneer panels don't actually weigh any more than ordinary leather and fabric and plastics. Under all of that, she's real enough.' He jerked a thumb at the window by his shoulder. 'I've got two supercharged flat-six Lycomings out there, and I can get 340 horse-power from each on take-off. You show me another plane that'll get six people off the ground in under two hundred yards.'

'*And* a bottle of Scotch, *and* the ice,' I said.

He grinned; we drank. Apparently the Nawab believed that good Scotch doesn't weigh any more than bad, either.

I said: 'I take your point. Maybe it's just that I've been too poor too long.'

'Count me in on that thought.'

We drank to it. The cabin was warm – not hot, she hadn't been standing on the ground long enough yet. The refuelling crew moved sluggishly around outside. Ken pulled out his cigarettes, glanced out at the petrol bowser and put them away again.

'How's Shirley?' he asked.

'Haven't seen her since.'

He nodded and looked serious. 'I still wish I'd – well, I don't know what.'

'I know. Skip it.'

I took a long pull at my drink, then said: 'I've been doing some dealing since you went away.'

He cocked his head sharply and frowned at me. 'Now, you wouldn't have done anything foolish, would you, while uncle Ken was busy elsewhere?'

'Depends on the point of view. Better hear me out, all of it.'

He nodded slowly. 'Go ahead.'

'I dealt the jewels back to the Nawab.'

He froze.

I said: 'One of the things I got in exchange was a couple of letters.' I took them out of my pocket and passed them across. 'It means you're off the hook. He can't press charges. You can come legally alive again.'

He skimmed through them. 'They can still lynch me, back in Pakistan.'

'They could have done that anyway.'

He tucked them away in a pocket. 'I hope you got more than that?'

'Maybe those letters are more important than you think. I, personally, find it's a great thing to be legally in the clear. Especially in our business.'

He laughed sharply. 'Legally in the clear? Since when?'

I shrugged. 'Well, let's say – up to a point. But that point counts. And yes – I got more. About £5,000 in dollars and Swiss francs. And a gun.'

He was staring at me. 'Five thousand? *Five?* Christ!'

'The Nawab gives five per cent rewards. I took less because of the gun and other things.'

He was still staring. 'It must be a damn good gun,' he said bitterly.

'I happened to need it. That gives it value. Anyway, I also got a look at the list of lost jewels. They didn't want to show it me, but they had to.'

'And now you're satisfied?'

'I think so. I now know where the rest of the jewels are.'

The inside of the cabin was very quiet. The noises of the refuelling gang outside were muffled and seemed very far away. A bowser ground its gears and chugged away out of hearing.

Ken watched it go, then took his cigarettes from his pocket and passed me one. 'How d'you know? How certain are you?'

'Reasonably. That list: it showed that the pieces I got, together with the first pieces that got picked up in Beirut, added up to just about every necklace, ear ornament and whatnot that were missing. All the stuff that was just gems and pearls strung together. The rest is gems set in carved jade or goldwork. Real craftsman stuff.'

'So?'

'Just suppose you had the whole lot on your hands – which would you try to market first?'

He blew smoke across the padded embroidery on the roof. 'I think I see: the necklaces and stuff. Being just stones, they'd be easy to break down and maybe re-cut. The jade and gold would be more difficult to sell – undercover, anyway.'

'Right first time. More than half the value of the jade and gold will be in the way they're carved or moulded – and that makes them too easy to identify. All right – so you'd hang on to them until you were dead certain of the market. First, you'd send just a sample, say three pieces, to see if you've found a safe buyer. That's the stuff that was picked up in Beirut. Then you'd send

151

out the rest of the easy stuff. Last the jade and gold. We came in in the middle of stage two.'

He frowned. 'So the rest is still somewhere around Athens. Have you got any idea where?'

'Not Athens. Mikklos went to too much trouble sending out what he'd got to leave any more lying around. The whole charade of sending them out to Beirut through Tripoli and the camel train was a panic measure – he thought the Nawab must have got his direct line to Beirut all stopped up. If he'd had any more, he'd have sent it out, too. No – he never got the rest. That's still where it first arrived – on the island with the crashed plane.'

He pulled a little silver ashtray out from the seat-arm and crushed his cigarette slowly down into it. When he looked up again there was a bright glitter in his eyes and a hard-set little smile around his mouth. He asked softly: 'When do we take off?'

'Nine tomorrow morning suit you? We'll use the Dak. We can get down on a road on Saxos; Kira's about half an hour by boat.'

He nodded: 'You've got yourself a new co-pilot.'

PART FOUR

24

I LEFT THE airport at about half past six, stopped at the hotel to change into my lightweight suit and went on down to the Uaddan. I was going to spend a nice, open, unsuspicious evening, and if anybody wanted to search my room – that was fine with me.

Ken was staying out of sight. If he suddenly popped up, the Nawab was sure to blow a gasket and do something amateurish. From now until nine the next morning I wanted no trouble at all.

The bar of the Uaddan was thinly populated at that time. Most of the guests were eating: there was a steady hum and clatter from the dining-room beyond. Rogers and Shirley Burt were sitting at a table in the middle of the wall.

I waved to the barman and went across to them. 'Evening, children. What are you drinking?'

Shirley lifted her head and blew smoke at my stomach. 'Scotch. I'll have a second gallon.'

Rogers gave her a quick, nervous glance and said to me: 'I'm going to eat in a minute.'

The barman came up behind me. I ordered two Scotches and sat down.

Shirley was wearing the same tan shirtwaister that she'd had on when I first met her back in Athens. It was still doing its best to make you want to start tearing it off, but she wasn't giving it any encouragement. She was staring fixedly through the top of the table, turning her glass in her fingers.

I offered her a cigarette; she picked a half-burnt one out of an ashtray and showed it me, without ever looking straight at me.

Tonight was Gloom Night at the Old Uaddan.

Rogers finished his drink and got up. 'I think I'll try some dinner. Good evening, Miss Burt. Jack.' He avoided my eye and went off towards the dining-room, not hurrying, but not wasting time, either.

The barman rolled up with our Scotches. Shirley finished her current one and shifted a large lump of the new. I stared; the last session I remembered in a bar, she'd had a foot on the brake pedal.

I said: 'Cheers, Sister Burt,' and swallowed my portion like a man.

She asked: 'How's our mutual friend? I don't suppose he happened to get eaten by a camel, did he? I'd have liked a shot of that.'

I got the message. She was washing away the Ken-that-might-have-been in Scotch, but not being able to stop talking about him, either. And in a way, she was giving me fair warning of what she was doing.

'I have an idea,' I said. 'Why don't we consume a certain amount more stag's-breath, then hie us to an Italian eating place I know yonder?'

'Stop being so goddam solicitous,' she snarled. 'If you want to stick around and drink Scotch, okay: If you want to make there-there-little-girlie noises, get to hell elsewhere.'

I said: 'It's not my job to help you recover from your men. I work out of sheer self-interest.'

She didn't believe me, but the thought did her some good, all the same.

'Apart from that bit about eating,' she said, 'you've got a good idea there. If you're ready to follow the Scotch bottle wherever it leads, stick around.' She gulped her drink, and beckoned the barman. We ordered two more Scotch-on-the-rocks, easy with the rocks.

She lifted her new glass at me. 'Cheers. I know something about you, Mr Clay.'

'Everybody knows something about me. Nobody knows quite enough to put me in prison. Cheers.'

'How long did you say you'd known Ken?'

'Knock it off,' I said harshly. 'Leave that alone. Won't do you any good.'

'It isn't just one thing or the other,' she said, slowly and very deliberately, 'it's the combination of both that is so irresistibly depressing. First I have to get sad because I think the guy's dead. Then I find he isn't dead, he's just run out on me. I could take one, just one: the two together are a bit much.' She stared at me very hard; she was still at the stage where she could do that. She'd had just enough Scotch to focus her attention on just one thing. 'I've got an idea that you knew all along he wasn't dead. That so?'

'I guessed it,' I admitted.

'And it didn't occur to you to tell me?'

'No. Why should it?' I was beginning to get angry. 'Who the hell are you, anyhow? A week ago I didn't know you existed. A week from now I'll have forgotten. If Ken wanted to play dead, that was his business. Not yours.'

'War-time buddies,' she said. 'Men.'

I stuck my elbows on the table and leant at her. 'That's right. War-time buddies. I was sharing a plane with Ken when you were still wondering when you were going to start growing a chest.' That reached her. She went red suddenly, and tears started in her eyes. But she managed to keep them there.

'All right, I'm being childish. I'm sorry. Give me a handkerchief.'

I gave her a handkerchief. She blotted her face, yanked out her powder compact and repaired the damage. I finished my Scotch. She noticed, and shoved her half-finished drink across.

'Finish that for me. It was a lousy idea anyway, getting tight.'

I swallowed it without arguing. She finished her work with the compact, tucked it away and said: 'Well, what about this Italian place?'

As we got up, the Nawab, Herter and Miss Brown came out of the dining-room. Miss Brown ducked her head gracefully at me. To the other two, I just wasn't there.

Seeing them reminded me that Yussuf must be on the loose somewhere. I asked the desk clerk to get us a taxi.

The Italian place was less than half a mile away, a ground-floor room on a corner with more tables than atmosphere. But they gave you a full plate and didn't throw you out if you licked it clean.

We had scampi, veal and white chianti, listening to Louis Armstrong from a jukebox in the corner.

Shirley said: 'It's a funny sort of business, being an American. Wherever you go, there's some part of America got there first. As often as not it's Louis Armstrong.'

'It's an American world. I fly an American plane. Ken's Piaggio was built in Italy, but it has American engines. There's an American base a few miles from here. An American world: drink your chianti and like it.'

She shook her head – both at more chianti and the idea. 'No, that isn't so. That's what a lot of people say, everywhere, and a hell of a lot of Americans believe it. But it's not so. A Dakota

157

belongs here, as much as it does anywhere in the states; Armstrong sounds right here, anywhere. But that's not *because* they're American – the fact that they're American has got sort of digested. Spent maybe, like you'd spend a dollar if a kind American gave it you. That doesn't make it an American world.'

'Is that bad?'

'Not from the world's point of view. But there's a lot of the Americans who like to think they hold a mortgage on world civilization and can foreclose whenever the world starts acting un-American. They'd hate to realize they don't lead the world – when the world goes on flying Dakotas and listening to Armstrong over dinner.'

'Hell, the world's full of countries who hate the idea of not leading the world. I could name you five in Europe, including Britain.'

She gave me a quick, odd, look and said: 'Easy: the colonial powers. But when they – you – were trying to run the world, they were never trying to sell the idea of being English or French or whatever. Not the same way we try to put over the idea of being American.'

'Well – we were trying to sell the idea, but nothing more. We were telling people they could become Christian, send their sons to Eton and Sandhurst, wear a topper at Ascot – but that wouldn't make you an Englishman. Nothing could. You had to be born an Englishman. You could be a better African or Indian, or whoever, by acting like an Englishman, but you couldn't actually join the club.'

She spun the last of her wine in the glass. 'You don't get to be a Philadelphia Kelly just by joining our club either, chum.'

'No. But you don't have to be a Philadelphia Kelly – a Philadelphia Kelly can't go that many more places or do that many more things that any steel puddler with a hundred million dollars. There'll always be clubs within clubs; you'll find one of the most rigid class structures on earth inside any fairly comprehensive jail.'

She nodded gently, watching the wine swing to a stop in her glass. 'On the other hand, you can always resign from being an Englishman. It isn't so easy to stop being an American. Have you noticed that?'

I shrugged, a bit stiffly. 'Maybe. That comes of having a strict club qualification: you can always slip below the requirements '

She glanced at me curiously, then nodded again and emptied her glass. I picked up the chianti bottle and offered it. She shook her head.

Then she said: 'Why did you and Ken give up English nationality?'

I tried; at least I tried. I put the bottle carefully back on the table again and said: 'You mean why are we flying for foreign masters? Well, England's pretty full of pilots —'

'I don't mean that. I saw the register at Ken's hotel this afternoon: you can't fool around there, you've got to hand your passport over. He's a Pakistani national. So I went round and looked at your registration. You're a Swiss national. All right – why?'

'Is this the journalist in you?'

'Don't be a damn fool.'

I tipped a little wine into my glass and looked at it. It didn't tell me a thing.

She stood up suddenly and said: 'Come back and have a drink at my place.'

'Your place?'

'I picked up a bottle of Scotch at the Rome stopover. I'd like an expert opinion on it.' She gave me a perfectly blank, guileless look.

I dropped three Libyan pounds on the table and followed her towards the door.

25

WE RODE in a garry back to the Uaddan.

She had a third-floor room, not big, not small, just a hotel room full of hotel furniture and lit by hotel lighting. The sort of room you can live a lifetime in and leave as much of your personality on it as you can scratch on a diamond.

I shut the door carefully behind me and turned around. She was standing a few feet away, braced and tense, as if she expected me to jump and wasn't sure whether to catch me or duck.

'You don't have to tell me anything,' she said. Her voice sounded too steady.

'You didn't have to invite me up here,' I said. 'Except you mentioned Scotch.'

She relaxed a little and smiled briefly. 'It's in the case under the bed. I'm going to clean up.'

I dug out the bottle; the label was so Scottish that it couldn't have been printed farther north than Milan. I poured doses into two glasses on the bedside table and took one with me into a pink wicker-work chair.

She came back from the bathroom with her hair a bit looser and her face a bit shinier.

We lifted our glasses and drank. It was battery acid with colouring.

She put hers away in two gulps, shuddered a little and sat down on the edge of the bed. I got up and went into the bathroom and trickled some water into my glass.

She was still sitting on the bed, frowning slightly and staring at nothing. I tried to think of something quick to say about photography, but she beat me to it.

'Had you and Ken really not met before that night in Athens, not for ten years?'

'About that time.'

'What have you been doing these past few days?'

I shrugged. 'Nothing.' A good, bright answer. Just the thing to convince an intelligent girl.

She said quietly: 'Ken runs off and pretends to be dead. You go off somewhere and roll back a few days later with a plaster on your face, not speaking to your co-pilot, and with a Greek cop treading on your tail.' Her smile had a sarcastic twist to it. 'This is nothing?'

I said: 'You asked me up here for an opinion on a bottle of Scotch. I'd say lousy.'

She said: 'I'll tell you what you're up to: you two think you can find the Nawab's jewels yourselves.'

I just shrugged.

She said in a tight, over-controlled voice: 'You don't know what you're taking on. You think you can lick the world, just because you were buddies in the same squadron once. Do you know what could happen to you?'

I said: 'Look, Shirley: skip it. Ken and I'll be gone tomorrow. Just forget it. Do your picture story on the Nawab and leave it at that.'

She said: 'I could stop you.'

I looked up at her.

She said: 'I could go to the Nawab now and tell him about you two. He doesn't know Ken's still alive, does he?'

I shrugged again.

'*Does he?*'

'Go ahead. I couldn't stop you.'

She stood up abruptly and stared down at me. Her mouth was set hard and her eyes were furious. 'You damned fools! Don't you know what Herter would do to you if he knew what you were doing? Did you know he beat a man nearly to death in Beirut to find out that the stuff had come from Athens? He'd murder you. Like that.'

I said: 'They aren't in Pakistan now.'

She jerked her head angrily, tossing the idea aside. 'The Nawab's never in Pakistan. He still lives in Tungabhadra – everywhere. He carries his own little princely state around with him. Herter's his private army and his own executioner and everything.'

'I've seen bigger armies.'

She just stood and smouldered at me. Then she dropped back on the bed and grabbed for her eyes and her face crumpled up. 'You damn, damn fools,' she whispered. 'Why d'you have to try and be crooks? Why can't you just leave it alone. Why, why, *why*?'

Then the room was quiet, with a stiff, fragile quietness, and her sobbing was a small, lonely sound. I emptied my glass and stood up and poured another and almost tiptoed away to trickle water into it.

When I came back she was still sitting there with her head down in her hands and her shoulders heaving.

She was crying over a lot more than a few smudges on my soul; I still felt like a man who makes a living out of kicking kittens.

I said: 'There's a reason why. For both of us. It goes back a long time, and it gets a bit complicated. Just accept it, and leave it at that.'

She looked up slowly. Her face was flushed and soaked; she looked about twelve years old. From the neck up, anyway. She said: 'C-can I have some more Scotch?'

I poured her some.

'Thank you.' She stared at me damply. 'G-go on. Tell me.'

'It's not brave and it's not noble and it damn sure isn't clever.'

She smiled wryly. 'That's true of any story any man ever told me. Go on.'

I stared at her a while. But you have to live with it – and that means talking to somebody about it sometimes.

I sat down and took a long pull at the whisky. The water tasted fine.

I said: 'This goes back over ten years, to Pakistan, just before Partition. Have you heard of the air-lifts there, then?'

'Something. It was carrying refugees.'

'Yes – mostly. We got out there about a year before it started, flying for a small Muslim airline out of Karachi. At that time, Europe was full of pilots looking for too few jobs. Out in India and Pakistan, the smart boys knew Partition was coming and what would happen when the British pulled out and the riots started. That's why they started building up the airlines.'

I took another pull at my glass. 'So – Partition happened and the smart boys were right. We were flying three, four trips a day, Muslims out to Karachi, Hindus to Delhi, and not a half the planes or pilots we could have used. But the pay was good.' It should have been, too, with the planes badly serviced and half the landing-strips just patches of dirt, and everybody who had a rifle loosing it off at every plane that passed.

'But we had big ideas in those days: we weren't going to be hired men for ever. We were going to get our own plane, our own airline: Kitson-Clay Lines. One plane, two pilots and a snifter of Scotch for everybody who lived through the take-off.' I grinned as I remembered it. 'It wasn't such a bad idea, at that. We could have built it up from one plane; it was the people who owned the planes that were making the money.

'So – after we'd been flying refugees about three months, somebody offered us a plane. It was just a beat-up old Dak that none of the other boys would touch – that's why we could afford it. So we patched it up – and we were in business.

'That felt good. We even painted the name on it: Kitson-Clay Lines. It didn't mean a damn thing, we were still right back in the refugee traffic. But it was our own plane.

'Then, some time into 1948, the Indian government started cleaning up some of the princely states. Hyderabad, Tungabhadra, the rest – places with Muslim princes and courts and Hindu populations.'

I took another pull at the glass. She hadn't touched hers yet. She was watching me intently.

I said: 'Now I think perhaps the princes and Nawabs would have done a sight better to get the hell out the first day of Partition. Still, it's easy enough to say that. They'd most of them been there a long time, and anyway, they weren't the moving-out kind. So one morning most of them woke up to find the mob beating on the palace gates and a piece of the Indian army coming down the road. That's when they started howling for an air-lift.

'So the next morning a lad comes out to the airfield and assembled the directors of Kitson-Clay and says what about a nice trip into one of the princely states just across the Kutch – not Tungabhadra, as it happens. Fly in with a load of boxes, out with whatever the local Nawab wants brought out – probably himself.'

She said quietly: 'And the boxes were guns.'

'They were.'

'You knew that at the time?'

'Yes. It said so on the outside of them.'

She nodded. I went on: 'It was about 500 miles as I recall, on to a small private strip next door to the palace. I know we weren't counting on any refuelling at that end, because we loaded the rear end of the Dak with five-gallon cans of petrol.

'We hadn't been to the place before and the strip wasn't marked on any maps, so we had a little trouble finding it. In fact, we never did find it. We were stooging around looking for it, and being a little careful because there was supposed to be an Indian Army brigade sort of besieging it and we didn't want to bump into them.' I took on more whisky. 'The hell we didn't bump into them. We went across them at fifteen hundred feet and one of them put a burst of tracer slap through our tail end.'

Ten years I've lived with it, and most of it is just a story by now. Just words. But not kicking open the cabin door to see what damage had been done and seeing the first flames begin to spill out of that pile of cans. And grabbing for the fire extinguisher and then just standing there, wondering what the hell difference it could make to 200 gallons of aviation spirit and slamming the door again and yelling for Ken to get us down, get us down *quick*.

We had the Transport Command habit of not carrying parachutes. Odd – I still don't.

And trying to strap myself in the seat with Ken dropping her in a 45-degree dive and sideslipping her to keep the flames blowing sideways, away from the tailplane. With both of us waiting for the bang that meant Kitson-Clay Lines had only half an aircraft to work with from now on. Fifteen hundred feet is low, on most days. Not that day.

It was beautiful, the way he did it, turning her in the sideslip to find a place to put her down, handling her as I didn't know a Dak could be handled (and I could have flown one sleeping, even then) and losing his elevator cables at the last moment to the fire, but pulling her nose up on the trimming wheel cables, slowly, horribly slowly, and just dropping her over the dyke of a flooded paddy field with a splash like the launching of a battleship. A splash that broke her weakened tail off, though we didn't see that until we'd slid clear across the field, throwing up a bow wave across the windscreen like a torpedo boat.

And that moment of lovely stillness when the screen cleared and showed us the tail lying fifty yards back at the end of a wake of burning petrol, and knowing we were alive again.

And then remembering we were still carrying a load of guns intended for use on the same characters who'd shot us down and were now coming belting across the fields to see if there was anything further they needed to do about us.

I lit a cigarette and breathed smoke on to the dregs of my whisky – not that that would help it. 'Most of them wanted to stand us up and shoot us right off, without benefit of a wall. Then one of their officers got the bright idea that we'd be good material for a trial. First-class international incident stuff.'

'How d'you mean, international incident?'

'British Imperialist spies smuggling guns to Muslim Imperialist princes. Good front-page stuff in America; you remember how touchy you used to be about the British and India? Maybe not; maybe it was before your time.'

She said stiffly : 'I'm twenty-eight and my father was editing a New Jersey paper at the time.'

I assumed that proved something. I nodded. 'Good. Then, when they got us to Delhi, they reckoned we'd be even better as blackmail material. So they started bargaining with the British government: either they got the trial, with full publicity and ending with us getting shot, or the British government leant on Pakistan a bit to try and stop the air-lifts into the princely states. The British government didn't like it. They didn't like us much, either; they were well out of India and they wanted to stay out. But in the end they agreed: no trial, they'd pass the word down to Pakistan and other British pilots there, and deal with us on their own, *trés* quiet.'

'How?'

'Well, that had them worried for a while. Anything we'd done crooked, we'd done in India or Pakistan, and Pakistan was making us out here as victims of Indian Imperialism. So they sorted around awhile – and then they got it.' I poured the last of the whisky down my throat. 'They took away our pilots' licences.'

'How – like that? Without a trial?'

'You don't need a trial. You need a trial to take away a man's driving licence, not his pilot's licence. A pilot holds a licence in Britain just as long as the Ministry wants him to hold it. After that, he doesn't hold it. Nice and simple.'

'But you're —' Then she nodded. 'Yes. That was why you changed nationalities.'

'Yes.' I stood up and walked across to the whisky. 'I told you it wasn't noble. Somehow, you don't just stop being a pilot. Least, Ken and I don't. And that was the only way, when we learnt they were going to make this permanent. Switch nationalities and earn new licences. I did it in Switzerland, Ken went back to Pakistan.'

I poured more whisky and tried it without the water. Not a good idea.

'Except,' I said, 'you don't ever get back, of course. Not all the way. With all of that on our records, no big airline would ever touch us. We're in the small time now, for life. But we're flying.'

'That's your story.'

I went out to the bathroom for more water.

When I came back, she said: 'Give me a cigarette, would you?'

I gave her one and lit it.

'Still,' she said thoughtfully, 'you were lucky not to have got shot.'

'I'm not arguing that. I'm not arguing anything. I'm just giving a reason.'

She frowned. 'For what?'

'Ken and me,' I shrugged. 'For anything we've done since then.'

'What were you doing, before you joined this Swiss airline?'

'Odd flying jobs.' A box to Beirut; a man to Tangier; a bar of yellow metal to a small strip in Egypt that hadn't seen a plane since 1943. 'Free Trade, I think they call it.'

It doesn't last. They get to know you. They don't have to prove anything, either; when they start trying to catch you out on visas, inoculations, maintenance standards – then you grow up, quick. You find a two-horse airline in Berne that's almost respectable and you get almost respectable, too. A pilot needs to be able to come and go. When he can't, he stops being a pilot.

From some places, Aircargo is a long way up.

She asked: 'Are you going to stay with this airline?'

I grinned: 'I'm with it yet because the boss hasn't been able to find me to fire me. I'm through there. But I've been thinking about South America. The airlines are expanding fast, down there. They could use pilots who're used to mountains, rough country, short strips. But most of them want four-engine men, and Ken and I are mostly twin-engined. If we had some time on the big Douglases, the DC-4s and 6s, we'd be their boys. But I'm not getting four-engine time here and Ken's not getting it with the Nawab. And on it's own it's expensive.'

'What sort of expensive?'

'At a guess, I'd need about £10,000 to get enough DC-6 time and qualify as an engineer on their engines and learn about some of the new radar stuff I haven't met yet. With £20,000 I could sink something into any line that was willing to take me on – that would help, with me being European. Let's say I'll settle for £20,000.'

She stared at me a long time, very serious now, and then asked in a low voice: 'The Nawab's jewels?'

'The Nawab's jewels.'

26

AFTER A while she said: 'Can you do it without getting yourself hurt?'

'Yes.'

'I don't think you know —'

I said harshly: 'Let it alone. Just remember I know something about this business. This is quite like old times.'

Her eyes got wet again. She shook her head slowly, then stared miserably at the floor. 'Why?' she whispered. 'Why did you carry guns? *Why?*'

Why? because you don't know what it was like out there, then. Because it was a crazy situation that screamed for guns the way an empty belly screams for food. Because if you gave a man a gun you might be saving his life. Because everybody was carrying guns. Because what difference could one load of guns have made in a madness like Partition?

Tell her that, Jack. Tell the little girl from New Jersey what it was like.

I said: 'Because it never even occurred to us there might be reasons why we shouldn't. The reasons weren't our business. We were pilots.'

She raised her head slowly and looked at me, then nodded. 'Yes,' she said. 'Yes.'

Then she stood up and walked straight at me and I reached and held her against me, warm and firm and full and seeming to flood me with new life.

I held her; it was one of those moments that hang in the air as clear and long as the note of a bell.

Then she lifted her head and I kissed her. Gently, then hungrily. Her hands dragged on my back.

She broke from the kiss and stared at me, without moving her body, just leaning her head back and looking at me with an almost puzzled look.

I looked at her face. A nice face; a bit battered by the evening's tears, but a nice face. Not Miss Brown's face, not Miss Brown's body, but Shirley Burt's. Another night, another room, another girl. Oh, you Jack.

'What do you want, Jack?' she whispered.

'You.'

She nodded.

I could walk across to that bed. And tomorrow I could walk away again.

'I want more,' I said. 'You're not in love with me and I'm not in love with you. Somehow, that matters.' I shook my head. 'Maybe I'm just feeling old.'

'Thanks.' Her voice had an edge on it. 'How d'you think *I* feel?'

'Lonely.'

I got my head half out of the way of her swing; the half that was left rang like a fire alarm.

She was standing with her hands on her hips, glaring. 'You bastard!'

I rubbed my left ear.

She said: 'If you're going to be a bright successful little gangster boy tomorrow, you'll need to duck a lot quicker than that.'

'Consider me in training.'

'Goddamn you.'

She grabbed for her whisky and swallowed it in a lump and glared at me again, defiantly.

Then she grinned. 'Oh hell. You're a bastard, all right, Jack. I suppose I mean thanks, in a way.'

I reached for my own drink, then poured myself more.

She said – speaking to her empty glass: 'And tomorrow he flies out of my life, never to return. Off on his endless quest. Just like Odysseus. Except that *he* wasn't so damn slow — Oh, hell. Give me some whisky.'

'Odysseus? Which airline does he fly for?'

'Uneducated creep. Give me whisky.' She held out her glass and I poured some in. By now, somehow, we were leaning side by side against the dressing table.

I said: 'I'll be around.'

'Oh? He says keep yourself pure for him, he'll be around when he's feeling stronger.' She gulped.

'Fridays are my good days. We could make a date.'

'In Rio de Janeiro, of course.'

'Of course.' I poured myself more. The bottle was showing signs of wear on the inside. The room wasn't looking too good, either.

'Give me some.' She held out her glass. I poured, and most of it went into the glass. She sipped, then said seriously: 'I might just keep that date.'

168

'I'll be there.'

She looked at me. 'Would you?'

'I'll be there, in Rio. I've got one or two places to go first, but I'll be there.'

'Yes.' She nodded. 'I think you will. Suppose I was – on a Friday?'

Somehow, we had turned to face each other. I put my drink down, more or less on the dressing table.

She said softly, 'I think I'll be there.'

We held on to each other, tight, wanting each other but wanting more than either could give, then. Rio was an idea, a vision, an excuse. But it was still a real place.

'Goodnight, Jack.' She was smiling at me.

I kissed her and made my way more or less through the door and in roughly the right direction down the corridor. The stairs were nearly much too easy, but I made them.

The night was tall and gaunt and quiet, except that somewhere the note of a bell still seemed to be reverberating through the stillness.

I woke with somebody trying to shake the door off its hinges. It was still dark, and I had been far, far down in sleep. I got my feet on the floor, myself on top of them and weaved towards the noise. I had the light on and the door off the latch before I thought of going back for the Beretta.

Ken came in with a rush.

'Get your trousers on,' he said. 'We're flying.'

I stared at him through the ground fog that had built up round my eyes. He had on his suède jacket again; he looked serious and a little ruffled.

He said impatiently: 'Your bright little chum Rogers – the Nawab hired him. They've just taken off for the island in the Dak.'

27

IT WAS nearly four in the morning and there was a loud-speaker somewhere down behind the back seat of the Chrysler and inside it the Modern Jazz Quartet were psycho-analysing *Stardust*. Bar that, it was cosy and secretive, the way the back of a big car is at night. The headlights caught glimpses of stone huts and raw sand beyond the verge of the road, but they didn't mean anything to me yet. I was wrapped up safe in metal and warm darkness.

From the front seat, Ken said: 'I make it 600 nautical miles. Maybe a bit less.' He had a map spread across his knees under the glow from the dashboard. 'The Piaggio cruises at 180 knots. Call it three hours twenty minutes. If we take off at four fifteen, we're there before eight.'

I asked, 'What's the wind?' – just to prove I was awake. I was, but it was no thrill. I had a stomach full of Scotch *Milanese* and only a layer of cigarette smoke to hold it down.

'I don't know the weather,' Ken said. 'The Dak cruises at 135, right?'

'Nearer 125,' I said. 'She ain't young no more.'

He went back to calculating. Let him; he wasn't going to prove we could get back there before them, no matter what.

'And turn off that damn radio,' I said. Ken snapped it off. The driver half-turned to make a hurt protest, then recalled how much he was being paid to be up and about at this time of night, and went back to keeping us on the narrow half-made-up road.

Ken said: 'Four hours, fifty minutes, they'll take. They took off about two o'clock, so they'll get there about seven. We'll be an hour later. Can they find the stuff in an hour?'

The Chrysler turned into the straight smooth approach road to the airport; I pulled myself up out of the cosy feeling of not belonging to my own stomach and considered.

'Not in an hour,' I said, 'they don't know where to look. But on the other hand, they may cramp our style, don't you think?'

Ken didn't say anything; he folded the map quickly and stuffed it inside his jacket. We swung past the roundabout by the empty sentry-boxes and sailed up behind the hangars to the control tower.

Ken hurried into the tower. I climbed slowly out after him, zipping up my leather jacket; under it, I was back in the khaki drill Aircargo uniform, and around me the night was a cold crystal blackness. Far across the airfield, a double line of gooseneck paraffin flares flickered along the main runway. I lit a cigarette and tried to think about the weather. It didn't do any good; I hadn't seen anything but a local forecast in five days. The sky could have fallen down into the Aegean and I wouldn't know.

I got a sudden sick feeling about Rogers trying to land the Dak on the Saxos road in a cross-wind. I wasn't at all sure he was good enough – but he was only trying to do his job, earn an honest dollar for the boss. From his point of view I'd gone off my head.

Ken came back with a Customs officer and a bunch of papers. We all climbed back into the Chrysler and headed for the end hangar. The Customs man hunched down into his coat and sat looking sour and sleepy and not saying anything.

The Piaggio was parked beside the hangar, fat and shiny under the headlights. Ken went up to it and yanked open the cabin door and the baggage hatch and left the Customs man to poke around. He brought the maps and forecast back under the Chrysler's lights.

Behind us, the driver had the radio back on again.

Ken said quietly: 'I got us cleared to Rome; I reckoned it might cause less fuss than if we mentioned Greece.'

'It won't fool that Greek cop, Anarchos.'

'Maybe not. There's still no point shouting out where we're going.'

'What's the weather?'

He unfolded the map and laid the flimsy forecast sheet on top. 'Not so good. There's a dirty big low in the Adriatic and an occluded front sticking down from it.'

'How big?'

'I don't know. It doesn't affect a Rome flight so they didn't go into details; I just saw it marked on the map up there.'

'Where does it run?'

He dragged his finger down the map along a line running nearly north–south about a hundred miles west of Greece.

'What time was this map?' I asked.

'It was the midnight situation.' His finger poked at the middle of the Adriatic, between Yugoslavia and Italy. 'Pressure was about 970 up there. You know the Med better than I do – what's it mean to you?'

It meant we'd have the wind roughly behind us until we reached the front itself, but at that point it could become a problem. A Med occlusion can be big and rough; something you go over, under or around. Not through.

'Depends where it is,' I said slowly. 'If it's still well this side of Greece, the islands'll still be in the clear. Supposing we want to go over it, how's the oxygen?'

'Not good. Nothing worth a damn left. I was going to get the cylinders refilled at Athens – I left in too much of a hurry.'

'So if we meet it, we'll be going under it.'

He nodded slowly, his face cut into harsh blacks and whites in the headlights. 'We'll probably pick up an accurate weather situation when we're airborne. Not to worry till then.' He tapped my stomach. 'And stick that gun down the back of your pants; it makes you look pregnant.'

He walked back to the Piaggio. I drifted out of the headlights and shifted the Beretta to the back of my waistband, leaving my jacket hanging open and innocent. A car whispered, back by the control tower, and lights swung briefly across the field.

One of the Piaggio's engines whined, wound up and blared; the cockpit and wing-tip lights went on. The second engine turned over, caught and settled down, the propeller an almost invisible disc behind the wing.

Ken came back with the Customs bird. 'I'll leave her to warm up. We've got to go back to the tower to get our passports blessed.'

We got back into the Chrysler and ran down in front of the hangars. Ken opened the map across his knees again.

A new thought struck me. 'Has the Piaggio got any automatic navigation equipment?' I asked.

He shook his head without looking up. 'Never needed it.'

Probably he hadn't – not out in Pakistan, where they wouldn't have the ground installations to go with most such systems. Here in the Med we could have used a bit of radar or some-such; it meant we would be doing the flight on what bearings we could find on the radio-compass alone. We couldn't risk transmitting to ask for bearings; to do that, we'd need to identify ourselves and where we were going. I hoped the storm, wherever it was, wouldn't louse up the radio too much.

172

The Chrysler pulled up at the tower and we piled out again. The Customs man led the way in, knocked on a door, nodded his head at it and went away. We went in.

Yussuf was sitting by a small stove opposite the door.

I was bent like a corkscrew trying to disentangle the Beretta from the back of my trousers before I realized there were two other men in the room and Yussuf wasn't threatening me with anything more than a big ratty grin.

Luckily Ken was part in front of me, so the others didn't get a good view of my Wild Bill Hickok imitation. I settled the Beretta back and straightened up.

The other two were Immigration Control and the Airport Authorities. We put our passports down on the trestle table and Immigration started to work them over. Yussuf went on watching me with the same ratty grin, his hand tucked inside his blue cowboy jacket.

Ken ignored him – probably didn't know who he was.

Immigration stamped my passport and looked at Ken's. When he had it identified as a Pakistani one, he asked if Ken had any connexion with the Pakistani gent who had departed a couple of hours before.

Ken explained sweetly that the gent was his boss, that he, Ken, had been supposed to depart with him, but had got caught up in the intoxicating delights of the so-beautiful city and had missed the connexion. We were to meet in Rome.

Immigration gave him a big, knowing leer and wanted to hear about the intoxicating delights. The Airport Authority didn't: the runway lights were wasting good oil and he himself was wasting good sleep and would Immigration kindly take a step towards salvation by shutting up and stamping the passport.

Immigration stamped it; we were clear to go.

I grabbed Ken as we went out of the tower door. 'Get into the car and keep the inside lights off,' I told him. 'I'll meet you by the plane. That Arab kid in there's going to try something.'

He caught on well. He dived for the Chrysler, slammed two of the doors and the car went away like a scared cat. By then I was around a corner, flat against the wall with my Beretta in my hand. I took a quick look around; there was an old Fiat jalopy parked a few yards away that hadn't been there when we first drove up. I heard the tower door slam and quick footsteps came towards me.

He cut the corner close and whizzed past within a few

173

inches of me. He saw, or sensed me, just as I started my swing. The gun-barrel caught him high on the left side of his face, he pitched with his stride and skidded face-down along the concrete. And lay still.

I stared at him for a moment, but there wasn't anything else I could do, and if he were going to be found unconscious it would look a lot better if I weren't around. I took off around the back of the tower and started running down behind the hangars.

The Chrysler's big tail lights were just pulling away around the far side of the hangar as I came up. I walked carefully around the starboard propeller at the rear of the wing and up to the open door beside the co-pilot's seat.

'Okay?' Ken shouted at me.

'I boffed him,' I shouted back.

He nodded and yelled: 'Stay there a minute. Chocks. I'm trying the switches.'

This was no time nor place to start any magneto run-ups and I started to tell him that, but by then he had both throttles pushed right up. I was too much out of breath to argue with two Lycomings at flat-out power.

He flipped the switches, one by one, without getting any significant reaction, throttled back and nodded to me. I ran round to the port wheel, grabbed the chock, ran back around the nose for the starboard chock, threw them both in over the back of the co-pilot's seat, and climbed in after them.

Two close-set headlights swung around the corner of the hangar, turned and came straight at us.

Ken said, 'Christ!' and grabbed the throttles. We lurched forward and turned left, towards the hangar. The car tightened its turn to cut us off. Ken swept the throttles against the stops, the engines screamed and we slewed around on the locked port wheel. But there was no way clear; we turned through a quarter circle and were facing slap up against the hangars. Ken jammed on the brakes. We stopped with a thump.

The car turned in behind us, slowing.

I got a foot to the door at my side, a hand to the Beretta and nearly broke my neck arriving on the concrete. But I was up and with the gun coming up in my hand as a thin figure weaved around the tail of the Piaggio and came at me.

There was a bright flash at its waist level, a thin crack above the burble of the engines. I jerked away, then steadied myself.

*All right, sonny, you promised you'd try. But this time I've got
a gun; this is what I bought it for.*

But the starboard propeller was spinning between us and a
steel slug might bend a blade.

He fired again, just as Ken bounced out behind me. I shot
back, low, just to shake his aim, then ran outwards, to get an
angled shot across behind the prop.

He thought I was running away. He plunged forward after
me, under the wing. Into the propeller.

There was a *thump*; the figure was flicked cartwheeling in the
air, twenty yards away, beyond the wing-tip.

The engine spun on, untroubled. I straightened up slowly,
with the *thump* still echoing in my head. Then, after a moment,
I walked cautiously across. But I knew I needn't be cautious.

Beside him a small gun glittered in the starlight. I picked it
up : the same little silver and ivory ·22 automatic. I put it in my
shirt pocket and walked back.

Ken was leaning against the open doorway, hunched, gripping his left arm with his right hand. The Walther lay on the
ground.

He straightened up as I came. 'Arm,' he said calmly. I saw
the small rip high up in his jacket.

I unbuttoned the jacket and peeled it off him. There was a
tear and a small dark stain in the shirt, above the elbow. I got
a finger in the tear and ripped it clear.

There were two holes, so it wouldn't mean digging for the
bullet; thank God for that.

'How's the hand?' I asked.

He lifted his arm outwards and moved the fingers. 'Okay, it's
all —' Then the pain hit, and his face tightened suddenly.

'Got a first-aid kit on the plane?'

He nodded. 'Galley, cupboard.'

I climbed in, found the kit and wrapped a dry dressing tight
around the arm. There was a morphine ampoule, one of those
ready-loaded one-shot needles that bomber crews used to carry.
I held it up. 'D'you want morphine?'

He made a fair imitation of a grin. 'Scotch'll do. Some of
that in the galley.'

'Ken – d'you want to go on?'

'Hell, yes. But you'll be doing the flying.'

'Yes. You sure?'

He nodded. I reached in and flicked off the switches and

175

pulled back the mixture cut-offs. The engines ground and died and the night seemed very quiet.

He asked: 'What's that for?'

I waved a hand towards what had been Yussuf. 'We've got to report that. It shouldn't hold us up long: we should be able to pass it off as an accident – if you can keep your arm out of sight. He hasn't got any bullet holes in him.'

'What about the marks on his head, where you slugged him?'

I said: 'What head?'

28

IT TOOK time, but not much else. We got Ken into my jacket and chucked his, with its bullet holes, into the plane. Then I went over the ground with a torch. We had both been using automatics, so there were cartridge cases to be picked up. I found all three. I also found the bullet gouge in the concrete from my shot and aged it with a spot of oil. After that I was ready to assist inquiries in every possible way.

After a period of running around treading on each other's tails, they dug up the local police – the same one who'd questioned me when I'd got back from Mehari and whose name I still couldn't remember. We told the story three times – once for him to get the general idea, once for him to follow it over the ground and once for the statement sheet. It came out the same each time, just what had happened except with no guns and no shooting. He didn't like it much: he felt there was something missing, something to give a reason to whatever Yussuf had been trying to do. But he didn't spot Ken's arm.

I helped things along by asking what the hell Yussuf was doing at the airport and why he'd been allowed in so easily. The Airport Authority gave me a dirty look and then joined in to try and get things played down a bit.

Finally the copper had a long word on the phone with somebody who sounded as if he didn't like long words at 5 am. Then he came and picked up our statements and smiled at us.

'Signori – you are free to go. Of course, you will come back if the inquest requires it?'

176

I said 'Yes' quickly, before Ken could object. I thought I had the drift: once we were out of the country and difficult to track down, it would be a good excuse for not making too much of the inquest. By this time, they would be mighty glad to see me go: if they had to start investigating me now, all they would find would be that they ought to have investigated me earlier.

But legally, I was still free to come and go. In my job, that was the important thing.

The copper came to the door and shook us both by the hand. Then he said: 'The same boy you brought from Athens, yes, Captain?'

I nodded.

He sighed and looked at the handful of statements. 'It is as I said to you. These boys, they are so impetuous.'

And that was about the truth of it.

There was nothing left now but the Piaggio standing awkwardly face-up to the hangar and a few marks on the concrete that looked like oil under the starlight, and some of which were. We pushed her back, climbed in and Ken led me through the starting sequence.

I put on a pair of lightweight plastic headphones that looked like a streamlined stethoscope, switched on the R/T, released the brakes and let her roll forward.

With a steerable nosewheel she taxied light and fast – but you can't tell much about a plane just taxiing. Ken sat still and solid in the right-hand seat, his left hand lying in his lap and his face stretched taut under the mauve cockpit lighting. An unlit cigarette moved gently in his mouth.

I crept her up to the end of the runway and stopped. 'Check list, please.'

Ken recited it for me and I ran my hands over the controls, checking and setting. The levers had a live little quiver from the engine vibration, but the plane itself wasn't alive yet. She would be alive when she was flying; now she was just a penfriend I hoped I knew, but couldn't be sure about. All I could be sure about was the stiff good manners of the pre-take-off check ... *mixture – auto rich; pitch – maximum rpm; throttle nut – tensioned; fuel tanks – select wing-tips; fuel booster pumps – on; flaps – 20 degrees; hatches – secure; harness – tight.*

177

Ken fastened and tightened his straps awkwardly, then turned down the cockpit lighting until only the instrument needles and figures showed. The reflection in the windscreen faded; outside, the night was still a translucent black. Several of the gooseneck flares had burnt themselves out by now, giving the flarepath an uneven gap-toothed look.

He looked across at me. 'Okay?'

I nodded. He pressed the radio transmit button on the wheel and said: 'Piaggio request take-off.'

The tower cleared its throat and came back: 'Piaggio clear to take off.'

I looked slowly around the cockpit and settled my breathing. I had been a Dakota pilot a long time – too long; now I had to find out what sort of pilot I was without a Dak. And I had to start with a night take-off and no proper briefing.

A nice little plane without vices. Put down 20 degrees of flap, give her 48 inches of boost and she'll come off at about 60 knots. There's a lag in the airspeed indicator, though, so better start pulling back about 55 knots. . . .

Ken said again: 'Okay?'

'Yes.' I released the parking brake and pushed the throttles slowly up.

She jumped forward and the engine noise came racketing into the cockpit, shriller and snappier than the Dakota's big Pratt and Whitneys. I swung the rudder bar gently, waiting for it to become effective as the speed built up.

It built up fast, maybe too fast. I needed time to adjust to her, to learn to sense and predict her. And she started to burrow her nose as she went.

Ken said: 'Okay, get her off.'

The needle was showing just over 55 knots. I eased on the stick. She stayed on the ground.

With the engines mounted high, you've got a high thrust line; that'll tend to hold her down – you'll have to peel her off.

'Get her off!' He reached out his hand for the wheel.

The needle was over 60 knots now. I took a firm hold on the wheel and hauled back.

She came away, soared off; flying, alive.

Ken dropped his hand back in his lap. 'Wheels,' he said.

I fumbled for the undercarriage lever and jacked it up, then checked forward her nose to hold her down until we had full

178

safety speed. When it came, I brought the flaps gently up. She paused, then lifted more freely. At 100 knots I let her nose come up into a climb and started easing back on throttles.

Ken reached for the transmit button. 'Piaggio clearing circuit. Thank you and goodnight.'

'Understand Piaggio is clearing circuit. Please contact Wheelus base if radio bearings are required. Goodnight, signori.'

We were up to 1,000 feet now, climbing at 100 knots and going more or less east.

'What heading?' I asked.

Ken shuffled his legs, loosened his straps and snapped a lighter to his cigarette. He breathed smoke at the windscreen. 'You want to be on about 070 magnetic. I'll give you something better in a minute.'

I eased around on to 070. Ken waited until I had steadied her, then climbed carefully back out of his seat. He came back with a handful of maps, ruler, protractor and a Dalton navigation computer. He turned on the map-reading light and started to work on the big map.

I started to feel her out with little movements of the controls and trimmers. She was light and sensitive, with just a touch of sponginess to remind me she had two engines and was built for six or eight people. After the Dakota, she handled like a fighter.

I pumped the throttles slightly. Taking off power didn't drop her nose as quickly as I'd expected; pushing on power didn't bring the nose up immediately, either. The high thrust line again. I wasn't going to be caught out by that next time.

Ken looked up from the map. 'You're rocking the boat a bit, aren't you?'

I let her steady into the climb. He went back to the map.

After a minute or two he looked up and said: 'Our track should be 068 magnetic. We've got an off-shore wind until we're past the coast in a few minutes. Steer 071 for the meanwhile.'

I grunted. I wasn't sure enough of her yet to keep a heading within one degree. I'd stick to trying to keep 070. 'Unless we raise some radio bearings on this trip,' I said, 'we're going to get lost, no matter what.'

He smiled. 'Realistic.' He seemed more relaxed now. Sitting and hoping I could manage the take-off couldn't have been much fun. It was an odd feeling for me, too – being first pilot when Ken was around. I wasn't sure I liked it.

He asked: 'How d'you like her?'

'Very nice. Any time I have £35,000 to spare I may invest in one of my own.'

'You keep a track of 068 for the next three-and-a-bit hours and you can start investing. Right now, you're about four degrees off course.'

I was, too. I hauled her back into place. Ken pinned a second map, a local large-scale RAF sheet, on to a map board and started transferring our track line from the big map. We passed 10,000 feet at 5.37 and settled down to a fast cruise speed of 180 knots.

29

THE SKY began to take on a tinge of blue behind the blackness and the stars dulled gently. Inside the cockpit it was warm and drowsy. The Piaggio was trimmed to a perfect balance and the cockpit lighting was a comfortable firelight glow. We were slumped down in the big leather seats, each with its own little hot-air blower breathing down from the roof.

After a time, Ken said: 'Like some coffee?'

I stared blearily at him. I'd rather have gone quietly to sleep, but if I had to be awake, then coffee was the sort of help I needed. 'Yes,' I said. 'Are these things fitted with air hostesses, too?'

'Just electric percolators.' He climbed carefully out of the seat and went aft.

I pulled myself upright and tuned the R/T to Wheelus base and switched on the radio-compass.

I was still waiting for them to say something when Ken came back carrying a percolator and two mugs, all in one hand. He put the percolator down on the engine control pedestal, then flipped out two little silver mug-holders from under our seat-arms and dropped the mugs in. 'We're out of sugar. You'll get it black and bitter and like it.'

Wheelus suddenly came on the air, advising somebody that

ground pressure setting was 1,018 millibars, that he had the circuit to himself and there was ham and eggs waiting on the ground. The hardships of military flying.

I estimated the bearing off the radio compass – 258 degrees – and Ken drew it on the map. 'That puts you about three to four miles north of track, laddie. On the other hand, the wind's probably still veering. Stay on 070 and see what happens.'

'Will do.' I sipped coffee and began to feel more at home in my own body. Ahead, the sky was a deep blue, with just a faint line of lighter blue along the horizon.

Ken twisted to take the coffee with his right hand.

'How's the arm?' I asked.

'Fair to middling.' He leant cautiously back, staring out ahead and sipping coffee. I went back to switching the R/T around the stations; nobody else seemed awake.

After a few minutes Ken said quietly: 'Here she comes.'

I looked up from the R/T dial just as the rim of the sun reached up over the horizon and flared a hard, colourless light across the sky, almost dead ahead. There were no clouds, no vapour trails, nothing to catch or stop the light.

I winced and looked down; the cockpit seemed suddenly small and drab in the brightness outside. Ken leant forward and turned off the instrument lighting. The sea, 10,000 feet below, was still dark.

He looked at his watch. 'When do we get any weather?'

'We should get Malta soon. But it won't tell us anything about the Greek weather. We'll have to wait till we're in range of Athens.'

He nodded and I went back to fiddling with the R/T.

The sun reached the sea ahead of us, spilling quickly across it in a run of gold sparks off the wavetops, then gathering into surging pools of light, then these joining and spreading until the whole horizon was a vast plate of dimpled brass. We sat and watched it happen.

I raised Luqa, in Malta, on the R/T and got a goodish cross-bearing with another transmission from Wheelus. It put us still north of track, having done just over 100 miles. Allowing for variations in my flying, that still worked out to give us a wind blowing from 220 degrees, about 20 knots. I would have preferred it stronger; it meant the front was a good way ahead of us yet.

Ken stood up from his seat and asked: 'Want any more coffee?'

I looked up at him. His face looked pale and taut in the bright horizontal light. For him, the coffee probably hadn't been such a good idea; it had woken up nerves that would have been better left sleeping. A hole in the arm isn't something you cure with an aspirin and a sniff at the Scotch bottle.

I said: 'Not right now, thanks.'

'I'm going to stretch out in the back. I can't snooze here – I keep watching the damn instruments.'

He clambered carefully back and lowered himself gently into the big aft-facing seat on the starboard side, his left arm uppermost.

I moved the trimming wheel a shade forward to balance out his shift of weight, then lit a cigarette and sat back. There wasn't any flying to be done. The Piaggio hadn't any autopilot, but the air outside was as smooth and clear as plate glass.

I wasn't worried about the long sea passage, not with two engines that could boast they were maintained by a Nawab's millions. And I wasn't familiar enough with the sound of Lycomings to scare myself into thinking they were going wrong by just listening to them. So I didn't bother to try. I just sat. A lot of flying is just sitting.

At about 6.20 I tuned in to Wheelus again, then got Luqa almost immediately afterwards. I drew the bearings on the map and they put us just about back on track again. I took three degrees off the heading, turning slightly into wind before it could blow us off again on the other side of track.

I left the R/T on Luqa and waited for their weather broadcast; when it came, it gave middling westerly winds over the whole Malta and Libyan coast areas, getting stronger towards the east. No cloud. And no mention of what was happening farther east.

The front had been through here, all right, scouring the whole sky clean and leaving a westerly wind-stream pointing after it. But there was no hint of where it had got to. By now it could be over the Greek islands, past them, or pivoted round and lost somewhere in the mainland mountains. I just couldn't tell, and at this range Athens radio wasn't going to tell me.

After that I went back to sitting. But it wasn't the same, somehow. I looked carefully all around the instruments, fuel gauges, engine temperatures. Then I tested the radio-altimeter, a useful little gadget that bounces radio waves off whatever's below and times the echo. We'd need it if we had to fly under the front; the pressure changes would make the standard pressure-operated altimeter useless.

It seemed all present and correct. I switched it off, and had another careful look all around the instruments. I was beginning to see just how the Piaggio was equipped – and why. The Nawab could have afforded to load her down with every new radar and radio device in the book. Instead, she was very sparsely equipped. Partly that would be the lack of ground installations out in Pakistan, but also almost every form of automatic navigation needs an extra man to make it work properly. Ken must have decided it was better to save weight by having nothing he couldn't use without taking his mind off the actual flying. I could see his point; I'd rather have trusted to his piloting than to Herter trying to tune a radar set.

I twiddled the cockpit heat/ventilation control a little, then went back to just sitting, wondering why I'd bothered to do anything else for the past twenty minutes. I knew why, though. Using the radio had reminded me how used I was to flying with full use of radio, full weather briefing and freedom to divert or cancel any flight. This flight was something different. The occluded front, wherever it was, could make it very different.

30

GETTING ON towards seven o'clock Ken stood up from his seat, said: 'Goddamn this arm,' and went aft. He came back a few minutes later with a fresh pot of coffee, went aft again, came back with an opened tin of peaches and a spoon.

'All yours,' he said. 'I'm not hungry.'

'Thanks. How's the arm?'

'Middling.' He was keeping his face calm, but he was having to work at it.

'Take over while I feed?' I suggested.

He shrugged with one shoulder and sat down. I got the idea

that he'd rather not have flown her at all than just half-flown her, but it might help get his mind off his arm.

He put his right hand on the wheel. 'I have control.'

'You have control.' The old flying training manners die hard.

After a while he asked: 'Did you pick up any weather?'

'I got Malta. You'll be happy to know we're flying through bright sunshine with a westerly wind.'

'They didn't say anything about Greece?'

'They never do. And we're still a bit far from Athens.'

He nodded. It was about 7.00 now and we had come nearly halfway, with 300 miles yet to go. I finished the peaches and balanced the empty tin on the engine control pedestal.

Ken said: 'Cloud ahead.'

I looked up quickly. It couldn't be the front – we'd get a lot more warning from a lot more cloud before we ran into an occluded front from the backside – but it might be a hint.

It was just a fragment of cumulus hanging white and ragged and innocent down around 6,000 feet. It didn't tell me anything.

He said: 'Apart from Athens, would anybody else tell us the Greek weather?'

'Sure, anybody would – if we called and asked them. But nobody else does a regular Greek forecast. Shall I take her?'

He nodded. 'You have control.' Then he leant back and put a cigarette in his mouth and lit it. Most of the tension had gone from his face by now. He had his left hand hooked in the zip of his – actually my – jacket.

We passed over another patch of cumulus, a frayed white puff-ball stretching from 6,000 up to around 8,000. Ahead, the horizon was lumpy with more cloud.

After a while he said. 'You estimate there's about a million's-worth left on the island?'

'That's if there's everything on the list that the Nawab hasn't got back yet – and if you were right about it all coming to near a million-and-a-half. *And* taking its open-market value.'

He nodded agreement. 'I don't suppose we'll be dealing on the open market, Jack. D'you know anybody who could help that way?'

'I know a bird in Tel Aviv. He handles some stuff.' I couldn't see him handling this stuff; he'd run screaming through the ceiling if I tried to dump a million's-worth of hand-carved jade in his lap. Still, that wasn't our nearest problem.

184

Ken was looking at me, a small twist of amusement around his mouth. 'You didn't know *that* sort of information when I last knew you.'

'I've learnt a lot since then.' I put a cigarette in my mouth. 'One thing: how did you get on to that first load, the lot I took to Libya?'

He shrugged. 'We got Mikklos's name in Beirut. From the chap he'd passed the first few pieces on to.'

'The chap Herter beat nearly to death?'

He looked at me sharply. 'Where did you get that from?'

'A mutual friend.'

He frowned, then nodded. 'Her. Yes; I can't say I approved of Herter's methods.'

'Who does?' I lit my cigarette. 'What put you on to my load?'

'Just asking around – with a handful of dollars. He'd had that cargo in bond at the airport for over a week – labelled for Beirut. The day we arrived in Athens he'd switched the label to Libya.'

'This, you didn't tell His Excellency.'

'My heart has been breaking steadily ever since. How do *you* like being a rich man?'

I just nodded and he went back to watching the horizon. Then he asked: 'What will you do with it – the cash?'

I blew smoke at the compass and said carefully: 'I was thinking of going to the States and buying myself some four-engine instruction time and some up-to-date engineering licences. Then I thought South America. Lot of room for a lot more air transport down there, and they're building up fast. Maybe I'd get in on an airline; maybe I'd help start my own.'

'Just like old times: climbing up some damn mountain in an old Douglas.'

'Not quite. Airlines are getting to be very big business down there. Real business; this isn't just refugee traffic.'

He smiled wryly. 'Nor just guns. You've lost ten years, Jack: could you run an airline?'

I looked across at him. 'I think so. Given the right help.'

He smiled again, still staring ahead. 'Could I wear four rings and walk up and down between the seats adjusting women's seat-straps?'

'You could adjust any straps you like within international law. But don't fool yourself: they don't want just public-

185

relations pilots. They want people who can help build it up. There's still a lot of rough country down there, and a lot of damn short runways. They need pilots who can fly that sort of country.'

He wasn't smiling now. 'We qualify there, all right.' Then he grinned suddenly. 'Hell, it's an idea.'

'What were you thinking of doing?'

'Hadn't really thought.' He ground out his cigarette, then collected the coffee pot and peach tin and took them back to the galley. When he came forward again he had a small blue travel guide with him.

The time was 7.22. I raised Benghazi, for the first time, on the R/T and got a nice clear bearing. Ken dragged the map board up on to his knees and drew it in. I tuned to Luqa; it was off the air for the moment.

Ken opened the guide and leafed through it. 'Saxos – population approx. 1,500. Silver mines, no longer worked. Some pottery making. Legend claims that this is the island where Odysseus encountered the lotus-eaters after having been driven by fierce storms for nine days and nights. Well, well. They really had weather in those days. Did you encounter many lotus-eaters?'

'Not hardly a one.' (Odysseus – now which airline did he fly for? Forget it. But – half *his* troubles were people wanting him to settle down in the wrong place. The hell with him; just a bad joke.)

Ken said: 'Well, watch it if anybody offers you anything to eat there. We want to pile the loot on board and get the hell out.' He shut the book with a snap. 'I'd hoped they'd have a map of the island. You're sure we can put down on it okay?'

'I got a Dak down there the other day.'

He nodded. Luqa started chattering faintly in the headphones and the radio-compass needle swung sluggishly.

The running fix put us about twelve miles south of track, having done 370 miles. Ken did some work with the computer and announced: 'We've got a fair piece of wind behind us: about due west, over 30 knots. Ground speed of 212 knots. Come left ten degrees on to 057 and we'll be back on track at about 7.40.'

I swung left. I was getting it right now, straightening out within a degree of heading.

It was 7.27 now and the cloud was still building up round us, soft and fluffy-looking until we came close enough to see the tops boiling and surging. Off to either side, there were occasional billows reaching to near 20,000 feet. Wherever the front was, it was leaving quite a track.

I didn't like that; it was getting too thick too fast, but without telling us anything about the front itself. It could be a weak one just over the horizon or a stinker 150 miles ahead. I looked at the map and didn't like that much, either. We were still 200 miles from Athens, too far to get any sort of R/T reception.

I asked: 'You've got a W/T set on board, haven't you?'

He looked at me, surprised. 'Yes. Why?'

'There's an Athens weather broadcast at half-past the hour. I want to try for this one.'

'Don't we get it in voice?'

'Not at this range. And the way things are going, we could be inside that front before anybody tells us where it is. Where d'you switch it on?'

He was studying the cloud outside. 'You couldn't read morse that fast – they send at professional rates, for wireless ops.'

'I can read twenty words a minute. Where d'you switch the damn thing on?'

'Under the R/T switches. You couldn't read twenty when I last knew you.'

'I told you – I've learnt a lot since then.' But we were neither of us fooling each other: twenty a minute isn't fast. I hoped the Athens operator would still have that early-morning feeling.

I found the W/T switches and muted the R/T. 'You'd better fly her while I write. Tell me – why d'you have a set if you can't read it?'

'For getting bearings when we're out of R/T range.' He put his hand on the wheel. 'I have control.'

The headphones came alive; I tuned gently round until I thought I was on the Athens frequency. There was a distant hum and crackle. I turned the volume full up and watched the second hand of my watch come round to 7.30 dead.

The crackle became a stammer of morse, clear enough for me to pick out the SWA identification letters. Then it dissolved in a crackle again.

I shoved the headphones deep into my ears and moved the tuning knob gently. We weren't close to Athens, but we weren't far enough away to make this sort of difference to reception on W/T.

The morse faded back in and I started scribbling. Weather comes across broken down into a figure code, so it doesn't have the immediate logic of words. I knew enough by now not to confuse the issue further by trying to decode it as it came.

After five minutes I had aching ears and a piece of paper that looked like an accident in algebra – but I hoped I had enough. Ken looked across and asked: 'How does it look?'

'Tell you in a moment.' I picked out the three reporting stations that concerned us most: Athens itself, Canea in Crete and Pilos, on the Greek Adriatic coast, and started to decode them.

I'd missed a lot of Athens, but there was enough there to give a general impression: it was still in the clear, with occasional cloud. Canea was about the same, winds south-east to east.

Pilos was farther west, nearer us – and Pilos had the front. Pressure down to 980, squalls with heavy rain, one kilometre visibility, cloud base solid at 500 feet. But I'd missed the wind report.

Ken asked again: 'How does it look?'

'It looks like somebody pulled the plug on us. Give me the map.'

He let go of the wheel and passed the map board across. I balanced it on my knees and started worrying.

Flying a straight course, we were due to be over the sea all the way to Saxos. But about 70 miles before we got there, we had to go through a channel between the southern tip of the Greek mainland and Crete. It was a good, wide channel – except that, as usual with any piece of sea around Greece, somebody had carefully filled it up with islands.

And that was where the front was.

I shoved a hand through my hair and did some quick measuring with a pencil. If we stayed on track, we should just about miss the southern tip of the most northerly island, Cerigo, which was marked with a spot height of 1,660 feet. Between that and the next big island southwards, Andikithira, there was a channel about eighteen miles wide. Only *that* had to have an island in it, too: just a blob of rock named Pori, too small to have any spot height marked, but likely enough, if I knew Greek islands, to stick up to near 500 feet without even trying.

Which left us about a ten-mile channel between Cerigo and Pori. No trouble in clear weather and no trouble in any weather if we stayed at 10,000 feet. But with the front there, we were going to be down at 500 feet in bad visibility and a shifting strong wind. And, with a solid pile of thunderclouds on top of us, a poor chance on any radio bearings.

Ken asked: 'Where will it be?'

'Take a look. I have control.'

'You have.'

I put one hand on the wheel; the palm felt just a little warm and damp. I passed him the map board with the other hand.

He studied it for a moment, then asked: 'It won't stretch as far as the island, Saxos? We'll be able to land there?'

'If we get that far. If we really want to be rich, why don't we go back to Libya and steal an oil well?'

'Would get the plane dirty.' He grinned suddenly. 'We're rich men already, chum. All we need is a little accurate navigation and a little accurate flying.'

'Yes.' I was trying to work out just where the front would begin. I couldn't; I didn't know how deep it was. But if it was as rough as Pilos had reported, it wouldn't be much less than fifty miles from front to back.

Ken turned his left wrist, lying slack in his lap, with his right hand and looked at his watch. '7.40. We should be back on track now. Come right to 062.'

I put the wheel gently over and brought us round five degrees. Ken drew, for the first time on our flight, a small square on our track line: the sign of a dead reckoning position. He wrote the time in beside it.

I looked across at the map. The last circle, marking a definite fix, had been at 7.25, fifteen minutes and over fifty miles ago. We needed something better than a dead-reckoning position before we tried that channel under the front.

I asked: 'How about a little of that accurate navigation you were talking about?'

He grinned. 'You find 'em and I'll plot 'em.' He hauled the computer, protractor and ruler out of the door pocket and started work on the map.

I turned up the W/T volume and tuned carefully around the dial. Athens came in again with a flurry of static. I switched it on to the radio-compass and the needle jerked erratically; no good to within five degrees. I tuned away.

Luqa was clear but weak; the needle was too flabby for an accurate bearing. Benghazi was off the air for the moment; so was Pilos. I turned down the W/T and unswitched the R/T mute. The time was 7.44.

Ken asked: 'How far ahead d'you think we'll see the front? Fifty miles?'

I looked out ahead. Around us, close now, the cumulus was beginning to stretch up like the first tall buildings of a big city, throwing us into occasional shadow. But this wasn't the front. The front, when we saw it, would be a solid wall of clouds with cumulo-nimbus towers – thunderheads – stretching up four times the height we were at now.

'Yes,' I said, 'we should see it at fifty.'

'Good.' He jabbed the pencil at the map. 'What d'you reckon on at the front?'

That wasn't an easy one. It would be different from the wind up here and I didn't know what it had been at Pilos. And it would be shifting: veering round northwards as we came into the front, then backing sharply south and south-east on the far side.

That backing was important: we needed either an east wind or a west wind, or near to one or the other, if we were going down on to the east–west road at Saxos.

Time enough to worry about that later.

I said slowly: 'Count on 40 knots from 280 degrees at sea level.' It was a guess. It couldn't be anything else.

'Right.' He twirled the dial of the little computer. I went back to switching around the R/T channels. I didn't find anything; anywhere close enough to be in R/T range was either under the front or on the far side of it. The time was 7.46.

A tall cumulus stood slap in our path. I turned a careful ten degrees left to dog-leg past it. Ken looked up, then made a couple of marks on the map and dropped the computer back into the door pocket.

'Stand by,' he said, 'plan of action coming up. We're about seventy miles short of the channel now. We'll stay at height as long as we can get whatever radio bearings we can, then we'll go down, on the same course, to about 500 feet or wherever we have to. We'll be down to about 120 knots under the front, right?'

I nodded. Reducing speed meant we wouldn't lose or gain so much height in turbulence, and we'd have more time to see anything before we hit it. But it also meant the wind would drift us more if I'd guessed it too wrong.

The cumulus was out square to starboard of us. I turned on to the second half of the dogleg to bring us back on to track.

Ken said: 'Ten miles before the channel I'll give you a right turn to bring us away from Cerigo. If we come on to 087 degrees we should make a track of due east and that'll put us smack down the middle of the channel. We'll hold that until we're sure we're clear of that lot of islands. After that it doesn't matter; there isn't anything else to hit in that area. Okay?'

'Give me the map a moment.' He passed it across and I studied the new line he'd plotted for us. The right turn was a good, simple idea – and a simple idea is always best when you're navigating simple instruments. Start flying fancy patterns and you start multiplying your errors. But any idea for going through a ten-mile channel assumed we couldn't be more than five miles off track. And that assumed we knew our position when we started the descent.

Ken said softly: 'There she is.'

I jerked my head up – and there it was, all right. It was distant still – near the fifty miles we'd guessed – but even so it was big; a rampart of great white thunderheads reaching to 40,000 feet, their tops dragged off into anvil shapes by the stratospheric winds. Eight-mile-high pillars of thunder stuffed with roaring up-and-down currents that could flip a 100-ton jetliner on her back and then tear the wings off her. To a little four-tonner like the Piaggio it would be like flying through a meat mincer.

But we weren't going through; we were going underneath. If we could find an underneath.

Ken made a quick measurement on the map. 'About fifteen miles this side of the channel.'

I was still staring ahead. Till now I'd hoped, despite the Pilos report, that the thing would somehow have moved farther east, or been broken and ragged, with good gaps around 10,000 feet. It wasn't. As more of it crept up over the horizon of cumulus, I could see it was solid up to at least 25,000 before it broke into individual thunderheads. And 25,000 was far too high for us without oxygen, even if the Piaggio could have made it.

Ken said contentedly. 'So it won't reach as far as Saxos; we'll be in the clear there.' He looked out ahead, then at his watch. 'About 45 miles to go; start descending in seven minutes. At 7.55.'

Seven minutes to fix our position if we were going to get something better than a square on the map before we started our descent. I muted the R/T and turned up the W/T.

Athens was stronger now, but the static was louder, too. The

191

radio-compass jerked nervously around the dial, giving me any of ten degrees to choose from. I turned to Benghazi; silence. Then Luqa again. Clear but over 350 miles away by now. It had been too distant before; I was fooling myself even trying it. I tuned to Pilos and left the dial there; the front should have cleared there by now. The time was 7.52.

Pilos came on suddenly, loud and sharp and the compass needle swung and held it. But it only gave us half a proper fix, and that the wrong half. Square to our track, it put us about as far along the track as I thought we were – but it couldn't help tell us whether we were out to one side or the other. For that, I needed a station roughly ahead or behind. Athens or Luqa. The time was 7.54.

I asked: 'Where d'you put us?'

Ken stood the pencil on the map, on track, just thirty miles short of Cerigo. 'Maybe a mile or two off,' he said, 'I wouldn't say any more.'

He couldn't be sure. There just wasn't any way to be sure. We hadn't had a fix in half an hour and in that time we'd done over 100 miles. If we were only five per cent off, we were five miles off – and that was all the safety margin we had.

We could be five per cent off and not know it, flying on guessed-at winds with no landmarks.

I said: 'Down there, visibility isn't going to be good. Once we're under the front I may be on instruments. That means you keep a look out.'

Ken nodded.

I said: 'That means don't worry about the map any more. Just keep a look out.'

He looked at me, a small amused look. 'You worried about something?'

I said: 'We don't know where the hell we are. And we're going to be at sea level through a piece of sea that's lousy with islands. Yes, I'm worried about something.'

He was still staring at me, still amused. I reached forward and turned on the radio-altimeter.

I said: 'Any way you look at it, that's just plain damn *bad* flying. Any other flight of my life I'd have turned round or diverted or started screaming for help on the radio.'

I could still do that; I could pick up the microphone and start asking for a fix. Somebody would hear, some plane, some ship. All I had to do was pick up the microphone – and identify us.

192

Ken shook his head. He said: 'No. Not any other flight.'

I stared at him. Then I nodded. Not any other flight. Not that flight out across the Kutch, more than ten years ago now. That had been a special flight, too. No radio calls, no diversion, no turning back. And now I was back in the same cockpit with the same man.

The time was 7.55. I looked out ahead. The front was standing up over us now, solid and deep-chested billows of cloud, less than twenty miles away now. I was going to fly under that front because I wanted to. Because I wanted what was on the other side more than I wanted to dodge the front itself. It was my own free will. Suddenly, that seemed important.

'Fasten seat belts,' I said, 'we're going down.'

Ken drew a small square on the map, on our track, and wrote in the time beside it.

31

WE DROPPED gently down through narrowing canyons between the tall cumuli, dog-legging to miss their turbulent centres. Fifteen degrees right – hold for fifteen seconds, thirty degrees left – hold for fifteen seconds – fifteen degrees right, back on to course. The sun died above us and the cloud walls got darker as they got closer. I held 180 knots with the throttles well back, descending at 2,000 feet per minute.

I still had the W/T on Athens and was trying to average out the swings of the radio-compass to decide on a bearing. There wasn't much hope in it. Ken got up and went back through the cabin buckling together seat belts, closing drawers, clearing the galley. Getting ready for rough air.

The canyons were becoming just rifts and our doglegs wider. Below, the sea was a steely-grey, gashed with white streaks. We went down.

At 6,000 feet I pushed forward the throttles to clear the plugs, then brought them back again. Ken sat down in the co-pilot's seat and fastened his straps.

We came to it at about 5,000 feet: a big one that I couldn't dog-leg around. Not the front, not yet, just a wide whiteness gradually swelling up to fill the windscreen, misty and delicate – but sure to be rough enough inside.

I steadied her firmly on heading and ducked my head to concentrate on the instruments just before the cloud broke around us. For a moment it was still, passive, just a piece of Hollywood mist. Then the vertical currents hit us. The Piaggio reared on a wing-tip, fell off before I could catch her. Then we surged upwards, hung and dropped. There was no point in fighting her; all I could do was try and dampen the movement a little and hope we'd average a descent, perhaps even a course. The compass was swaying wildly.

Then, oddly, she steadied. That frightened me: for a moment I thought we'd broken a control cable. Then we came into the clear again.

I stayed on instruments, pulling her back to a heading and the right speed and descent.

Ken said: 'Just where the hell have you got us now?'

I looked up and out. We were in a cave. Above and around us the cloud was cut into huge ragged arches – dark, but with a dim, sourceless light that gave the whole thing the eerie stillness of an old engraving. The engines seemed quiet, the air passive. We just drifted, and it was a long creepy moment. I could no more have turned into one of those cloud walls than I could have flown willingly into a cliff. I was frozen on the controls.

I got my head down at the instruments again. They gave me back my balance; the dials were real and familiar. But I was still glad the compass showed we were going the same direction as the cave.

Ken said: 'And the Met boys would just never believe it.'

I just nodded. 4,000 feet now; I shoved up the throttles again to clear the plugs. Ken suddenly cocked his head on one side and said: 'Hold it – something on the R/T.'

I pulled back the throttles, turned off the W/T and flipped off the mute switch on the R/T.

An American voice blasted into the headphones at foghorn power: '. . . at 4,000 feet descending on course 070 degrees at 200 knots, identify yourself. I say again, unknown aircraft descending on course 070 degrees at 200 knots, identify yourself.'

He paused to give us a chance. Ken looked at me, surprised.

I said: 'The long arm and loud voice of Uncle Sam. American Sixth Fleet; we must be pretty close to them. Jumpy, aren't they?'

I glanced at the radio-compass: the needle was quivering with the power of the signal, coming from the north-east.

Ken asked: 'Will they shoot?'

'The Med wasn't a private American sea, not the last I heard.'

The voice came on again; I turned it down. Ken was peering down over the nose. There was nothing but dark billows of cloud and something that could have been the sea.

'You know,' he said thoughtfully, 'they must have damn good radar to spot us accurately in all this stuff.'

'Big ship, probably. Carrier or a missile cruiser.'

'Could we ask them for a fix?'

I shook my head. 'They're too helpful, those boys. Once you ask them for help, you're stuck with it. They'd broadcast us all over the Med. And we'd still have to identify ourselves.' I was watching the radio-compass, still stiff on almost the same bearing. Something about that troubled me.

Then the voice went off to chase us on another channel and the needle sagged away.

Ken looked at me wryly. 'Well, if you see a guided missile heading our way, you go ahead and identify us.'

'Wilco.'

He picked up the map board. 'We're about twelve miles from Cerigo. Prepare to come right.'

We were down to 1,500 feet now and the air was darkening, and heavy, as though the dimness were thickening it. The cloud walls were narrowing, closing in on us. We were going to run into cloud again before we dropped below it.

Then the end of the cave, where the walls met, glowed a sudden yellow-green with internal lighting. The radio screamed static into my head.

I snapped off the switch, pulled back the throttles, pushed her nose hard down and smashed through the last sill of cloud out into a dingy wet space between sea and sky at 400 feet.

I pushed up the throttles as the speed fell off to 120 knots, and looked carefully all around. There was nothing to see. There was no horizon; sea and sky merged at an indeterminate distance. Above, the base of the thunderclouds hung like a vast, cobwebby ceiling, trailing occasional white wisps. The sea below was hard and without depth, just a surface of sluggish grey metal, heaving slowly to a peak and then ripping off in little bursts of spray.

A squall hung ahead of us, a grimy lace curtain trailing from the cloud ceiling and dragging along the sea. The Piaggio swayed heavily, lurching either side of heading.

Ken looked at his watch again. 'Turn right now. Steer 087.'

I hauled her around. She wandered past the heading, back past it, then settled down somewhere near it, swaying uneasily. At low speed in the uneven gusty air she needed positive control, but I was overcontrolling her, not yet able to tell when it was a gust moving her or when it was me.

We slid into the squall. The Piaggio shook herself, and a thousand little hammers rattled on the cabin roof. Water smeared across the windscreen, then blew away in a starburst of tiny streaks.

Ken nodded at the screen. 'No windscreen wipers. The airflow's supposed to be strong enough to keep it clear. Usually does.'

The squall was heavy, too heavy for the rear sector of the front. What was ahead must be a waterfall. And I was worried about how it had seemed to jump at me suddenly; with no horizon and in drifting scud and rain, my judgement of angle and distance was all gone.

The rain hammers stopped; I looked out. Visibility was getting to be a meaningless word. I could fly us into the sea while I was staring at imaginary islands.

'I'm going on instruments,' I said. 'You've got the look-out.'

'Aye, aye.'

I checked the engine revs and temperatures, then hunched myself down and started concentrating on the blind-flying dials. Six of them: airspeed, artificial horizon, climb-and-descent – jump to the radio-altimeter, off the main blind-flying panel – back to the compass, turn-and-bank. Start again: airspeed. . . . Two circuits with the eyes every second. Then again. Pull up that wing, get back that height, drain off the speed . . . start again. Just a problem in figures, just a big reaction-testing machine. Pull the levers the right way and get the right readings on the dials. Nothing to do with flying. Nothing to do with staying alive or getting killed. Just a nice, cosy little crossword puzzle of reflexes. Two circuits every second. Start again. And you live.

The dials don't tell you if you're flying into a Greek island. The radio would tell me . . . no. Too late for the radio, down here at this height. The only way was to turn the hell round and get the hell out. *Just what was cautious Jack Clay doing in a circus set-up like this? Any other flight of my life. . . .*

The Piaggio was making little jerky movements under my hands. I released the wheel, then clenched on it again. My palms were damp.

Rain rattled on the cabin again. Beside me, Ken made a slow fumbling movement. His lighter clicked and the flame was very bright in the dim cockpit. Smoke drifted across.

He passed me the cigarette; I took it without looking up and drew a deep, deep breath, sweet and cool. I passed the cigarette back.

The flare of panic had passed. But something still troubled me.

The rain stopped. I was getting her steadier, staying around the 400-foot mark and within a degree or two of heading. But degrees didn't matter much now; we were too close. We wouldn't hit or miss something because of just a degree or two. And if we were in the wrong place we needed a big chance of heading.

I asked: 'How far to Pori?'

'I'm keeping a look out.'

I didn't say anything. Then he passed across the cigarette and shuffled the map board. 'About eight miles. Nearly square to starboard.'

'Suppose we were south of track, well south, maybe five miles?'

'Then, about two miles dead ahead. Why the hell should we be?'

I passed the cigarette back. Why should we be? Because I had a feeling, that was all. And one of the first things you learn in flying is to mistrust your feelings, your instincts. But one of the last things you learn, after fifteen years at it, was a new set of instincts. Some part of you learns to add up and balance the factors, probabilities and hints . . . and you have a feeling.

Mine said south of track, well south. *Why?*

I had been too busy with the flying to think it out, too busy keeping clear of cloud, listening to that American ship. . . .

I said: 'We're turning north.'

'What?' He stared at me. 'What the hell for?'

'We're south of track.' I put the wheel positively over to port. The compass hesitated, then began to swing north. Another squall broke over us.

'God blast it, Jack!' He slammed his good hand on to the map board. 'You'll really get us loused up and lost, just because you've got some idea —' Then: *'Break left!'*

I pulled the wheel full circle, stood her on a wing-tip, reached and cracked the throttles wide open. She screamed and hung in the air and pivoted.

I yelled: 'Tell me when I'm clear!'

He was hanging on to the side window, peering up over the sill. 'Yes – now. Now you're clear.'

I loosed the wheel, let the wing drop back, reached for the throttles.

'What was it?'

'There.' He pointed out to starboard. 'Your damn island. Pori.'

A flat, ragged grey shape slid aft through the squall, maybe two hundred yards away.

We were heading west of north now, almost due into the wind. I levelled her off and then started a slow, wide turn back towards east. 'Well, we know where we are now. Give me a heading for Saxos.'

He watched the island out of sight behind us, then turned back to the map. He had a tight, puzzled look. 'We're clear from here on. No more islands before Saxos. About fifty miles.' His voice sounded taut. He glanced at me. 'Your winds must be wrong.'

I said: 'Very probably; they were guesses. Call it 45 knots from 290 degrees and give me a new heading.'

He nodded and killed the cigarette in the ashtray. 'Why did you turn then, before I shouted?'

I said: 'That American ship. The bearing on the radio-compass was just about steady the whole time he was speaking, so they weren't all that close. And they were north-east of us. Between us and Cerigo, when we were supposed to be only twelve or so miles from Cerigo. A big ship, carrier or something. Carriers just don't do that, not that close, not in a storm. He must have been coming through the same channel we were trying for – and we were south of him.'

He looked at me, then nodded slowly and went back to the map. He drew a circle around Pori and wrote the time in alongside it.

I went back to watching the dials. The air was getting rougher as we got deeper into the front.

PART FIVE

32

THE BREAK came fifteen minutes and something over thirty miles later, suddenly, the way it does with the forward side of an occluded front. The steady rattle of rain faded and I looked up and found the screen blown almost clear. There was still no sun, but the clouds had lifted to a long upward slope of alto-stratus and cirro-stratus. Ahead, there were still wisps of scud and occasional fat heaps of cumulus. We were through.

I pushed the throttles forward and the plane lifted and ran away up the sky. I sat back and stared ahead at nothing. My eyes were dizzy with instrument flying and my arms stiff with fighting her through the last thirty miles.

Ken said: 'There, I think.'

I leant the plane the way he was looking. Off to starboard, shadowed under a cumulus, was the grey lump of Saxos and its smaller lump of Kira.

Ken picked up the maps and navigation gear and threw them into a passenger seat behind us. Then he leant forward to study the island. 'Which way does the road run?'

'East to west.'

He jerked his head around at me. 'Christ! Why didn't you say?'

We weren't going to get an easterly wind. We weren't even going to get a south-easter, not that close to the front. We were going to get a wind that was more south than anything, blowing 45 knots almost square across the road.

I shrugged. 'Now, just what good would it have done if I had? You have a friend who has a friend who knows the man fixes the winds?'

He shook his head sadly. 'You just should have told me. I was feeling rich; now I have to start feeling dead.'

'Jack Clay has control. No smoking, no panic. We'll live.'

The cumulus was easing away northwards as I came round at the island. I pulled back the throttles again and went into a long, shallow dive. The island began to grow colours, shapes of houses, the rim of foam around the shoreline, the touches of green on the ground above the harbour. I couldn't yet see the Dakota.

Then, as I came in across the harbour, I could: it was parked half-way along the road and standing crossways on it. For some damn silly reason, Rogers had parked it pointing north, facing out of the wind. Then I saw he hadn't parked it: he'd crashed it.

Not too badly. It was lying flat on its belly, with the undercarriage wiped off or bent back and the props gone. The wind must have swung him as he came down; the road was torn and scored a hundred yards behind it.

I went in low overhead. There didn't seem to be anybody about.

Ken said: 'He bent it.'

I pulled up and away. 'Yes.' I had a small, sick feeling back in my stomach.

Ken said: 'Well we might get down in the same state. I wouldn't guarantee anything. This job wouldn't have the stability on her belly that a Dak has.'

'We don't have to try.'

He jerked another look at me. I banked south, towards Kira, and nodded downwards. 'Down there. Morrison managed it – and he was in a Dak.'

Ken stared down as I came around in a right-hand turn. Kira's beach and short valley back between its two small hills showed up clearly; it looked very short indeed. But it pointed south of south-east, into the wind.

Ken said: 'Is that where the Dak came in?'

'That's the place. It's there, in the trees.' But I couldn't see it.

'Did he get killed – Morrison?'

I reversed the turn to look down on my side. On either side of the valley the slopes were almost cliffs, rough and jagged, the raw rock showing through the soil and touches of May green. The valley itself was just a sharply tapering vee, first fifty yards of sand, then another hundred and fifty of rough grass before the grove of cypresses and the sweep upwards.

There were a couple of small boats, pulled well up to and to one side: nothing the Nawab and party would have used to get across in.

Ken asked again: 'Did Morrison kill himself?'

'I don't think so.'

We circled again. To the west the front was a jungle of grey cloud only ten miles back, creeping towards us. The tops of the thunderheads were hidden by the slope of thin stratus, but they were still there. And in half an hour we'd have them back on top of us.

I turned in for a dummy run, high but slow, to feel the drift. At a guess, the wind was about fifteen degrees off the line I'd have to take into the valley. Not bad – but the island itself would be causing all sorts of cross currents.

Ken had been studying the island. 'There'll be one helluva down-draught into that valley. You might manage to —' he looked at me doubtfully, then back down at the island. 'Maybe there's a bit of a road on another island. We could sit out the storm there, then get in afterwards.'

'There isn't,' I said. 'I've seen them all.'

He looked at me again. 'Would you like me to try it? I could handle everything but the throttles. You work them when I —'

I said: 'You want to walk, then get out and walk. If you're staying, give me the landing check.'

He recited it for me.

I committed us at 400 yards, dropping full flap and holding up her nose as the speed dribbled away off the dial. The valley still looked very small and very, very final. I was going to come in as slow and steep as I could get. That way, I could pick my spot more accurately and she wouldn't roll so far when she hit. But that way she would be balanced on the thin edge of the stall all the way down, ready to topple at one good gust that I couldn't hold.

Ken said: 'D'you think they'll let us off angels' basic flying, training, seeing we've already got licences?'

'You can't take it with you.'

'How true.' His voice sounded brittle and absent; he was staring ahead and down.

Then I was alone, just me, just the plane and an unmarked spot on the beach, as close to the water as I could get.

I let her sag downwards in a nose-high stance, bringing up the throttles as she slowed further, trying to balance power against her reared-back attitude. As she got slower she got heavier and my arms were old and tired after the storm. I held her up. The first cross-gusts from the island reached her and she swayed soggily; I had to swing the wheel full circle and stamp on the rudders to keep her in line.

A wave stumbled and exploded soundlessly on the beach ahead; spray jumped and hung in the air . . . by the time the next wave broke, I would be down, somewhere, somehow . . . *I was high, too high for the beach, too low to miss the trees . . .*

Then the down-draught had me, rushing me down towards the beach. The trees and slope reared up to overtop me.

I pushed on the last inch of power to flatten the descent, hauled back her nose for the last time, snatched back the throttles again, clamped both hands on the wheel and slammed her down on the hard wet sand.

33

THE PROPELLERS ground, jerked and stopped. The systems faded with little tinkling, running-down noises; the needles drifted down off the dials. Gently, the whole plane died around us.

We sat there awhile. The sound of the engines faded in my head and I began to hear the wind scouring along the cabin sides, and to see the cypresses, twenty yards ahead of us, swaying gracefully.

Ken took out his cigarettes, passed me one and lit it. We breathed smoke into the still air of the cabin.

He said quietly: 'I'd forgotten about you. You do forget about people.'

I nodded and the cigarette waggled limply in my mouth. I unsnapped the seat straps and stretched slowly and slid open the side window. Sweet damp air pulsed in; suddenly the cockpit smelt of oil and stale warmth.

I stood up and walked back between the seats; my legs managed to feel both stiff and shaky at the same time. I opened the cabin door and stepped down and the wind rushed at me. I leant against the plane and looked back.

We had left almost no trace through the grass, but leading across the beach beyond were three little ruts, blurred on the dry sand near the grass, sharp and clear on the damp sand near the sea. The first flurry of our impact was gone already, washed away by a new wave. I must have got her down pretty close to the sea's edge. I had got it right.

I felt cold; the wind was cutting through my shirt and drying the sweat too quickly. I climbed back into the cabin and found Ken's suède jacket, with the little bullet holes high on the left arm, and put it on.

He came back and we both got out. People were coming down the hillside from the village, slowly, curiously.

Ken said: 'It's in there, the Dak?' He was looking at the cypresses.

'Yes.' Knowing how it lay, I thought I could just pick it out. He couldn't see it yet. 'Go and have a look,' I said. 'I'll get the plane turned around.' We would have the front and a north-west wind on us soon. She'd do better facing into it. And for take-off, of course. I looked at the short stretch of grass and beach again and my knees gave a new shiver.

Ken was off in the trees by the time the first people reached us. I asked for Nikolas and then saw him coming down the slope. I waited and answered questions with shrugs or nods until he came up.

He recognized me; we shook hands. 'You are all right?'

'Yes, fine.'

He pointed to the Piaggio. 'Wrong? Trouble?'

'Of a sort. But I want to turn her round. Can you help?'

'Of course.'

I climbed back in and worked the brakes while he and a couple of others shoved on the nose. We got her turned and run back as far as she'd go, within ten yards of the trees. I put on the parking brake, dumped chocks in front of all the wheels, locked the controls and shut the door behind me.

Nikolas was looking towards the grove. He gestured. 'Your friend —'

'I'll find him.' I started off, then turned back. 'Has anybody landed here this morning?'

He shook his head. 'Nobody comes. The sea, the waves . . .'

'Nobody would go out in these waves?'

He looked a little offended. 'They are sailors. But no use going —'

He shook his head and the wind jerked his fair hair across the scars on his forehead. I nodded and walked up to the grove.

Again, it was just like walking through a door. The air grew still and quiet about me, with just a distant, detached, rustling in the treetops. The trees and the cool ground and the lichen-coloured aircraft had the same ancient calm; even the patch where I had rubbed the Pakistani emblem clear on the fin looked old now. I found myself walking softly and carefully.

I couldn't see Ken. I walked around to the nose of the Dakota and then saw him through the windscreen. He nodded to me and came back and out of the fuselage doorway.

'What d'you think of it?' I asked quietly.

He shook his head slowly. 'It's the damndest thing I ever saw. It's like a piece of a temple. I wouldn't —' he shook his head again helplessly. 'I just don't get it. I feel like I'm walking on the souls of dead pilots.'

I nodded.

He asked, almost whispering: 'Are the jewels around here?'

'I don't know.'

I walked back and he followed. Nikolas was waiting outside the trees. There were a few children standing on tip-toe to peer into the Piaggio's cabin, but everybody else seemed to have gone home out of the wind. The clouds overhead were sliding across fast. A few spots of rain came down over the hill from the village.

I said: 'Nikolas, meet Mr Kitson. Ken, Nikolas Dimitri.'

Nikolas said a little stiffly: 'I am happy to meet you.' They shook hands.

I said: 'Nikolas was a German soldier stationed here during the war. He liked the life, came back and settled afterwards. That's right, isn't it?'

'That is so.' He nodded gravely.

Ken glanced at me, frowning. Out in the wind, he was getting restless with diplomatic formalities. 'Well, where now?' he asked.

I said: 'Perhaps Nikolas can help us.' Ken lifted his eyebrows. Nikolas looked at me curiously.

I ploughed on. 'It all starts with the Dakota in there. It all goes back to that. Ken, what did you say about what it felt like, in there?'

He looked up at me, gently rubbing his bandaged arm with his right hand. 'Like a temple, a bit.' He glanced over his shoulder at the trees, as if to remind himself it was still there, a few feet away.

'That's right,' I said. 'That's what it's supposed to be like, in a way.'

They both looked at me.

I said: 'That Dakota's been there just over ten years; we know that. Those trees are at least twenty-five years old.'

Ken looked back again. 'It can't have crashed into them. There'd be —' He turned back to me.

'Yes. So somebody got half-grown trees and planted them there afterwards.'

'Why? Why should they?'

'Well, now I start guessing. I don't claim to know a lot about Greek islanders, but I know they aren't savages who'll make a fetish out of a piece of machinery. And if they just wanted to hide it, then it would have been a sight easier just to chuck it into the sea. There's only one sort of person I can think of might turn a cracked-up old Dakota into a shrine. A pilot.'

'Morrison,' Ken said. 'The character who flew it in here.' Then he shook his head. 'Ah, it's crazy.'

'Don't tell *me* it's crazy. We already *know* it's crazy. We know the first jewels took ten years to reach Athens from here. We know somebody got trees and planted them around that Dak. The reason *has* to be crazy.'

'Yes. Yes, maybe so. So you think Morrison stayed on here?'

'That's what I think.'

Ken turned to Nikolas. 'Is there another man, an Englishman, here – on the island?'

Nikolas spread his hands. 'There is no man. The man – the pilot – of the aeroplane, he went away.'

'*When?*' Ken demanded.

I said: 'Morrison would be a man about our age. Anglo-Saxon, so he probably couldn't pass for a Greek. And he might have scars on his forehead from where the Dak cracked into that rock.'

Ken was staring at Nikolas. Slowly a hungry grin spread across his thin face. He said softly: 'Hello, Morrison.'

Nikolas said: 'I am German. I came here in —'

I said sharply: 'Skip it. Ten years ago, becoming a German would have been a good idea; nobody would think of an Englishman doing that. Now we're all good pals again.'

Nikolas looked slowly from one to the other of us. The

wind gusted stronger and colder and with another spatter of rain in it.

Ken said: 'There's a real German waiting across on Saxos. He'll have you sorted out in ten seconds flat and he won't be polite about it, like we are.'

'It takes time,' I said more gently. 'After ten years, it takes time. But not too much time; we haven't got too much.'

Nikolas said: 'All right. What do you want?' His voice sounded tired, but more natural.

'The jewels,' Ken said.

He shook his head. 'I sold them – to a man in Athens.'

'No,' I said. 'I won't bother to explain why I know you didn't – not all of them – but just take it that I know. We'll do a deal with you for the rest.'

He shook his head again. 'I promise you —'

I got angry. '*Don't* promise me! The man you stole them off – the Nawab – he's over on Saxos waiting for the weather to clear. He'll be down on our necks in a few hours. You can deal with us or you can talk to him – but you *can't* deal with him. They're his jewels – remember? Hand over the rest to us and he needn't even know you're still alive.'

He stared at me. The wind stabbed at us again. The horizon across the end of the valley was a pile of dark cloud.

Nikolas said slowly: 'You'll buy them off me?'

'You'll get a share of what we get for them.'

'What sort of guarantee have I got?'

'You haven't got any guarantee,' I said, 'but you've got a hell of a lousy alternative.'

He stared at his feet for a moment. Then: 'I will meet you in the café.'

34

THE CAFÉ had a little oil stove burning and we were sitting hunched over it, steaming, and sipping cognac. The front had caught us before we reached the bar; outside, rain was clattering against the windows and beginning to trickle in under the door and down the steps.

The proprietor was standing over us with the bottle in his hand. He seemed to assume we must have been in trouble to try the landing, and it brought out in him all the islander's hospitality for the shipwrecked mariner. To him, that meant cognac. I agreed with him up to a point, but I reckoned the point had come and gone. I was on to my fourth glass now.

I finally got across to him that what we could use, if he was feeling generous, was some food. It struck him as a brilliant, if unconventional, idea, and he stumped off into the back room to do something about it.

Ken leant back against the wall and closed his eyes. It was dark and peaceful in the bar and the sound of the rain outside made it even cosier. I looked at my watch: 10.15. The front would be overhead for another two or two-and-a-half hours. The Nawab wouldn't be here until after twelve.

After a while the proprietor rolled back with plates, cheese, honey-cakes and a loaf of bread. I thanked him and offered to pay for it; he wouldn't hear of it. I thanked him again.

Ken pulled himself off the wall and started to eat. The room filled up with a damp, oily heat. We unzipped our jackets as far as we dared without showing the guns shoved in our waistbands.

I lit a cigarette and sat back. 'How's the arm?'

'Stiff. But I think it's okay.' He leant carefully back against the wall, closed his eyes and went limp. He had the pilot's knack of doing nothing when there's nothing to be done.

At eleven, Nikolas – or Morrison – came in. He was soaked through, smudged with wet oil and looked exhausted. The proprietor looked at him wonderingly. Nikolas threw him a few words and slumped down on the bench beside us. The proprietor came across with a glass of cognac.

Ken asked: 'Well?'

Nikolas stared at the stove, his face blank with exhaustion. 'They are at my house.'

'We'll go down when you're ready,' I said.

He put the cognac back in a lump and went on staring at the stove. Then he said quietly: 'I thought everybody would have forgotten about them by now. It seemed a long time. I thought nobody would care any more. That's why I started to sell them.'

Ken said: 'People don't forget a million-and-a-half that quick.'

Nikolas looked up at me. 'How did you know about me?'

I said: 'For the reasons I've given you. And because when I first came in here, a week ago, and asked you if the pilot of that Dak had been killed, you had to ask the proprietor here. That's the first question anybody would have asked as soon as they knew about the crashed plane; everybody on the island would know the answer straight off.'

He nodded and went back to staring at the stove. Then he said, quietly but very bitterly: 'Why did you come – after this time?'

I said: 'Somebody was coming, some time. You should have known that.'

He ignored my answer. 'You don't know why I planted those trees, do you? You don't understand, do you?'

I shrugged.

He said: 'Those trees are Morrison's grave.' I saw Ken stiffen. Morrison was watching me, smiling, waiting for me to say something. I didn't. He said: 'I am Nikolas Dimitri, now. Morrison is dead. But you wouldn't understand.'

Perhaps I did, perhaps I could guess, but now he was going to tell me anyway. After ten years, he had to tell somebody. I know.

He looked away, at the stove, and said quietly: 'You've never been rich; you don't know what it's like. I was rich. I was rich when I took off with those jewels. I looked down to the back of the plane and I knew I was *safe*, nothing could touch me. Everything was going to be all right, always.

'I landed in Arabia, at Sharja, and refuelled; then I was going on to Beirut. I'd heard that was a good place to sell them. I was going to sell them, and take off – and nobody would ever have heard of me again.

'Then when I got near it, I thought – if I try to sell them in a hurry, they'll cheat me. They'll give me just a little for them. And I wanted everything, all of it. So I decided to go a bit farther, to Rhodes. I thought I could make it.'

The voice was all Morrison now, not Nikolas. He still had a trace of the phoney German accent – he'd practised that too long to forget it in a few minutes – but the vocabulary was coming back.

Ken lifted himself slowly up off the wall, watching Morrison, not saying anything.

Morrison said: 'I must have missed it somehow. It was night by then, and I didn't know the winds, and I couldn't get any weather on the radio. I was lost. But I was still safe; I *had* to be safe. I knew it was all right. So I turned north. I knew there'd be land there sooner or later.

'Then I began to run out of fuel. I must have been very much west and south. The starboard tanks ran dry and the engine stopped and there wasn't anything worth pumping across from the port. . . . Then the port engine started to miss. And then – I knew I was going to be killed. I was lost, nobody knew where I was, nobody would come looking for me. I was going to be killed.'

I said: 'I know just how you felt.'

'No, you don't!' He brushed me aside. Then, calm again: 'Then I saw this island. And the beach – and I knew I wasn't going to die. But' – he swept us with a triumphant look – 'but Morrison died. You see that? He crashed into the sea and was killed because he thought he was rich and safe. And *that* was what the trees are for. His grave. Like candles. And the Dakota still there – I wouldn't let them touch it, except a few pieces they could use. I wanted to make it beautiful, I wanted to *give* it to the island. *Because* of the island and the people – because of what they are. They didn't know about the jewels – they never knew. I buried them under the plane and they don't know yet. *That's* what sort of people we are here. *That's* why Morrison is dead and I'm Nikolas Dimitri – do you understand *that*?' His voice ended almost in a shout.

Nobody said anything. The proprietor was standing by the counter, smiling awkwardly and not understanding a word.

I looked at Ken: he was watching Morrison intently, his hand resting in the gap of his jacket zip.

Morrison shook his head and went back to staring at the stove. He said quietly: 'You don't understand.'

I understood, all right. We were Morrison, now, we were the pilots, the sort of people he used to be, we were after the jewels. Now, we were the guilty ones.

He said: 'You can't take them away. They belong here now. Morrison stole them and Morrison is dead. We need them here.'

Ken moved his hand under his jacket.

I said quickly: 'Too late now. You started digging them up again – that made it too late. All you can do now is let us handle them.'

He turned his head and stared at me. For a long time he

stared at me and there was something behind his eyes that might have been hatred, or contempt or just plain weariness. And he probably didn't know himself. Then he shrugged and said again 'You don't understand.'

'No,' I said, 'I don't understand.' I could let him keep that much.

He stood up and said quite calmly: 'The rain is nearly over. We'll go down to my house.'

I stood up after him. He started for the door. Ken stood up slowly, still watching Morrison. He said quietly, to me: 'Well, you said the reason had to be a crazy one.'

I nodded. 'Part of it.' I was thinking that if a man carrying a million-and-a-half's-worth of jewellery was about to crash into the sea, it might occur to him that he himself stood a chance of surviving – but he was certainly going to lose the jewellery. An unworthy thought. I tend to get unworthy thoughts.

I said: 'Would you say he would have been more crazy or less if he'd simply chucked the lot into the sea, where he couldn't ever get it again, rather than burying it?'

Ken nodded, gave me a quick bleak smile, then followed Morrison out of the door.

35

WE GOT no more than spattered reaching the house, just thirty yards down the main alleyway, up a side alley and through a courtyard. We were in the hind sector of the front by now and the rain was easing.

Morrison pushed open a door of heavy old planks and we followed him in.

It was a small, almost square room, with thick plastered white walls, and a stone floor with a few faded rugs scattered across it. The furniture jarred with the solidity of the walls: it was cheap city stuff, a table, chairs and a glass-fronted cabinet, finished in a bright shallow stain. The top of the cabinet was covered in stand-up chromium photo frames. A pressure lamp roared softly at the ceiling, giving me a sudden twist in the stomach as I remembered the same sound and smell from the police post at Mehari.

In the middle of the floor, with the rugs pushed back from around them, stood two earth-stained wooden ammunition boxes. Morrison closed the door gently behind us.

'There they are,' he said. We stood and stared down at them.

Then I asked: 'How did you meet Mikklos?'

He shrugged. 'I went to Athens, looking for somebody who could sell them for me. I said I wanted somebody who could sell anything, anywhere. A captain on one of the island boats had heard of him.'

'A lot too many people had heard of him,' I said. 'What terms did he give you?'

He just shrugged again. 'I am going to change.' He went through an inner door. We went back to looking at the boxes.

After a while Ken stuck out a foot and tried to rock one of them. It didn't budge. Then he said: 'Well, this is what we came for. Let's get rich.'

He stooped and pulled at the lid of one; it came away easily. For a long time we both seemed to stop breathing.

The box was nearly full – and it was straight off the Nawab's list, all right. Most of it was mutton-fat jade, a milky grey colour, carved into delicate fern-leaf turban ornaments or curved dagger handles and sheaths or little cosmetic jars decorated with reliefs of temples, landscapes or just grill patterns. By itself the carved jade was terrific. But it wasn't by itself; an Indian Prince might not have appreciated fine carving, but he knew gems when he saw them. Every piece was daubed with patterns of diamonds, rubies and emeralds, some with gold wire insets as well, making shapes of flowers and stars and Islamic moons in contrast to the shape of the carving.

There were a few gold pots, not so well worked, looking as if they had been put together from strips of metallic plasticine. Every joint had a ruby sunk in it.

The whole lot was damp and dribbled over with mud. It still looked a good million's-worth.

Neither of us said anything. Neither of us touched any of it. Alone, each of us might have scooped it up to handle, to fondle, to feel the richness of it soaking into our hands. But that was too naked, too much an act of love.

We didn't even open the second box.

Ken took out his cigarettes and passed me one, then turned away to the window. 'Clearing,' he said.

I looked at my watch. 'Should be right through in half an hour.'

'Yes.' He walked back and put the lid on the open box. 'They'll have seen us land from Saxos. They'll be across as soon as it's a bit clearer. Let's get this stuff out of here.'

Morrison came back in, wearing a clean shirt and trousers and with his face washed and his hair combed. He looked at the boxes, then at us.

'You've looked at them?' he asked.

I nodded.

'What will you do now?'

'Get them out. When the Nawab rolls up here, he needn't even know you ever saw them. Just go on being Nikolas.'

'When will you —'

Ken said : 'Let's get them down to the beach.'

Morrison just looked at him.

The boxes had had rope handles at each end. These had rotted away, but, recently, Morrison had replaced them with wire loops. He had carried them himself from where he'd had them buried in the grove, so three of us could carry the two of them easily enough.

I took a handle of each, Ken used his good hand picking up the other handle of one of them, Morrison took the other and opened the door with his free hand.

Herter walked in through it, wearing a damp trench coat and carrying a Luger in his hand.

Holding the boxes like that, Ken and I could have had tommy-guns in every pocket and we'd still have been as pacifist as a statue of Gandhi.

Herter must have counted on that, must have been waiting outside for it, listening. He came into the room sideways, watching us carefully, with a small tight smile on his face. He looked pale and wet – the sea crossing couldn't have been much fun – but he was steady on his feet and he was holding the Luger as if he knew about Lugers.

I know about Lugers. I stood very still, wishing quietly that I'd remembered the Nawab's habit of sending the Master Race on ahead to do the dirty work.

Herter said 'Hello, Mr Kitson. We have missed you.'

Ken didn't say anything. There was a little glitter behind

Herter's glasses that I hadn't seen there before. Now he was out on his own, on his Master's business, doing the bits his Master probably didn't want to watch.

He looked like a man who wanted to kill somebody.

He said: 'Put the boxes down, slowly.'

We put them down slowly.

He said: 'Put the hands up, please.'

We put them up.

Then the inner door opened and a woman came in. Herter whipped round, his hand going white on the Luger. I swayed forward, opening my mouth – but the gun jerked up, pointing clear of her.

She was built small, with tan skin and hollow cheeks and very black hair pulled tight into a bun. In her middle thirties, dressed in a black skirt and white blouse and with a heavy black shawl around her shoulders.

Somehow the idea of Morrison marrying hadn't occurred to me. But in ten years' of trying to belong on the island, that was one thing he was sure to have done.

She was staring at the Luger with wide, dark, worried eyes. Morrison said something in Greek; the gun swung back to cover him.

'She will stand by you,' Herter ordered.

Morrison translated. She moved almost timidly across the floor to his side, glancing quickly between him and Herter.

Herter turned to Ken and me. 'The Walther and the Beretta, please,' and he grinned at knowing exactly what guns we had. 'Mr Kitson first.'

Ken unzipped his jacket and took out the Walther carefully, holding it between his finger and thumb, and put it on the table.

I put the Beretta down after it. Then we backed off while Herter collected them left-handed and stowed them away in his coat pocket.

'Now,' he said, 'we will carry the boxes to the beach.'

There was nothing else to do. We picked up the boxes as before and Herter followed us, all four of us, through the door and the courtyard and into the main alley.

The rain was about over now, bar a few spots and a feeling of dampness in the air, and the wind was less gusty, steadying from the west. The white walls were grey and streaky and fat little streams zigzagged between the cracks in the paving. We seemed to have the village to ourselves; if anybody saw us go, they didn't do anything about it.

We came out of the village and started on the stepped path down to the beach, the Piaggio sitting down below, looking clean and crisp among the rocks and grass, like a fashion model against a gimmick background. The path was hard, slow and awkward with the boxes.

There was no boat on the beach. The waves were still high, maybe not quite as bad as they'd been when we landed.

We bumped our way across to the Piaggio.

Herter said: 'Put them down, now.'

We put them down and I straightened up slowly and looked carefully around at Herter. I still had Yussuf's little automatic in my shirt pocket – but it was in no position for a quick draw. I needed time to get it out and time to use it; there were only three shots left in it and it was an unfamiliar gun. Unless I used it carefully, a ·22 might not do Herter much harm – but a 9 mm. slug from the Luger, wherever it hit me, would change me.

'Open the door,' he ordered Morrison. Morrison opened it.

'Kitson and Clay – put the boxes inside.'

We picked them up, one at a time, and swung them into the Piaggio's cabin. I might do it now, get the little gun out, while I had my back to him. As we lifted the second box I glanced at him.

He had Morrison's wife standing just in front of him.

I shut the cabin door and turned back, the gun still in my shirt pocket.

Herter nodded and started digging inside his coat. He brought out a Verey pistol – the one from *my* Dakota – stepped back and fired into the air. A red flare zipped up, well higher than the rises on either side of the valley, and arched down beside the grove. Mission complete, no danger now, all right for His Excellency to come across and count the takings.

'Now,' Herter said, 'we will wait.'

I asked: 'How badly was the Dakota damaged? Was Rogers hurt?'

Herter smiled sourly. 'Undoubtedly you would have managed better, Captain, but nobody was hurt.'

I said: 'I asked about Rogers. I wasn't worried about anybody else.'

That nearly got me killed. The smile fell off his face and he bent slightly forward, balancing the Luger, ready for its recoil. It seemed a very long, quiet moment.

But he had no orders to kill me and he needed a better reason than a dirty crack. He straightened up slowly, but went on watching me carefully.

Ken asked: 'D'you mind if we smoke?'

Herter said: 'You do not smoke,' without glancing at him, and went on watching me – as if he were trying to remember something about me.

Then he remembered it. A wide thin grin stretched across his face and he held out his left hand. 'The money, Captain, please.'

'What money?'

The grin got wider. 'The dollars and francs. For the first jewels. Please.'

I looked at him, then lifted my hand to my shirt pocket. I went for the pocket with the money in it. The Luger was lined up on my stomach; I wanted better odds than that.

I threw the rolls of bills down on the grass in front of him. He slammed a foot on them, bent slowly and picked them up.

He took a step back. 'Now,' he said, 'we wait.'

36

WE WAITED more than twenty minutes. Occasionally Morrison said something to his wife in Greek; the rest of the time we were quiet. The wind was still blowing cold and I wanted to zip up my jacket, but that would have put the little automatic right out of reach. We just waited.

Then a small fishing caique came bouncing around the point into the bay and waddled up to the beach. The fisherman managed the landing well, timing his beaching between waves, but everybody in it still got pretty wet.

Herter let them find their own way; the Nawab wearing a gabardine golfing jacket that for once looked fairly costly, Miss Brown in a white belted mackintosh. They came slowly up through the long grass towards us, both looking damp and pale and a bit shaky. The jewels must have had more drawing power than I'd guessed at.

Herter made a gesture of a bow without moving his gun hand. 'The jewels are in the cabin, Your Excellency. Perhaps you would wish to check them against the list.'

The Nawab was looking at Ken; a slow, careful, satisfied look. 'I see,' he said thinly, 'that it was stupid of me to think of one with your very special talents getting himself drowned, Mr Kitson.'

Ken went on looking elsewhere. Herter stiffened and brought the Luger up. The Nawab frowned and shook his head. 'We will talk about Mr Kitson's disloyalty later.' He turned to me. Herter and the Luger turned with him.

'And Captain Clay.' He gave me a brief smile. 'As I recall, you drive a hard bargain, Captain. What are you asking for this part of the jewels?'

'The usual terms,' I said. 'Five per cent – in cash.'

He smiled again. He wasn't getting full value out of having us under the gun – his stomach was too much of a distraction – but it was a happy reminder of the good old days when Nawabs were really Nawabs.

Miss Brown said abruptly: 'Do we have to stand out in the wind any longer, Aly?'

He glanced at her hastily. She was standing with her hands deep in the pockets of her white mac, her head hunched down, looking cold and bored.

He said: 'Would you like to look over the jewels?'

She shrugged. Herter reached inside his coat and passed her the list. She took it, threw back her long black hair into place with an impatient jerk of her head and sailed straight past me into the Piaggio.

The Nawab watched her, then looked carefully around the little valley and beach. The boatman was hauling his old tub up clear of the surf; it probably wasn't doing the propeller much good, but he would want to stay with the cash customers. The waves behind him were still coming down with a full-blooded wallop.

The Nawab frowned at them and turned to Morrison. 'How long will it take for the waves to die down?'

Morrison shrugged. 'Completely, at least twenty-four hours. But they'll ease quite a bit in the next three or four.'

I held my breath. He had spoken in his best English.

But the pseudo-German accent was still there, and the Nawab didn't notice anything. He nodded and turned back to Herter. 'Can you keep them here for another couple of hours or so?'

Herter gave a stiff little nod. 'Of course, Your Excellency.' He hesitated, then asked: 'What does Your Excellency wish me to do with them?'

Thanks, chum. It just needed that.

The Nawab swung slowly around to glare at us. 'I would like to see them shot down like pigs!' he spat. 'I want them to see how I deal with treachery like theirs. I want them to realize how much trouble they have put me to!'

His stomach must have been recovering fast. He felt safe to work himself up into a rage without coughing up his dignity all over his feet.

I wanted to laugh out loud. I didn't. He meant just what he was saying – we had nearly fooled His Excellency the Nawab of Tungabhadra, and that was the worst thing we could have done. The jewels themselves came a bad second.

'Unfortunately, we are on foreign soil here. So perhaps we shall have to be kinder than I would like.'

The Piaggio's door swung open and Miss Brown stepped down. She looked a lot fresher and brighter. 'They're all there, Aly.'

That spoiled his rage. He just nodded, glared at me and said: 'I wish we were in Pakistan, Captain.' He turned to Herter. 'You have my permission to do whatever is needful if they try to misbehave, Herr Herter.'

Herter gave another jerky little nod and smiled bleakly.

The Nawab looked at Miss Brown: 'Shall we go up to the café in the village?'

She nodded and started immediately. The Nawab started to follow, then turned back and looked at Morrison. Then he said to Herter: 'How did this man Dimitri come to be involved?'

'The jewels were at his house, Your Excellency?'

'How did they get there?'

'I do not know, Your Excellency. Shall I find out?'

The Nawab shrugged. 'If you want to.' Then he pattered away across the grass after Miss Brown.

Herter took a few steps back to get the regulation distance between him and us and waved the Luger to bring us back into a group.

I said quickly, hoping to distract him from the Nawab's last idea: 'Can we smoke now?'

Herter shook his head. 'You will not smoke, Captain.'

I said. 'Oh, for heaven's sake —'

'Be quiet!'

I shrugged. 'You might let the woman go back. She can't do any harm.'

'We will wait.'

His eyes had that hungry little glitter in them again, and the Luger was lined up on my stomach. He had been given full permission to shoot us down if it seemed necessary, and that was a message you didn't have to tell him twice.

Ken said: 'I'm sorry about all this, Jack.'

'Skip it. You couldn't help it.'

'Well, I don't —'

'I said to skip it.'

Herter said: 'Be quiet!'

Ken went back to stroking his bandaged arm. We waited. At least I seemed to have got Herter's mind off Morrison. I was wrong.

The sun suddenly flared out from the passing front, warming us the moment it hit us. The rocks and sand began to take on bright colours again.

Herter adjusted his position to keep the sun over his shoulder, keeping us in a little group, me on the extreme left, Morrison on the right and himself a good fifteen feet from any of us.

Then Herter said to Morrison: 'Why were the jewels at your house?'

Morrison looked up at him slowly and shrugged.

'Why?' Herter barked.

Morrison didn't say anything.

Herter levelled the gun and took a couple of paces forward. Morrison's wife stared at him fearfully.

Herter said: 'You are Nikolas Dimitri?'

Morrison nodded slowly. He seemed tired, disinterested in the whole business.

Herter frowned, thinking back to something. I hoped he wouldn't remember it. He did. He said: 'You were born German, *nicht war*?'

Morrison just looked at him.

Herter snapped: *'Und bei welchem regiment hast Du gedient?'*

I said quickly: 'For God's sake, he isn't German, he's French, and he hardly speaks a word of English anyway.'

But I had talked Morrison out of pretending, just a few hours before. He shook his head wearily and said: 'I'm English. My name's Morrison – I brought the jewels here in the first place.'

Herter took three quick steps and stopped, bent forward, the Luger levelled. He said, almost unbelieving: '*You* stole them from His Excellency?'

Morrison just nodded.

Herter shot him three times in the stomach.

I jumped him.

The Luger whipped around at me and I clouted it with my left hand, knocking it across and past me, and it fired somewhere under my right armpit. Then I had my right hand on his gun wrist and dropped my whole weight on his arm.

We crashed down with me still lying across his arm. The Luger bounced out of his hand. I swept it farther away, jerked myself clear and rolled after it.

The woman started screaming, a single continuous sound.

I rolled and came up sitting with my right hand around the Luger, but not in the right places.

Ken was going for Herter, but coming in between us. I had the gun now. I howled: 'Keep clear.' Ken checked, glanced at me.

Then I saw Herter wasn't even trying to get up. He was on his knees and was tugging Ken's Walther from his coat pocket. I had forgotten about that.

My hand was slow and ponderous as a steel grab fitting itself around the Luger. Herter ripped the Walther free of his pocket and fired as it was coming up. Sand blasted in my face.

My fingers clamped into place around the Luger. I fired. And again. The slugs thumped him back on his heels; the Walther jerked and fired over my head.

I stretched out my arm and fired a third, careful shot.

Herter toppled slowly over backwards and spread himself in the wet grass.

I stood up slowly, with the sound of the Luger still in my ears and the jolt of it tingling in my arm. The woman had stopped screaming. I walked over to Herter and took the Walther out of his hand and then the Beretta out of his pocket. And that was that.

Morrison was down on his back with his wife cradling his head in the crook of her arm. The belly of his shirt was torn and soaked dark with blood – much too much blood.

I said to Ken: 'Get the first-aid box.' I put guns out of sight in various pockets and knelt down beside Morrison.

He was still alive, but only just. He had three 9 mm. slugs through his stomach and one of them had opened the main artery. After that, your life is counted in seconds.

Ken brought the box and opened it beside me. There was only one thing in it that was any use and that was the morphine.

Morrison opened his eyes as I lifted the ampoule, recognized it and croaked: 'No morphine. Let me – let me —' The woman looked at me and said something sharp and I put the ampoule back in the box.

She wiped his forehead with her shawl, gently, and whispered to him. He said something to her, then turned his head slowly to me again.

'You're Jack Clay – aren't you?' he whispered.

I nodded. 'Yes.'

'And he – he's Kitson?'

'Yes.'

He smiled very faintly. 'I remember about you two.' He closed his eyes again and the sweat broke out on his forehead. She wiped it clear. 'You two – they used to – talk about you two. Two best – transport men – in the business. Always – worked together.' He looked back at his wife, but spoke in English. 'Funny, those two – here.' The sweat started again and he closed his eyes.

I stood up, slowly. After a while he opened his eyes and spoke gently to her in Greek. She whispered back. He said something and smiled again and died.

I stepped softly back under the wing beside Ken. The woman laid Morrison's head back gently, making him comfortable, then spread the black shawl over his face.

Then she stood up and stared at us, a look of blazing dry-eyed hatred.

There was nothing I could say. In any language she would have hated me for anything I said. I had brought his death to the island and that was all that mattered to her. And she was right.

She turned away and walked, slowly but erect, to the stepped path and up towards the village.

Ken said softly: 'Get on board, boy. Now, quick.'

My knees felt dizzy. I sat down on the Piaggio's doorstep and took guns out of my pockets. 'Not now.' I shook my head. 'There's two dead men to be explained away, now.'

He stared at me. 'My God, isn't that reason enough?'

I handed him the Walther. 'Your pistol, I think. No, that's the wrong sort of reason.' I looked at Herter, sprawled untidily, less stiff dead than he had even been alive, and Morrison lying neatly only a few yards away.

I asked: 'What date was Morrison's last flight, when he whipped the jewels?'

Ken stared at me. Then he said. 'February 10th. Why the hell?'

I just nodded. That had been just a week before we had gone down burning into the paddy-field in the Kutch. Morrison had never heard that about Kitson and Clay.

I stood up and walked across to Herter and bent down and dug the big wad of notes out of his pocket. The top few were slightly bent and crumpled: my dollars and francs. I took them and put the rest back. There must have been over £25,000 there, in various currencies.

Then I said: 'I'm going up the hill to make a deal.' I turned away, leaving him just standing there. But after a few steps he was up with me.

37

WE MET a bunch of villagers at the top of the path; Morrison's wife wasn't one of them. They stopped and would have let us go past except for one old boy who seemed to feel it was up to him to try and do something. Just what, he probably wasn't sure himself, and I wasn't helping. He tried me in Greek, then a rough brand of French, but I didn't know any French that day. He just looked at me. There was more between us than the language difficulty, and he knew it. Then he shook his head, more hopelessly than angrily, and stepped aside. We went on up into the village and nobody tried to stop us.

The door of the bar was unlatched. I kicked it open and

stood back. After the glare of the sun on the white walls it was very dark inside, but I could make out a dim splash of white. I went carefully down the steps with Herter's Luger in my hand.

They were both there, sitting at a table in the far corner, where we'd sat an hour or two before. The Nawab seemed surprised to see us. The proprietor wasn't around.

I put the Luger in my trouser pocket and reached across the bar for the cognac and poured two small glasses. Ken shut the door behind us.

Miss Brown said softly: 'We heard shooting.'

'And you came running to see who'd got shot,' I said. 'Cheers.' I finished my cognac in one.

The Nawab was watching me with small, nervous eyes.

'Herter's dead,' I told him.

He winced slightly and seemed to shrink. 'You killed him?' he whispered.

Miss Brown said calmly: 'Somebody had to, sooner or later.'

'That's right,' I said.

The Nawab didn't hear us. 'You killed him, just like that?' he whispered.

'What d'you mean, just like that?' I said harshly. 'The last time you saw us he had a gun on us. He shot down an unarmed man. He did it because he thought you'd want it done. He was being your executioner; I expect he died happy.'

The Nawab winced again.

Ken put his glass down on the counter and unzipped his jacket, showing the Walther jammed in his belt. He looked at me and lifted his eyebrows in a question.

I poured another cognac and walked across and leant on the back of a chair across the table from the Nawab.

Ken stayed leaning against the bar.

The Nawab asked: 'What are you going to do now?'

Miss Brown laughed shortly, a rich little sound.

I said: 'I've come to collect our reward on the rest of the jewels. They're down there, and you've counted them. Now I want our reward.'

There was a long silence while they all stared at me. Then, behind me, Ken said softly: 'You're crackers, sonny.'

Miss Brown asked: 'Is that what you want, Captain?'

I nodded. 'That's what I came for.'

224

Suddenly she laughed again, a clear full-blooded peal this time. The little room rang with the sound. She shook her head. 'Excuse me, Captain. You're a man of very limited ambitions.'

'That's me.' I kept looking at the Nawab. 'Well?'

He was getting some colour back in his face. He leant away from the table and studied me, then smiled. 'That's what you want – your five per cent?'

I nodded. 'What valuation did you have on the whole lot? Around a million-and-a-half sterling?'

He bowed his head gracefully, still smiling. 'It came to about that, I believe.'

'Fair enough. For argument's sake, would you say the load down in the Piaggio represents about a million?'

He ducked his head again.

'Fine,' I said. 'That leaves our share at £50,000.'

His smile got broader. 'That sounds eminently fair, Captain. Unfortunately' – he spread his hands – 'you cannot have it in cash. As you know, I never carry cash myself. But, of course I will give you a cheque.'

Ken said harshly: 'And stop it as soon as he gets to a cable office.' He slammed his glass on to the counter. 'Okay, the parade's over. Let's get airborne before we lose the wind.'

Miss Brown looked at him, then me, and seemed to be smiling with genuine amusement.

I said to the Nawab: 'I'm not too happy about flying off and trying to sell this stuff privately; it wouldn't be easy. But I'm not too happy about taking your cheque, either. So unless you can think of something better, I might be inclined just to heave the whole lot into the sea, just so that nobody could hold me liable for it.'

The Nawab shrugged and said nastily: 'Mr Herter carried all my cash – but obviously you'll have got that already.'

I shook my head. 'Oddly enough – no. That stays with him. It'll look better for my story if the police find a large piece of money on him. So – what else d'you suggest?'

The Nawab just shrugged again.

I looked at Ken and said: 'So it looks like we take a cheque.'

He was staring at me. 'Christ Almighty!' he said, '*I* don't.'

I pulled the chair out and sat down in it.

'There was always this risk,' I said. 'That he just didn't want the stuff back badly enough. He's just not money-hungry; he's never been without it enough to feel hungry. He just wants the satisfaction of doing us down. And, you know, he can.' I watched the Nawab; his eyes grew small and bright and he had a little secret smile on his mouth. I said, to Ken: 'We can shove him around here, because we've got guns and nobody's watching. But once we're off the island, we go back to being Kitson and Clay and he goes back to being His Excellency. And once we fly off with that stuff, he'll chase us to hell and Hyderabad because he'll think we've cheated him. Hell, you know him.'

Ken nodded. 'I know him, all right,' he said grimly. 'That's why I'm not taking his cheques. *You* take a cheque for £25,000 if you're so mad keen, and give him one of the boxes. I'll hang on to the other.'

I asked: 'What'll you do with it, Ken?'

'I'll manage.'

'How? What dealer, what city, what country? D'you know these things? D'you know who'll handle that sort of stuff?'

He looked at me steadily for a long time, then walked across and sat down in a chair just a few feet away. He picked a cigarette out of a packet Miss Brown had left on the table, lit it, frowned at me and said: 'This is getting to be a deal between you and me, Jack.'

I said softly: 'It always was. It was always coming to that.'

38

THE ROOM had drawn in with him, had shrunk down to no bigger now than a cockpit. Somewhere, there was a beautiful girl in a white mac and a little millionaire in a golfing jacket – but that was somewhere else.

I said quietly: 'That jade down in the Piaggio – it's not worth anything. Not to us. We couldn't sell it; that's why it's still here. Most thieves wouldn't lift it off a bedroom table – and we don't have their advantages: the Nawab will *know* we've got it. All he has to do is send descriptions of it and us to Interpol and it would be ten years before we could try and shift it.'

'Thanks,' he said bitterly, 'for putting the idea into his tiny mind.'

I shook my head. 'He doesn't count. Forget him; it wouldn't matter if he never said a word about it. You just walk into any jeweller's shop in any town in the world with that stuff and everybody would know it was stolen goods. You and I simply aren't the sort of people who own that sort of stuff honestly; just having it would make us crooks. You couldn't sell it honestly, and for the same reason you couldn't sell it crookedly. There isn't a professional crook who would touch anything so distinctive.'

'Your boy in Athens, Mikklos, touched it.'

'Ken – Mikklos got killed.'

He stared hard at me, leaning forward in his chair with his left arm cradled in his lap. Then he nodded. 'Okay, I take your point. So there's a risk – I'll admit a big risk. But there's still a chance of a profit. We hand it back to him for one of his cheques and we've got a guaranteed loss.'

I said: 'You know, half an hour ago I'd have settled for just having nobody pointing a gun at me; I'd have reckoned that a good bargain. Now, I want a little more. I need a little more. There are two dead men down on that beach and I killed one of them. I killed him in front of witnesses. That suits me, because I think I had a good reason to kill him. But I've got to stay here to prove that reason; if I run out now, I'm a killer. The same goes for you. You run out with those jewels and you're a crook. We couldn't either of us come back, ever. And in our job, we need to come back.'

'Perhaps,' he said gently, 'perhaps I've had enough of this job. Perhaps I'd settle for a nice quiet, warm place and one of those boxes. Risks and all.'

'Crack up on some nice lonely island and bury the jewels under the plane and just sit around ten years?' I sneered. 'It's been tried.'

'Yes,' he said, 'and perhaps I'll try it, too.'

I said: 'Take it from me – it just won't work.'

He leant back slowly and crumpled out his cigarette in a little pottery ashtray. He stared at me. Then he said: 'It goes back ten years, doesn't it? It all goes back to that. We had a chance, then, when we got our own plane. With that, at that time, and being as good as we were, we could really have made something.' He shook his head. 'But that's over, Jack, over and done. We got a dirty deal; got on the bottom end of a political stunt and lost the plane and our licences.'

He leant forward in his chair. 'Face up to it, chum – that finished us. We'll never make it now, not the way we could have then. Now – we've got another chance. A different one, but a chance. Certainly there's risks; there were risks that time before, and we went down on one. But it's a chance.'

Then he said: 'There's ten years of my life in one of those boxes, Jack, that and more. Ten years that we've waited around being small people in small jobs. So' – he shrugged – 'maybe you're happy there. Not me. So don't tell me not to take it. You don't have to, but don't tell me not to.'

I said: 'You really still think we got a dirty deal back there, then?'

He leant back and looked at me, frowning slightly and breathing smoke slowly.

I said: 'We didn't get any dirty deal. We were lucky to get out of that one alive; losing the plane and our licences was the least we earned. That flight was a mistake. We made it because we were young pilots who thought they were tin gods. We learnt that we weren't. We should never have carried guns in other people's countries – or at least we shouldn't bitch about what happens when we do. Haven't you learnt that yet?'

He was sitting tense, watching me from under his brows. 'Go on,' he said softly, 'go on.'

'So now you want to try another duff flight; another wrong cargo. It doesn't work, Ken, it never does. You think you've had ten lost years flying limousines out in Pakistan? You should have had some of the jobs I've flown. I've been on the wrong side of the sky the whole damn lot of that ten years!'

His face twisted into something like a smile. 'And that puts you in control now?'

'Yes. I've seen what can happen; you haven't.'

'And you don't want it to happen to me?' he asked coldly. 'Just because we shared a cockpit ten years ago. I suppose you've just been stringing along to protect me from myself.'

I said: 'Ken – did you ever think why the hell I bothered to come to Mehari and get mixed up with the boys there, when I already had the jewels?'

He frowned and thought why. Then he looked at me and asked carefully: 'This – all of this – wouldn't just be because

228

you were huffed that I didn't invite you in on this at the beginning?'

'You didn't.'

He smiled. 'But suppose I had? Suppose I'd come up to you that morning in Athens and told you I'd got a clear line on to the jewels and suggested we went after them together? What then?'

I said, very precisely: 'You didn't, Ken. What you *did* was find out I was supposed to be carrying them and then try to beg a ride in my plane with a gun under your jacket.'

The room was very quiet now.

He leant back again, frowning slightly. There might have been a touch of worry in his eyes. Then he shook his head. 'I wasn't going to shoot you, you dope.'

'*Weren't you?* How the hell d'you know *what* you were going to do? You were prepared to try and take something off me in my own plane, with a gun. Nobody does that to me; you were damned well going to *have* to shoot me.'

He shook his head again, still frowning. 'No,' he said quietly. 'I wasn't going to. But . . . I don't know.' He looked down at his feet. 'I'd sort of forgotten about you, Jack.' Then he looked up. 'This isn't the point. I'll grant anything you say; I'm not trying to push you into anything. But I'm still taking one of those boxes. I've got a good reason for taking it.'

'Not good enough.'

He said flatly: 'I'll take just one box, and the boat. That you didn't go along with me will strengthen your story more. You can put all the blame you like on me.' He stood up. 'If that's the way you want it.'

'It's not the way I want it. Sit down.'

He stepped back from the chair and spread his feet firmly. Then he moved his left hand cautiously until it was hooked in his belt well clear of the Walther. 'No,' he said. 'Call it a day, Jack. I'm going to walk out of here now. So leave it at that.'

I unhooked the zip of my jacket, moving slowly and deliberately, and let it flap clear of the Beretta. He watched me intently, his body arched, his face stretched tensely.

Then I leant back slowly and lifted a cigarette out of the packet on the table and put it in my mouth. 'There's more to this than you know, Ken. So I still have control.'

'Don't try it!' His voice was anguished. 'You've seen me use a gun. Don't try it!'

'Fifteen years,' I said softly. 'Fifteen years – and it was all coming to this.'

'*Don't!*'

I shrugged. The Beretta was plain in my belt; there was an unlit cigarette in my mouth. I moved my hand carefully, to my shirt pocket.

I pointed the little ·22 at him.

His right hand had jerked as far as the butt of the Walther, but he stopped it there, not gripping the gun. For a long time he stood frozen, staring at the little gun.

I said: 'I have control.'

He let his right hand fall slowly away, without looking up. 'You have control,' he said grimly. He seemed to relax a bit. 'Fifteen years,' he said. 'Fifteen years – you sentimental bastard.'

I nodded and stood up carefully.

He looked up at me. Then he smiled.

'You know something?' he said. 'It's a damn funny thing, but I feel a lot better with you pointing a gun at me than I'd have felt pointing one at you.'

I shrugged.

He shook his head slowly. 'I wouldn't have liked shooting you, Jack.'

'You sentimental bastard, you.'

We grinned at each other.

39

I MOVED DOWN the counter where I could see everybody; the room seemed to widen again as I moved. I looked at the Nawab.

'Deal's complete,' I told him. 'Write the cheque.'

He smiled a little wanly. 'Are you sure it's necessary, Captain?'

'I'm sure. You write it or I'll chuck the whole damn load into the sea.'

He frowned and reached under his jacket. He might have had a gun there – Kira was getting to be the arsenal of the Western world – but he didn't carry his own guns. He brought out a cheque-book and a pen. He wrote the cheque and blotted it dry and tore it out. He looked up at me again.

I said: 'Now write a receipt, saying you've got all the jewels back in good order and that you've paid a reward of £50,000 for their recovery.'

He frowned at that idea, mainly because he couldn't see where it led.

I said: 'That piece of paper' – I waved the gun at the cheque – 'may not be any good, but at least I've gone to some trouble getting rid of the jewellery. I don't want any claims from you later that I hung on to any of it.'

He still looked suspicious, but he dug out a piece of paper and wrote it out.

I said to Ken: 'See how they look.'

He picked the cheque and the receipt off the table and glanced at them. He shrugged. 'As good as you'll get.'

'Fine. Now,' I said, 'there's the Piaggio down on the beach for whenever you can find somebody to collect it. That just about concludes our business – except for this.' I held up the little automatic, then walked across and put it down on the table. Ken stared at me. I said: 'Yussuf was carrying this around. I imagine he got it from you, since he gave you the only gun he brought back from Mehari, and he wasn't a lad who liked to go around gunless.'

The Nawab reached and poked the little gun delicately with his fountain pen. He looked up. 'Did you kill him, too?'

'You and me,' I said, 'between us. I won't ask why you left him around Tripoli with that gun. Personally, I'd say it was a sort of insurance against my following you here – but, as I say, I won't press it.'

I thought he looked a little relieved; I could have been wrong. He might never have been worried.

I said: 'What I will press, is the business of Mikklos's murder.'

Ken said softly: 'For God's sake.'

I stared at him, then looked back at the Nawab. 'It concerns me. Anarchos thinks I know something about it. That means I can't come back to Greece, not officially, without going up for a police grilling. Maybe even a sentence for concealing evidence or whatever.'

He smiled faintly and spread his hands. 'I'm sure your natural resilience will see you through that, Captain.'

'Perhaps. I'd still like something more. The trouble is, I do know something about it. I know how he was killed. I found his body.'

He stood up and put his fountain pen away inside his jacket. Miss Brown stayed where she was, watching me carefully.

The Nawab said: 'That could be dangerous knowledge, Captain.'

I said: 'I'll let you judge. He was killed with five shots from a ·22 automatic.'

He couldn't help it. He jerked his head in one snap glance at Miss Brown. Then he pulled back quickly to look at me. His smile was gone.

'Thank you,' I said.

Nobody said anything. Then she made one quick graceful movement and was standing back from the table with the little gun in her hand. It swept slowly across the three of us.

Beside me, Ken sucked in his breath sharply.

I said: 'You told me he liked his employees to carry guns; I thought that one looked a bit light and fancy for our Herter.' I looked back at the gun. 'Don't throw them around the way you did last time, honey. It's not fully loaded now.'

She smiled at me, almost sadly, across the gun. 'Everybody keeps on underestimating you, Jack. Even me. Well, what were you going to do about it?'

I said, very seriously: 'There's only one thing I can do: turn you in to Anarchos, with that gun. He'll match it up against the bullets they dug out of Mikklos.'

Perhaps her smile got just a little sadder, no more. 'You'd really do that, Jack?'

'It's as I keep on saying: either I do that or stay out of Athens, for good. And I need to be able to go places. That' – I stared at her – 'and that I'm not convinced Mikklos needed killing.'

The Nawab said suddenly: 'Why should she kill him?'

I looked at him. He seemed small and shrunken and lonely. I said: 'You sent her there, didn't you? You knew Mikklos had been handling the jewels and you wanted to know where he'd got them. You could have known he was a womanizer, *that* was no secret. And so if anybody could get anything out of him, she could.' I shrugged. 'So she tempted him and he grabbed and she was just defending her honour.'

That seemed to convince him. He looked at her a little more hopefully.

'Yes,' she said, very seriously and emphatically, 'that's how it happened. But I'm not going into court for it. You're going to have to explain it to that Greek policeman yourself, Jack.'

'Oh, he knows how it happened,' I said softly.

She gave me a sharp, hard stare. Then it faded suddenly into a smile. She just stood there, smiling calmly, almost mischievously, and understanding exactly what I meant and pointing the little gun straight at me.

Then she said gently: 'Goodbye, Jack. I won't tell you to look after yourself: I think you know how.'

I said: 'Goodbye, Dahira.'

She smiled and then jerked her head at the Nawab and her voice was different. 'Come on, Aly.'

He stared at her, then us, then started to say something, then didn't, and went slowly across to her.

She pulled open the door behind her back. Sunlight flared in, outlining her with light and giving her, with her long hair and white coat, the sudden blazing purity of a Renaissance angel.

Then the door slapped shut and she and he and the little gun were gone.

40

THE LITTLE room was very dark after the glare from the street. I looked at Ken; he was standing away from the counter, staring intently at the closed door.

I sprinkled cognac into two more glasses and held one out to him. 'Wrap yourself around this and start thinking. We've got to get our story worked out; the Athens cops'll be down here in a minute.'

'Did she?' he asked fiercely. 'She really killed him?'

I nodded. 'Yes.' He turned to me and took the glass. His face looked suddenly old.

I said: 'Anarchos knows it; it's just that he couldn't do anything about it in Tripoli. I saw him take a set of her fingerprints – on his lighter; she probably left a set around Mikklos's office. And I wouldn't be surprised if he's got a witness who saw her go in or come out. She's somebody people notice.'

I took a pull at the cognac. 'He knew damn well I'd been in that office, even if he couldn't prove it. That was what he was on to me for: he thought I might have picked up the murder gun if she'd left it there. If he had the gun, he had a case.'

His eyes blazed at me. 'You made damn sure he'd find it on her, didn't you?'

I said harshly: 'You don't believe that stuff about Mikklos making a pass at her, do you? That was just for the defence counsel. I saw what had happened: she sat down and drank a glass of *ouzo* with him and then she stood up and emptied the whole magazine into his chest. Across the desk. He was sitting down when he got it. That was how she killed him.'

He stared at me, then emptied his glass and put it back on the counter. Then he shook his head. 'I still don't see it. I don't see why. She couldn't have been trying to make him talk, not like that.'

I said: 'It was a good way to stop him talking, though.'

He jerked a look at me.

I said: '*You'd* found out that Mikklos was shipping the next load through Tripoli. She was stopping the Nawab and Herter finding out.'

He stared down at the counter for a long, long time. Then he asked: 'Did you mean that – about the cops getting here?'

'Yes. Anarchos will have guessed we'd be coming here – if we didn't arrive in Athens. They'd be here but for the front. We're only eighty to ninety miles from Athens.'

He nodded as if that decided something. I poured more cognac into my glass. I'd had more than I wanted already; but I hadn't finished talking, and I needed something to help me along.

I said: 'She was part of your reason, Ken. She had to be: she was the only thing that gave it any sense at all. She knew damn well that Herter and the Nawab weren't going to find those jewels, not by themselves. But you stood a chance. So when you found them, you and her and them would be away to some quiet place.'

I gulped cognac and went on tearing his dream to bits. 'But

234

it was the jewels she was after: they meant freedom, a new life, all that. She was ready to ditch the Nawab for them – but she'd have ditched you, too. When you didn't find them and I did, she tried to switch to me.' He was staring at me. I ploughed on. 'She came up to my room in Tripoli and made me an offer. Oh, it was nicely tied up, but the message was there: hang on to the jewels and you can have me too.'

He was still staring and his face was weathered stone.

Then he nodded and said simply: 'Yes, she would have done that.'

I gaped at him stupidly.

He said: 'I loved her.' Then he opened his fingers neatly and let the empty glass drop and smash near his feet.

I moved my head slowly up and down without really knowing why. Then I said: 'She'd gone back to him, Ken. When you and I didn't turn the stuff up, she went back to him. You told her last night where we were coming – and she told him. That's the only way they could have known.'

He nodded. The roar of a Piaggio engine shook the room.

I listened to it without realizing what it was; then I jumped for the door.

Ken said: 'Hold it.'

I had my hand on the latch when I looked around. He was pointing the Walther at me.

'He'll kill himself,' I said. 'And her.'

'Get away from the door.'

I let go the latch and stepped slowly back.

'He's got a chance,' Ken said. 'He's got a good wind. And he can fly that thing. I taught him.'

The second engine caught and roared up.

I said: 'It isn't much of a chance. She'd stand a better one in court.'

He wasn't looking at me, though the Walther still was. He was staring at the door, listening to the beat of the engines.

He said: 'I don't want her in court.' The engine note sagged; he nodded.

I jerked open the door and stumbled out into the sun. In the alley the noise was louder, hammering back and forth between the walls. People were staring out of their doorways; two children were running ahead of us.

Ken had the Walther back under his jacket. We started to run, slipping on the irregular paving.

The engines started to build again as we came clear of the village and on to the hillside. There were people crowding down on the path.

Below, the Piaggio hadn't moved. As the engines climbed to a scream the nosewheel pressed down into the grass. Then the brakes came off, the nose rose and dipped again and she started to move.

She seemed to go very slowly, lurching as she ploughed through the grass. Then she came on to the thinner grass and started to run, sand flicking back from the wheels. And then she was on clear sand and racing, driving straight and trembling at the sea. The nosewheel lifted, hesitated, she ran on her main wheels for a moment and lifted heavily into the air, her nose straining for the sky.

Ken whispered: 'Nose down, nose *down*.'

She wasn't flying yet; she was mushing along, reared back timidly from the sea in a near-stalled attitude, struggling for height but not getting any because she was at too steep an angle to get any speed. Because the Nawab wasn't pilot enough to know that you always sacrifice height, no matter how little you've got, to find speed. . . .

Then the wave had her. It slapped the port wheel and exploded through the propeller like smoke from a gun. The Piaggio staggered and skidded; the nose jerked higher, a wing dropped into the wave trough and for a second the whole plane hung there, shuddering.

The next wave rose and flipped almost lazily at the wing-tip and the plane cartwheeled suddenly, wing over wing, and smashed into the sea.

The spray fell back and we saw it, just a glint of the belly and the hard shapes of the wheels in a circle of foam. Then the foam rose on a wave and the wave passed and the Piaggio was gone.

The wave broke loudly on the beach.

Something like a sigh rippled through the groups of villagers. When I looked at them, they looked away quickly, and stirred uneasily, then began to shuffle back towards the village. Down below, two men were running for the boat.

Ken said: 'I could have done it. With one arm, I could have done it.'

I said: 'She didn't ask you to.'

He nodded and went on standing and staring at the sea and

236

rubbing his left arm. 'So nobody gets rich, after all.' I thought he was talking to himself until he said: 'What did you say you got for that first load?'

'Five thousand sterling. Some of it goes on repairs to the Dakota; some better go to Morrison's wife.'

He nodded. 'So nobody gets rich.'

I reached and took the Walther out of his belt; he didn't try to stop me. I walked to the edge of the cliff and pitched it far out, into deep water. The sight of it hitting the sea made me wince. I threw the Beretta shorter. Then I walked back. Anarchos was going to jump on us for a lot of illegal-entry counts, but he needn't get us for carrying firearms, too.

I still had the Luger – but I would need that to explain away Herter.

Ken said. 'Will they believe our story?'

I shrugged. 'They don't have any others. Not now.'

He looked at me and smiled crookedly. 'You know something, Jack? She came as damn near taking it with her as anybody ever did.' He laughed briefly, then his face set hard with pain.

I just nodded. She had been that sort of girl. But she had been a lot of other sorts of girl, too.

Later I would tell him about the three 20-carat Golconda diamonds that I'd snipped off the big necklace in the first load and sewed up safe behind the badge on my uniform cap. At a guess, I'd say £30,000 apiece on the open market. We wouldn't get that in Tel Aviv, of course – but we wouldn't get just ten per cent either. Not for three single stones that nobody could trace, not when I had a piece of paper saying the Nawab had got back everything he'd lost.

I'd settle for anything over £40,000 in all. That would be enough. For both of us.

They had the boat out by now, but there was nothing for them to find. The sea had no mark on it but from waves and wind. Down there, it would be as still and quiet, and soon as old, as in any grove of tall trees.

Gavin Lyall
The Most Dangerous Game 70p

'Gavin Lyall writes with zest and bite, and splendidly, his triumph in *The Wrong Side of the Sky*' NEW YORK TIMES

Blame the Dead 60p

'Superior, tough yet pensive thriller, full of twists and turns from Harrow schoolboys to Norwegian alcoholics' OBSERVER

Judas Country 70p

'Skilful mixture of aging flyers, with planes to match, battling their way through arms smuggling, Middle East intrigue and the tale of a fabulous sword which once belonged to Richard the Lion-Heart... Must be contender for the best crime book of the year' DAILY MIRROR

Midnight Plus One 70p

'Motor dash from Brittany to Austrian border; cars crumple, bullets fly... a magnificent cliffhanger' SATURDAY REVIEW

Shooting Script 60p

'The vortex of Caribbean politics made even more turbulent... by one of the most compelling of contemporary storytellers' NEW YORK TIMES

Venus with Pistol 60p

'Works up to beautiful tension and ingenuity in Vienna – via London, Amsterdam, Zurich and Venice' TIMES LITERARY SUPPLEMENT

Martin Woodhouse
Mama Doll 50p

The adventures of Giles Yeoman

Amanda Grayle was Giles Yeoman's first concern – and the second casualty in the Westlake affair.

Then Francis DeFray had his head blown off in front of ten million viewers, and Yeoman began his search for the death-by-gadget killers.

Pulling no punches, the action races from Iceland to the Canaries, the West Indies and home to a hail of bullets on Salisbury Plain.

'First-class thriller' EVENING STANDARD

'Unusually crisp and witty, with a hard and fascinating scientific centre' SUNDAY TELEGRAPH

Blue Bone 50p

The further adventures of Giles Yeoman

Kate came out of the Thames under a rain of shotgun fire and into Giles Yeoman's houseboat.

Someone badly wanted a shipment of plastic dog-bones.

Finding out why involves kidnapping a Czech scientist from East Berlin and a whole mess of trouble on a tropical island.

It was fun – until they chopped off Kate's finger . . .

'Absolutely splendid thriller' SUNDAY TIMES

'So good . . . intelligent yet racy, tense and packed with action. stylish and funny with excellent characters and dialogue' SUNDAY EXPRESS

Selected bestsellers

☐ **Jaws** Peter Benchley 70p

☐ **Let Sleeping Vets Lie** James Herriot 60p

☐ **If Only They Could Talk** James Herriot 60p

☐ **It Shouldn't Happen to a Vet** James Herriot 60p

☐ **Vet in Harness** James Herriot 60p

☐ **Tinker Tailor Soldier Spy** John le Carré 60p

☐ **Alive: The Story of the Andes Survivors** (illus)
Piers Paul Read 75p

☐ **Gone with the Wind** Margaret Mitchell £1.50

☐ **Mandingo** Kyle Onstott 75p

☐ **Shout at the Devil** Wilbur Smith 70p

☐ **Cashelmara** Susan Howatch £1.25

☐ **Hotel** Arthur Hailey 80p

☐ **The Tower** Richard Martin Stern 70p
(filmed as *The Towering Inferno*)

☐ **Bonecrack** Dick Francis 60p

☐ **Jonathan Livingston Seagull** Richard Bach 80p

☐ **The Fifth Estate** Robin Moore 75p

☐ **Royal Flash** George MacDonald Fraser 60p

☐ **The Nonesuch** Georgette Heyer 60p

☐ **Murder Most Royal** Jean Plaidy 80p

☐ **The Grapes of Wrath** John Steinbeck 95p

All these books are available at your bookshop or newsagent:
or can be obtained direct from the publisher
Just tick the titles you want and fill in the form below
Prices quoted are applicable in UK

Pan Books, Cavaye Place, London SW10 9PG

Send purchase price plus 15p for the first book and 5p for each
additional book, to allow for postage and packing

Name (block letters) _____

Address _____

_____

While every effort is made to keep prices low, it is sometimes
necessary to increase prices at short notice. Pan Books reserve the
right to show on covers new retail prices which may differ from
those advertised in the text or elsewhere